The Last Witch on the Knock

Aimée MacDonald

The Last Witch on the Knock

JOHN MURRAY

First published in Great Britain in 2026 by John Murray (Publishers)

1

Copyright © Aimée MacDonald 2026

The right of Aimée MacDonald to be identified as the Author of the Work has been asserted by her in accordance with the Copyright, Designs and Patents Act 1988.

All rights reserved. No part of this publication may be reproduced, stored in a retrieval system, or transmitted, in any form or by any means without the prior written permission of the publisher, nor be otherwise circulated in any form of binding or cover other than that in which it is published and without a similar condition being imposed on the subsequent purchaser.

All characters in this publication are fictitious and any resemblance to real persons, living or dead, is purely coincidental.

A CIP catalogue record for this title is available from the British Library

Hardback ISBN 978 1 399 82127 8
Trade Paperback ISBN 978 1 399 82789 8
ebook ISBN 978 1 399 82129 2

Typeset in Sabon MT by Hewer Text UK Ltd, Edinburgh
Printed and bound in Great Britain by Clays Ltd, Elcograf S.p.A.

John Murray policy is to use papers that are natural, renewable and recyclable products and made from wood grown in sustainable forests. The logging and manufacturing processes are expected to conform to the environmental regulations of the country of origin.

Carmelite House
50 Victoria Embankment
London EC4Y 0DZ

www.johnmurraypress.co.uk

John Murray Press, part of Hodder & Stoughton Limited
An Hachette UK company

The authorised representative in the EEA is Hachette Ireland, 8 Castlecourt Centre, Dublin 15, D15 XTP3, Ireland (email: info@hbgi.ie)

For Colin and Sheila

Part I

Milk Teeth

1715

I came into this world a sweaty hot mess a mass
no hair until I was three at least
this big big thing
and my mother took one look and said
my girl
seems like a devil child
but I think I will love her
love me she did and does
strong strange lady
and I have a little brother now and
I helped the midwife and Mother deliver him
blood on my hands and some white thing
and skin and skin then skin on skin
her holding him
small gummy bud mouth
toothless doglike beauty
black lashes jaundiced skin
the midwife said
he slid out like an apple
but apples don't slide they are plucked from trees
so maybe he wasn't ready to come and
a hand ripped him out anyway
a baby, good enough to eat
my mother free and me
deciding, no matter what, I would protect him
and her and us

she, who is the type to say:
the sky is a painting tonight, eh?
and he, who is the type to say:
you have never seen a painting, Ma
and me, who is Kate
in sixteen ninety-six
a heavy red newborn
with two balled fists and a turnip head
and a mouthful of teeth
yes
teeth
little white pearly bits
and my mother, straining
stooped with me on her back
I have made her ancient and beautiful
in her odd way
And I knew it then, even
long nose long hair hard fingertips and deep creases in her
    neck
feet like leather so sometimes she walks
shoeless in hot weather
and I look on thinking, oh
me, personally, I don't ever want to look like that
even though I love you so, I love you so
when I am cruel my brother tells me I have snakes for hair
and I turn to my scaly strands shrieking
BITE BITE BITE
but there are just these limp locks
reminding me to clean
to brush
I need to do these things so I have my looks
and my personality
you need both for The Big House

Kate, says my mother
Kate, I think we can get you to The Big House
and she says it like it's a game
which, obviously, makes me want to play.

One

I like to watch Leo drive and Leo likes to be watched while he drives. Tanned forearms brushing the wheel, shiny black sunglasses. His blond hair is a cloud around a smooth face, and he looks sort of American, whatever that means. You look sort of American, Leo, I say, and he says: What does that mean?

He turns the music up and I feel it in my throat. He puts the windows down and the outskirts go by in a haze of summer.

We speed through the grey, out of the city and into the flat hot green. I thought everything would be muted pastel, dappled pale greens and wildflowers, like a painting. Instead, there is no definition and the sun touches everything. The countryside in summer is like the big felt panels I used to play with as a child, arranging felt animals and felt trees just so, little bits of primary-coloured felt fluff under the nails and a big blue felt river running through it all. I think this but I don't say it because I don't want Leo to laugh at me or tell me I am strange again.

It's only an hour from here if we go the quick way, Leo says. He is looking at the map now, small blue arrow tracking our progress away from everything, and I know better than to ask him to put the phone down.

How about we go the tourist route, actually? he says as he turns off the main road and onto the tourist route.

I ask him to put the windows up, because when the windows are down I worry that an insect will get in and then be trapped and we will be unable to pull over so it will buzz and sting in panic and it will go for our faces, probably, and Leo will find it all funny and dab at his tiny pretty wounds with tea tree while mine will swell into lumps that make me a monster.

I ask again, and he ignores me. I try to put the window up myself but nothing happens when I press the button because he has put the child lock on. I press again and again until he slaps my wrist and shouts over the music: Stop messing with the car, for real, Thomasin.

I stop messing with the car.

A few minutes go by and then he says: American as in, like, an actor?

In the shower that morning I watched a tiny moth crawl across the wet tiled wall. It was right by my head and I'd just shampooed my hair and the soap was running down my shoulders and arms. I was right under the stream of hot water and the shampoo went in my eyes, even, but I just stood and tried to look at the moth as it writhed in the damp. My face stung but I wanted that sting. The water started to run cold and I took the shower head off its stand and sprayed the moth and watched as it slid down the mouldy grouting, circling the drain once and vanishing with the bubbly water. I let the shower head go and it crashed onto the plastic. Water shot out all over the bathmat and then the floor and then the ceiling too, so everything felt like it was dripping and peeling and melting and I couldn't quite breathe right so I was taking in air in heaving gulps and my feet were grey and numb. The window was ajar, opening out onto the stairwell, and I could hear Leo's footsteps coming up and the shudder of my spare keys in the old lock. When he found me I was still standing there, naked and soapy and shivering. In the chipped porcelain sink – a disposable razor, pink plastic handle and hair between the blades.

If you took a knife from the kitchen, even the bread knife, the scissors from under the sink or the keys in your hand, and pushed them into my feet, the soles or the bony tops of them or whatever, I don't think I would feel a thing, Leo, I said.

Thomasin, he said, and his voice had that mildly disapproving tone. Come on now, Thomasin, not today.

Thomasin? he says now, my name a question. I think he's been speaking for a few minutes and I just haven't been listening. We're not going to do this today, are we? We're going to be normal, yeah?

We're going to be normal, Leo.

If we are a 'we' instead of separate entities, this 'we' might be OK because Leo will be the dominant force and he is more stable than I am.

We are going to be normal today, my darling, I say again.

Leo has never really felt like my darling, though. Leo is muscular but slim and he is older than me and conventionally very attractive. When we kiss, it's like my lips are on fleshy plastic, which is not entirely off-putting because it takes my mind off the other things.

Leo pulls out onto the right side of the road to overtake an SUV. He stays there for a little too long and I grip my seat, picking at the cream leather. A van is approaching, horn blaring. At the last minute, he swerves back to the left and the horn is an eerie sort of music, an elongated note hanging for a second in the sticky heat.

The note fades out and Leo gives a sharp laugh.

Did you think we were going to die just there?

I nod and he rolls his eyes and I feel deeply, disgustingly embarrassed.

You're, like, especially intense today, you know that?

Just nervous.

I watch the blue arrow on Leo's phone again. We move further and further away from home, closer and closer to something else. I look away.

Just nervous, he throws back at me, imitating my awkwardly high pitch, the crack in my voice.

Just nervous, Leo. I haven't seen her in forever and it all feels a bit weird.

We are in trees now, big firs arching over a sunken road. Light flickers in from an opening ahead and it is like the car is carving its way through a tunnel.

Well, my truest-ever love, Leo says, we really are in the sticks now.

I say that yes, we really are, and I am embarrassed still but this time because he has to give me a lift in the first place, and because we are going to a town where my family will be and I don't need to know them at all to know they will be different from him.

We come off the forest road – we burst out of it, into blinding light – and we are in the town. There is an old visitor centre in a big brown box building, cartoon thistle emblazoned on the sign, and stretches of pruned grass and flowers leading to neatly sectioned fields. There are stone walls and hedgerows. There is a warehouse with a big sign that says: CHRISTMAS SHOP: OPEN ALL YEAR ROUND. On the plastic doors is another, smaller sign that says: CLOSED. The aunt of my imagination does not belong in this sort of rural orderliness.

We pass a Co-op – big car park, old people milling with tartan trolleys, children on colourful bikes and teenagers lounging on the hoods of souped-up little cars – and suddenly we really are in the town, or at least the town I imagined. Cottages low to the ground, wilting flowers in window boxes, peeling paint on wooden garden gates, B & B signs flapping like useless limbs in the heat. Patches of grass bordered by trees, goalposts and white paint, a tour bus branded with the logo of a local firm and splattered with mud, a Victorian hotel looming by the hill that overlooks the town.

So this is where the infamous Agnes lives, Thomasin?

Apparently so.

The aunt of my childhood wore sarongs in winter and had long straggly hair and lived on the other side of the city to me and my dad and, when she was invited to the house, she would bring strange snacks that we would throw out when she left and she would sit on the hard floor instead of the sofa and this, my dad would tell me, was a good thing because my sister spreads dirt wherever she goes, Thomasin. Then she moved away and we never saw her again and I started to think of her as though she was just a figment of my imagination, and then I stopped thinking of her altogether.

Leo looks vaguely disgusted, or maybe bored. I stick my head out the window.

On the streets are people, or rather, not people. Scarecrows in children's jumpers and jeans, in dated fascinators and long hand-knitted scarves, or old-fashioned button-down summer dresses and men's dress shirts, sitting on benches, propped up against lamp posts and at street corners leering at us with button eyes and dead mouths as we pass. They scare me a bit, these bags of straw in human clothes, and I tell Leo as much.

He says: Everything scares you, Thomasin.

Two are tussling in the grass at the side of the road. I decide I want to lighten the mood. Look, Leo, they're kissing.

He rolls his eyes. That's so hot, babe.

At the corner of the little high street – colourful cafés and dated clothes shops and fishing supply stores and takeaways with their shutters drawn and a butcher letting a salty, dank scent out the open door – is a woman. Her dress is dipped in mud and her hair is tangled and long and brown and she is just standing there, hands hidden beneath ripped linen. I feel something strange when I look at her. Or maybe I am confusing simple disgust or boredom or the other things that Leo and I like to feel together for strangeness, or whatever.

I lean further out into the hot air, towards her. She is stooped over slightly as though she is searching for something on the ground or like she is going to fall, and part of me really wants her to hit the kerb but in the end she seems to steady herself and we drive past and I see her face and she is made of straw too.

Oh my god. Her nonexistence sort of feels like a betrayal.

That one doesn't even look remotely realistic. Leo is laughing at me. I laugh too. Do you think good old Aunty Agnes will be made of straw as well, Thomasin?

He drops me off at my aunt's. It is a small flat at the end of the high street where the shops and people and straw people have tapered off into brown pebbledash. The last time I saw Agnes I was still too young for school. My dad skirts around the topic of her like she is a freak, which is maybe why I chose to remember her as eccentric and uniquely special. The town I imagined for her is one of sprawling Victorian mansions with creepy vegetable gardens, or weirdly shaped newbuilds with big windows and outdoor pools with a scum of countryside debris. I thought, too, that she might have money. Maybe because my dad has money. Maybe that is the only reason. I try not to let my disappointment show, especially when Leo says: Welcome to your luxurious retreat, my lady.

I ask him to come in with me, because I am scared to go up and ring the buzzer. If I go in with Leo, he will start a conversation so that, by the time he leaves, my aunt and I will have been chatting for a while like we are old friends. My aunt would probably be begging Leo to stay, making eyes at him over the dinner table. He has that effect on people. If I go without him, I will probably sit in silence fiddling with a tassel on a cushion or a curtain and then throw up on the living-room floor.

Will you? Please.

I would rather – what is it you say sometimes? he replies.

I would rather stick a screwdriver in each eye.

I would rather do that, Thomasin, if I'm being perfectly honest. And then: You can be absolutely disgusting sometimes, you weird bitch.

Before he leaves, though, he pulls me in close and I am enveloped in his aftershave and the washing powder his mum uses and he tells me to text and I can even phone, if I want, and send him pictures if I do anything cool or interesting like go hiking or wash my hair without having a breakdown.

In this moment, I think he is going to tell me that he loves me but instead he says: Don't do anything stupid.

Sometimes, when Leo talks, it is as though he is just reciting lines from films he has watched. He is a leading man. I watch as he jumps into his car and I hope he doesn't see the tiny hole I have picked in the seat, the spot where my littlest finger finally broke the stitching and sunk through the leather deep into the foam. I know he will see it, though, and I know it will make him hate me and he will cut contact for days and I will be miserable when he doesn't text and even more miserable when he eventually does. For now, though, my mouth is still fresh from his last kiss, the sharp mint of his gum and his mouthwash and everything that makes him shine.

I love you, I love you baby, I love you.

I stand on the street staring at the double wooden door into the stair and the buzzer marked with my aunt's name. The idea of a summer here is so entirely unfamiliar that it almost feels relieving. The sound of Leo's engine whirring in the distance is gone now and that is relieving too.

This summer might be the right thing for me, or at least it will be something, anything at all. This is what I tell myself as I press the buzzer. It is a stupid, weak, non-thing to think.

I can hear the sound of my arrival reverberating upstairs in the flat. I can hear a woman's voice, hint of a raspy city accent: Hello? And then: Hold on a sec, would you? Finn? Finn! Go and stop that. And then: Nina? Nina! And then: Sorry, hold on, are you still there?

Yes. Yes, I'm still here. But already the voice is shouting again for Nina. Nina! You wouldn't go down and get that, would you?

My dad phoned my aunt and asked if I could stay with her for the summer. It was the first time they had spoken in years, apparently. Not because they fell out but because some people are just not made to like each other. These are not things he has told me, because he tells me nothing. They are just things I have picked up and created and made true. The only correspondence between me and my aunt is a text I sent upon his request: Thank you in advance for having me, Aunty Agnes. XXX.

I hear a door opening and a dog barking and music spills out and then the door slams and I hear footsteps coming down the stairs and the main doors open and there is a little girl in a turquoise leotard and matching tutu with a plastic pack of gold sequins in her hand.

I am Nina, she says. You are my cousin, yes? Hello.

Hello, I reply, and I start to ask where her mum is because I am sort of awkward with children, like they can see right through me, but already Nina is marching back up the stairs and the dog is still barking from somewhere and I can't hear the music but I can feel the bass vibrating and I can do nothing really, nothing but follow.

The stairwell isn't winding stone like the tenement flat I share with Claudia and Elaine. Claudia, now back at her parents' place down south, sweet Elaine holding the fort with her café job in the city until we're both back. You will be back, won't you, girl? she texted this morning. A string of little hearts at the end of each message.

This stairwell is brown-carpeted, ending in two doors on either side of a short hall. One has a few empty plant pots and a doormat that says *Welcome Home* in cursive. The other has a million pairs of tiny colourful shoes and tall leather boots and sandals with big gold buckles and cork heels, and a row of hooks on the wall laden with vintage denim and cropped corduroy blazers and little leather jackets with glittery embroidery and silver zips. If these fit me, I will steal them, I think.

I like this one, I say, brushing the sleeve of a suede shearling coat. Nina sticks her tongue out, fumbles with the door handle: Then you're going to love Mum.

Nina opens the door and from down the hall I can hear my aunt saying: OK, Finn, we're going to be good now, aren't we? Good, you hear that? Good.

You have a little brother or something? I ask Nina. There could be a million little brothers and I – and probably my dad too – would be none the wiser.

Something like that. She is scowling and her stern little expression is so at odds with the rest of her appearance – wispy ponytail, small round face dotted with freckles and maybe just a little sunburn – that it makes me smile.

She leads me down the hallway, trailing gold sequin confetti. The floor is a dark brown too, but mostly obscured by overlapping rugs, a lot of small Persian carpets in beautiful deep gem colours and shaggy cream rugs and bright green ones too. Tufts of synthetic yarn as fine and soft as hair obscure my feet as I walk. The ceilings are low and even lower hanging lamps brush the top of my head – big squares of coloured glass suspended on exposed wire. Pictures line the haphazardly painted walls – strange little things, like they've been randomly bought from charity shops and estate sales or ransacked from a dead granny's house. A small wooden cabinet sits at an angle by the living-room door. On top of it is a pistachio telephone set and a matching velvet stool. It is plugged in, so I gather it isn't just for show. An old mobile sits charging next to it too, and a pair of wired earphones in a ball. I imagine sitting at that table and making phone calls, but I can't imagine the voice of anyone I know on the other side.

It's an odd place – I have been consumed by something strange and bright and I suppose, if I was a writer for an interior-design magazine, I would call it 'eclectic' or something, but all I can really envision when I first see my aunt's place is Leo saying: What the fuck is this hellhole?

The music is blaring as we enter the living room. More rugs fill the large low space. A cracked leather sofa and a linen one piled high with cushions are pushed against opposite walls. A TV sits flickering by the big window, which looks out onto the high street. A small bookshelf in a corner buckles under the weight of children's books and romance and crime novels with names like *Last Stand* and *My Lover, My Killer* in big block lettering. The glass coffee table has been pushed to the side of the room and in the centre, my aunt Agnes and a giant grey dog are dancing. Giant is an understatement – it is the most gigantic dog I have ever seen. On its hind legs it is taller than Agnes, maybe as tall as me.

She drops its front paws and the dog lands on all fours. It looks at me and starts to howl. Not a low bark, but something blaring and repetitive like a siren. The only thing my aunt does is press some dried meat strips into my hand.

Offer them to him.

I hold out the rubbery brown things and he quietens and advances towards me, sniffs my hand and takes the treats, appeased. He clambers onto the linen sofa, a clear line of drool dripping onto the fabric. He looks sort of regal there, the kind of dog that might fetch game for a hunter or warm beds or pose dutifully with a lord clad in red velvet.

He is really pretty, your dog.

He is Finn, says Nina. He is a wolfhound but he acts like he is just a wolf.

My aunt looks at me then as though she has just registered my presence. Her pink mouth splits into a yellow-toothed smile.

Thomasin! Here at last!

My aunt Agnes has peroxide hair and shimmery blue eye shadow and frosted lip gloss and because fashion is cyclical she looks stylish again with her bootcut low-waisted jeans and her ribbed halter neck. She has big earrings tangled in a mass of hair and a little dot on her nose where a piercing once was. A few loose cigarettes stick out of her pocket and she is beautiful and odd and just like her apartment and she is nothing like my dad, really.

Aunt Agnes, I say, and she says: Oh no no no please never call me that again it makes me feel about a hundred and four.

She goes to extend a silver-ringed turquoise-polished hand, hesitates and pulls me into a close hug instead. She smells like the sort of perfume you can buy behind the counter at the chemist – sugary, wonderful. Everything here is a sensory overload.

You have to call me Nance. My face is buried in her hair and I feel her jaw move against my shoulder as she speaks. Usually this is the sort of thing I would try to pull away from, but I let her hold me.

OK, Nance. Saying this name is like uttering a secret I have just been let in on. My dad has only ever called her Agnes.

Go and stick the kettle on, Nina, Nance says. And stop chucking your sequins around.

Nina asks for a Coke instead and Nance shrugs. Crack on, but it's your health at stake. She looks at me and rolls her eyes conspiratorially. My girl is a bit of a sugar fiend. Don't let it corrupt you. Then: Hey, you don't mind if I smoke, do you?

It's your house, I reply.

Ah but it's yours now too, Thomasin, for as long as you need it.

I sit on the leather sofa and Finn jumps down from his perch and jumps up onto mine. He brushes his rough tongue across my palm, long face looking up. He is trusting, almost instantly. All it took was some food.

Good boy, Finn, I say.

Got him when Nina was really wee off a farmer in the town over who wanted him as a working dog. Turns out he's lazy and he hates working so we got a good deal.

He looks like he's finally doing what he was meant to be doing all along.

Another lick. This time it is my knee. I've never really been around dogs – not in the flat with the girls or at Leo's or in the big empty house with Dad. I pat him lightly on his head and then scratch behind one of his flat straggly ears. You are sort of a sweet boy, I say, and through a cloud of smoke I see Nance grin.

Nina comes through with two cups, milky tea sloshing on the carpet, and a can of Coca-Cola stuffed into the elastic waistband of her tutu. She wants to sit beside me too, and she asks me my age and tells me hers and then she asks me what I do and I think that is a very weird question for a ten-year-old.

What do I do? I ask. You mean, like, in life?

She nods, sits with her legs crossed and her hands clasped.

I tell Nina that I am in training to become a famous author, because I think that is the sort of thing children like to hear.

She pats me on the arm. That is so nice for you, Thomasin. And then she leaves.

Nina is sort of the worst person in the world right now but also I love how confident she is, says Nance. She's kind of everything I should be as her mother. I'm not oblivious to that fact. She taps ash into a tiny green glass tray.

I sip my tea and watch Nance's growing colder on the side table.

The curtains are bright orange and patterned in large uneven circles. I think about how I could perhaps comment on their brightness, the way they frame the window and the slightly grim view beyond it so nicely, and then Nance speaks again.

There's no point tiptoeing around it, Thomasin.

There's no point tiptoeing around it, I repeat, picking at the skin around my fingernails. This is something I started doing when I was nineteen. It's a weird habit to pick up as an almost adult, I think.

My phone is in the back pocket of my jeans and its sudden vibration makes the whole couch groan.

When your dad phoned he didn't say much, but he did say you've been having a bit of a rough time and that third year was a bit rubbish for you.

Yes, that is true.

As the semester was finishing, when I was meant to be doing things like revising and writing and going out, I started going home a lot and just climbing into my childhood bed and my dad would come home from wherever it is he goes now he is retired and just find me lying there.

I say: I think I weirded out my dad a bit.

He did say he got a bit weirded out. He didn't say it in those exact words, though.

I'm sorry if it feels like he's palmed me off onto you.

You're an adult, honey. You can palm yourself off wherever you choose.

Nance, I say, I like your curtains. Did I mention that before? How much I like them?

I am staring at those orange curtains and thinking about the days and nights of not eating or stuffing my face with all the delicious things. Mostly I would stuff my face and not go outside and pick at myself in the bathroom mirror and try to heave my guts up over the sink so I could at least take out what I was putting in. Always failing, always Claudia banging down the door: Dude, we are going out and my stuff is in there, can you hurry up? Little girls' night intervention over supermarket cocktail cans and microwave meals. Them saying: Come on, girl, you're not really yourself any more. But meaning: You are boring and unlikeable now and we can no longer idolise you. Me, out into the meadows curling my toes in the grass in the dark snot running out my nose and into my mouth and this saltiness goes on for days and days and it feels like there is no end even under strip lights in seminars tearing at the pages pressing the metal of the ring binder into the soft flesh of my hand or my leg and then not showing up to class at all and then Leo, scowling, where's my girl gone where's my fun Thomasin and my girls agreeing kind of looking at him with big shimmery eyes and saying yeah yeah you were always the loudest and the funniest and the most confident was it something we said or he said or your dad said or what? Me, picking at skin.

Yes, I think you mentioned the curtains. Or maybe you didn't until just now. Everyone seems to like those curtains.

I think, Nance, I say, my aunt's name still strange in my mouth, I think I just want to be back to myself, you know? Especially for my final year. I just want to be, like, a person.

I slide my phone out without standing up and the message is from Claudia: You left on kind of a weird note so just wanted to make sure you're there and you're fine and stuff. Elaine wanted to text but she was too scared. I told her to suck it up so expect something from her soon. Please reply this time. XXX.

Sometimes I try to sabotage my friendship with the girls, push their limits a little. I reply: Need some space. Don't be a bitch Claudia. XXX.

She replies almost instantly, a long message I can't be bothered to read.

I type: I really don't care, and then I press send.

It's not that I don't ever want to go back. It's just that right now what I want to do is slide into the soft furnishings of this colourful place, wrapped in fluff and hidden from sight, living off the crumbs between the couch cushions.

Thomasin? Nance is sitting next to me, just sort of staring into my face and holding out a cigarette. Just this once. Don't tell your stupid old dad or he might literally kill me.

Finn on one side, sleeping now, and Nance on the other. I take the cigarette and Nance lights it and I breathe it in and she puts an arm around me. When I moved here I wondered how a place could be so boring and so bizarre at the same time, you know? There's some weird things and weird people and I know you'll be an old hand at weirdness coming from the city, but things here are different.

Different is probably good, I say.

But then I think of the straw girl on the high street, swaying. I wonder whether I really am an old hand at weirdness. Already I am starting to see the countryside not as this free place, cool fresh air and rolling hills, but something hot and tiny, contracting. I reach for my aunt's hand to check that it is real.

You know that outfit Nina is in, Nance says. She's part of this wee dance troupe at the local church and they sent all the girls home with leotards and a pack of sequins and an order for the mums to get to work. Sew every individual sequin onto the stretchy spandex, they said. I think not. And Nina won't take the bloody thing off so it's a constant reminder of my inadequacy. I'm going to try and just glue them, I think, but if all else fails she'll just have to be the little troupe weirdo in blue.

When Nance laughs her big earrings ring and she says: Oh, Thomasin, and I think she is sort of like a big bright bell herself, clanging a weird old song that makes me feel like a child. She asks me if I want to watch reality TV and I tell her I do and I rest my head on her shoulder and we scream at the screen.

Two

I wake up in Nance's spare room – fold-down camp bed laden with patterned blankets, tiny wooden desk against a window looking out over what I initially think is a back green. Actually, it is marsh land, stretching on and on up to a walled field boundary. Everything outside is green and brown and purple and dewy and even though the sun hasn't really risen yet, there is a sort of eerie paleness to it all. There is a framed picture of Nina and Finn in a bare forest up a hill somewhere. Between the trees there is a town and it may well be this town but it could also be anywhere around here. It is winter, which is a far-off dream, and a younger Nina is in a pink puffer with her hair in ratty pigtails, a puppy version of Finn has a tartan bandana around his thick neck.

Winter in the city is frost on the meadows and on the monkey puzzles in big front gardens and rows of boxed white hedges and delis in town with preserve hampers on display and misty glass in overpriced cafés cluttered with tourists in snow suits and gift-shop jumpers and it is the big market filled with tat and the Ferris wheel going round and round, clammy children with their gloved hands pressed to the glass looking out on the old smoke-logged monuments, and red-lipped women on screens outside shopping centres and girls in sequins clustered outside pubs bouncing from one bare goose-bumped leg to the other and tarmac that cracks in the cold and buses filled with people, the windows steaming up so from the outside it is all just indistinguishable colour. Or, inside, a stranger is pressing himself against you as the double-decker hurtles down the mound and a middle-aged lady is asking you and the leg you smashed on the ice and the cast you are wearing and the crutches you are holding to give up your seat for her and her terrier. You say yes, obviously, every time. Everyone is watching you.

I lie there for a while as the sky lightens and then Nance appears at the door with a mug of coffee and a plate of toast with jam. I won't wait on you hand and foot every day, don't worry. She takes a bite out of my toast and then sets it on the bed.

I call this room my office but I don't do anything official so it just sort of exists in its own wee world.

It looks very official to me, I say. And then I tell her I like the space, because I do. I like the glass candle holders and colourful candlesticks along the windowsill, the stack of books on the floor by the bed.

Move stuff around however you want, obviously. She toes a different stack of mass-market paperbacks until they look dangerously close to toppling.

I take a bite of my toast and the jam stings the back of my throat when I swallow. I cram the toast into my mouth and then I lick the crumbs and the jam and butter smears off the plate and Nance nods approvingly.

Hungry?

Starving.

Finn comes in then, howling, saliva dripping at the corners of his mouth. He stands over me, a grey giant, and I pull my knees to my chest. After a moment, he seems to remember who I am and he snorts slightly and climbs up onto the bed, which creaks under his immense weight as he nestles under the covers beside me.

You don't mind if he chills with you for a bit, do you? Nance asks. I need to get dressed but I've got the day off work thank the good lord and I've got something nice planned for us. She puts a hand on my cheek and says: Ah! Ah! This is so exciting!

She disappears in a cloud of blonde and perfume and deep-teal dressing gown and I press my nose into Finn's back, who sighs but accepts me, and chew the last crumbs of bread in my mouth into a pasty pulp.

I hear Nance clattering about in the bathroom and I need the toilet but I don't want to move, don't want to disturb her or take up more space in the already small flat, so I just sit there swathed in covers, fiddling with one of the books from the stack by the bed. My phone is just out of reach. The last thing I did before I went to bed was send a text to Leo: Goodnight, Leo. I still love you even though I am really weird right now. XXX. Always, drifting off staring at the screen, waiting for his response.

Now I zone out for a minute, trying to pick the plastic cover from the paper. I stop, drop the book onto the bed. I imagine my dad coming in, looking around, saying nothing, walking out.

Nance returns, Nina in tow: So, I know you've just got here and all, but how do you fancy a swim?

I used to like swimming but I don't think I have tried it since gym classes in the high-school pool. I had a body I really felt good in then because I wasn't fully developed.

OK, sure, if you want.

Sensational, Nance says, and I think she really means it. We'll drown your sorrows in the icy water, Thomasin.

Nance drives us up to the reservoir, me in the back clutching Finn so he doesn't try to jump out. When I get in, the car seat is boiling and he recoils into me. We are rounding the side of the hill past the big old hotel when the back door on Finn's side flies open. Finn hisses and clambers over me to safety. I cling to Nina's headrest and stare at my feet. The ground is wrappers and old cans and scrunched-up napkins.

Oh, the door always does that on an incline. Nance laughs. Poor guy hates it. He once just jumped out and wandered home, you know. Can you believe that? Can you?

I can actually sort of believe that, I reply, door still flapping, car spluttering on.

I brace myself, one hand still on the seat in front, and grab the open door, pull and slam it shut. A group of boys in the hotel car park are watching and laughing. I stick my finger up at them and it makes them laugh harder.

God, it's not that funny, is it? I say, and Nina says: But it is so embarrassing, Thomasin, and it is always like this.

Finn Finn Finn. Nance, in another world, sings his name. We have been jostled in the back of the car for the past fifteen minutes and his claws have dug into my exposed thighs and now he licks my fingers apologetically, guilty boy, and I kiss his leathery snout.

Turn the radio off, Mum, says Nina. It's all just adverts. You always make us listen to the adverts. And then: The sun is extra yellow today. Do you guys think the same thing?

I quite like the adverts, says Nance as we pull up to a small patch of gravel car park that is already half full.

Because I have just got here and haven't seen the town outside of cars and the apartment, I feel as though I am in some sort of limbo between the city and here. A temporary hold on being. The thought makes me breathe a little easier as I remove and fold up my old jogging bottoms and sweater and stand in nothing but one of Nance's slightly too small swimming costumes, staring out at the nearly still surface flickering in the morning sun. I could be anywhere or nowhere or everywhere, even.

Nina squeals with joy and runs across the muddy bank. She is wearing her turquoise leotard, and the few sequins Nance has managed to attach come loose in the water.

Mum. Nina points to the flickering gold, and Nance, cigarette between her manicured fingers, says: Ach love you'll stand out now, won't you? They'll stick the wee blue girl in the front of the class.

So embarrassing, Nina says, but she is smiling and wading out through the thick mud into deeper water and she isn't even flinching at the cold so I suppose the sun has warmed up the shallows. I can't remember ever swimming in open water that wasn't the sea.

The reservoir is wide and flat and one side is bordered by the big concrete dam and the other is green and wild, two halves equally marred by heatwaves. The sun sends lights across my vision.

There are other families at the reservoir too. Children with plastic buckets and spades as if we are at the beach and blankets spread out over the grass and I see packets of slimy meat and cheese slices and cans of beer and wine in plastic cups. There is a baby in a pop-up tent clutching an iPad.

A ginger-haired girl on a pink blanket is lathering sun cream onto her freckled skin. She looks about my age. There is a hardback beside her and, when she is done, she lies down and picks the book up and holds it open above her head, casting her face into shade. She's wearing a pale pink bikini top and little denim shorts and I think these colours look nice against her hair and skin.

I look over to Nina and Nance and Finn and they're all standing in a row in the murky water, smoke puffing from Nance's small frame. When I turn back to the girl, I expect her, for some reason, to be looking at me but instead she is laughing at her book. She is wearing wire headphones and the white cable trails down her stomach and into her shorts pocket. I am jealous of her because I haven't laughed at a book in a long time, but also because she is in a bikini top and shorts and I have left my grey sweater in a pile by the car and Nance's costume is emerald green and I feel grotesque and, as I stand there just looking, I start to convince myself she is laughing at me.

The water is up to Nina's waist now. It is like quicksand, she says, and this makes her want to go in further. She squeals, wades out.

Oh no no no, Nance is saying. Nina, sweetheart, I love you and all but not a chance I'm going out any deeper and Nina is pulling her hand and she puts her cigarette out on a rock and tucks the half-smoked thing into the strap of her swimsuit and that single act is obsolete anyway because they are wading out out out until all three of them are in deep and they're treading water shouting: Thomasin come in COME IN.

I leave my towel up the shore and start to walk towards them. My feet aren't used to being without shoes and I feel every twig and stone and hear every crunch and it sounds like my bones. I shiver and go to wrap a jumper around myself and realise I don't have one and realise, too, that this is the first time in a long time I have been without a big baggy thing to cover myself.

The ginger girl really is watching me now, sucking on a Capri-Sun from her family's cooler. I walk into the water and it is biting so I can barely breathe and it stings my skin at first but it is a nice respite too, and the ground is soft and mushy underfoot. I am starting to sink in, lifting my feet is an effort. As a child, I assumed quicksand would be one of my biggest concerns as an adult. Quicksand and piranhas and maybe boys. I wonder how deep I would sink if I stood still and let myself go.

Instead, I walk on towards Nance and Nina. Finn paddles over to greet me and he jumps up to lick my face, paws on shoulders, and this pushes me in and I go right under and for a second everything is really, really dark.

Thomasin? You OK? I break the surface into blinding light and my damp fringe hangs in my face and I am laughing and I imagine the ginger girl has sucked her juice dry so that there is nothing but the crinkled silver packaging and she is crushing it between her fingers and looking at me and I propel myself along with my hands and my arms, lifting my feet so they don't touch the ground.

I'm still a little way away from Nance and Nina. Finn paddles back and forth between us. Nance hoists Nina onto her hip and Nina squeals and Finn, covered in the tendrils of some sort of underwater plant, jumps up onto her too and they topple.

I reach them as they emerge, clutching each other, Nina's little arms around her mother's neck.

I watch them for a moment and then I continue to swim out. I swim past them and their screams sound the way I think a memory would sound and that thought doesn't really make sense to me and I keep going, my strokes getting more forceful, angrier even. I push out against the water and it rolls back and slaps me in the face and I do this again and again. I realise I am quite near the centre of the reservoir because I can't hear any cries from the shore, can only see Nina and Nance's costumes as bright dots in the distance. The girl on the towel is an orange and pink and blue spot. Nance's hair catches the sun. Or rather, it is the sun.

I am treading water because although my arms and legs are tired and I'm not sure I can go any further, I don't want to go back either. There is just the rippling of the water and birds high above. They screech, dive-bomb the shore and every noise sounds like it is on the other side of a sheet of plastic, or at the opposite end of a tunnel. The tiny dot that is Nance has her back to me, I think. There is just me and nothing else for a very long stretch.

Then I see her, and it's like she is right next to me but also too far away to reach.

The straw woman from the high street is floating in the water. Just bobbing at the surface on her side, button eyes hanging by a thread and wet linen trailing in the murk. There is hardly a breeze, but it is as though she is gliding towards me on some invisible current and this is when I become most aware that there is no one else here and I try to swim away, to the shore, but I am so tired and I don't want to take my eyes off her because it feels as though she will gain on me if I do. The straw hair comes apart and drifts away from her and she is just this big mouldy bloated sack and I try to keep myself above the surface but my head dips under and there is a current under the water that is holding my legs, dragging me, and I swallow a big gulp of cold water and I feel it behind my eyes, on the bridge of my nose, and I push myself up and gasp in the stifling air but I know this is the last time I can do that and if I go down again I will really go down because I can't swim against that current and I start to cry and I am tasting my own snot again and I scramble and kick but my panic makes me sink and the straw woman is bobbing towards me and I can't see the shore at all now, not even the trees lining it, and I go under again.

I open my eyes underwater and can make out the concrete mass of the dam stretching down into the earth. I can't see where it ends or begins so it is just this colossal wall moving towards me crawling through the deep reservoir undergrowth through Nina's quicksand through time, which is slowing. There is a tight feeling in my lungs, a rawness like a layer of me has been scraped off. I breathe in water and my body gets heavier. I try to kick myself up or twist myself from side to side but my ankles tangle in the reeds.

Drowning has never really been something I have considered seriously. Only in a romantic sense, maybe. I would have to die in a white dress, and only once I've grown my hair long. It never really seemed feasible, though. If you're drowning just swim, is what I think I thought.

And then I see the straw woman above me blotting out the light and I am floating up up as though my body is filled with air again and if I didn't already have my own ideas of what death would feel like, I might be thinking: Oh, this is it then, this is how death feels.

And as I break the water my arms grab for this odd figure and I wrap myself around her waist and clamber on as though she is some sort of life raft and my eyes are stinging and I throw up in the water and it stays floating on the surface, watery pale peach pink chunks of toast and jam and there is no breeze still, so my breakfast collects around me and the straw woman, and I throw up again because of it, eyes streaming so I can't see but I can feel it right down my front.

I am slipping and I don't want to slip, don't want to go back down, but then I feel this tightness this sharp firm feeling just below my chest to the left in the ribs like something is grabbing my waist and digging in and holding me upright and my vision is blurred but I am on the straw woman looking down at her from above, and she is a girl with translucent hair and a long narrow face and big sunken eyes that look colourless and watery. Pale pink skin, a set of teeth.

I scream and push out from her but her fingers press deeper into my side like she is trying to puncture my flesh.

Trying to roll off her now. I would rather be alone in the water and in my sick, I think, but I am breathless and I can't fight her and my eyes hurt and I can't see.

I hear movement nearby and after a moment arms wrap around me. At first I think it is the straw woman tightening her grip but it is Nance – I know from her smell – and I can hear Nina hyperventilating and I am hyperventilating too and I can hear Finn and another dog barking and a man's voice shouting and a woman hurrying her children away from the scene – you just go and wait in the car now, my doves, go on – and every voice feels so loud and immediate and then I feel sand and pebbles on the back of my legs as I am dragged out and when I've caught my breath I start to sob right into Nance's chest and I am crying: How did I get back to shore how did this happen what happened?

Jesus fucking Christ, Nance is saying, and I still can't see but I am trying so hard to wipe the reservoir from my eyes and Nance is shouting now: Someone come and help me get the bloody thing off her.

I realise that I am still holding the straw woman and she is real. Not real in the way I saw her for that brief moment, though. Nance and a man are prising my arms from her waist, which is coming apart. I slip from her, my fingers still grappling for the linen. I hold and they pull and her dress rips in my hands and they are still dragging me from the mud further up the shore and I am lying there on my side coughing up water and Nance rubs my eyes with her tasselled sarong and the first thing I see when I properly open them is the straw figure drifting off, back out into the centre of the reservoir as though moving of its own accord.

Three

Nance and I are sitting under a tree at the side of the reservoir. I can smell my own sick in my hair. Nina and Finn are in the car with the doors open and the engine on so they can listen to music and every so often I hear words and sounds from the charts.

We sit in silence for a while, me wrapped in her sarong, and I watch the people high up and far away on the dam wall wandering up to the edge and looking over into the water. A bird dips its tiny red beak into the reeds. I look out to the centre of the reservoir for the straw woman but the sun hitting the surface of the water obscures my vision. Where I was is bright white negative space now.

Nance sighs and tosses a cigarette butt into the tangled mass of tree roots. She lights another and takes a long inhale. She offers it to me but my lungs are still stinging and I am panting a little so she just holds it there, between us, and I watch the smoke do a stagnant dance in the heat.

After a while, Nance sighs again. What was that, then, Thomasin? What the bloody hell was that? There is a deep line between her thin brows.

She is angry. This is not what I expected and it hurts, deeply.

You were so far out we couldn't see you, and it's not like I'm a strong swimmer and it's not like Nina or Finn would've been any help and you know people have died here before, Thomasin, every summer people die here and just, just what if that had been you? What the fuck, Thomasin, what the actual fuck?

Nance. But then I can't say anything because although I want to please her I don't feel I should have to apologise. All I want is to be held, to bury myself into her swimsuit and feel enveloped in the sarong, have its softness draped around us like a tent.

What? She gets up and brushes dirt from the backs of her legs. I want this to be a good summer for you, Thomasin, and I like you and it's not fair you feel like this and I want to do what I can for you, but there are some things I just can't do.

Nance, please don't be angry at me. It comes out whiney and I feel like a big simpering slug just clinging to her, to her leg, to Finn's fur or her daughter's hair.

Just go and get yourself dried off, all right? You can get changed round the side of the car. I'll take Nina and Finn on a little wander. I think I should try and explain to her what happened.

I wish someone would explain to me what happened, is what I think at first, but then I watch her walk away and the numbness settles in and I can stand and walk, too, and I make my way over to the car. I feel OK now, I think. My empty stomach gurgles and what was fear is now hunger. I am OK, but I am also ravenous. The radio is off but the doors are open. Nance's costume sagging and stinking, I start to strip.

I use the sarong as a towel, half wrap it round me and shimmy out of the sticky one-piece. I grip the post of a large metal sign to steady myself. The sign says: BE AWARE UNDERCURRENTS, WEEDS, ALGAE, DEBRIS, STRUCTURES! DEATHS HAVE OCCURRED AT RESERVOIRS. OK, is what I think. The sun beats down on my naked body and part of me wants to throw my wrap to the ground and run back into the water and go deeper this time.

Instead, I pull on my pants and my big sweater, too, because even though it is so hot I have nothing else, and I am about to get into my jogging bottoms when an old lady with a short perm and a set of hiking sticks comes round to my side of the car and lets out a cackle and says: Just checking if the coast is clear, dearie.

I open my mouth to respond but I don't really know what she means, and as I am fumbling with my trousers, trying to pull them up my damp legs under her strange gaze, an old man that looks like her twin but is probably her husband appears, laughing too.

Just getting the wife to check you weren't naked or anything. He winks and that wink makes me feel like I am about to throw up again.

Instead of saying anything, I give them a wide dumb smile like my body is a thing to look at and laugh about, like I am in on the joke, but like I should be embarrassed, too, and I am embarrassed, and I feel my face flushing and I tug on my waistband.

They are walking away, both laughing still, and I finally get my trousers round my waist when the man turns around and his smile is a leer and he says: Part of me didn't want to see you naked, but part of me absolutely did.

This time, when he looks at me, his face flickers, briefly. It is as though his features have distorted, his expression rippling from his own lecherous smile into something other, something with intent.

I jerk backwards and the movement shocks him, the uncanniness dissipates.

Everything OK, my dear?

Um, is what I manage to say, and I can feel that I am smiling because my face hurts from the strain and that smile is not my own.

Another wink and they are gone and I double over, palm on hot car metal, like I've been punched in the gut.

On the drive back to the town, Nina sits in the front again and I am thankful for it. I catch Nance looking at me in the rear-view mirror, but I refuse to meet her gaze. Nobody says a thing and there is no music and the door doesn't fly open on an incline this time and I wish it would because I want Finn to clamber over me so, so badly.

OK, says Nance when we get up the stairs and into the flat. Let's just watch something, yeah? I don't think I have the capacity for anything else right now.

Silently, almost solemnly, Nina drags her duvet into the living room and the three of us sit on the leather couch. Finn is delighted, sprawling out on the linen one, grey head resting on a cushion in a very human way.

I think about offering to make a pot of tea, to grab Nance's cigarettes and lighter from the side table in the hall, even. I know how bad I must smell and I want to wash the reservoir and the sick from my body but I am wedged between Nance and Nina and I don't want to move.

We watch a programme where they take a haggard woman and put her on an extreme diet and cut up her face and file down her teeth to snap on veneer caps and give her streaky highlights and send her back to her family swaying in a bandage dress and kitten heels. The woman's name is Maureen and they give her so much surgery that by the end she has forgotten everything she has had done so she just stares at the camera and she says: They sorted out my nose, I think, and did some sort of sculpting thing around the jaw. About halfway through, she manoeuvres around her house, white bandages obscuring her face like a mask. She grips onto the kitchen counters because she is unsteady on her feet and she takes prescription painkillers with water from a plastic sippy cup and she lowers herself slowly onto a rigid couch and her blue eyes peek out from behind the white, which is stained with yellow face fluids, and she tells the camera: I'm just so excited for the future. It feels like everything is finally opening up to me.

Ach that's actually really nice, says Nance. She's empowering herself.

When Maureen, shiny without her bandages, is reintroduced to her family, at first her children don't recognise her. It is me, she says, lowering herself down to them, big white smile pleading: It is me.

Go and pause it, Mum. I need a wee. Nina gets up and takes the whole duvet with her. She drags it across the rugs like she is a little queen.

You're OK, Thomasin, OK? says Nance when her daughter is gone. She looks at me closely. You're OK.

The straw woman.

What?

I've seen that straw woman before, Nance. She was near the flat, like, on the street.

I've never really got used to them. But that one, I mean, it was good she was there, you know, because at least you had something to cling on to.

It's just, I say, it's just I sort of felt like it was her clinging on to me.

Without it, I mean, god, Thomasin, I think we both know what could've happened. Underwater currents are no joke. You are a lucky girl.

I just feel like it is quite weird that the same straw woman was in the high street when I arrived and then in the water and, I don't know, do you not think that is a bit freaky?

It is bored teenage boys, probably, dumping her in the water because they have nothing better to do. When weird things happen around here, they usually just happen because of bored teenage boys. And then, again, she says: You really are quite a lucky girl, though, Thomasin, oh my god.

Yes, I mean, I guess. I don't know.

Nance stares at the screen so she doesn't have to look at me, I assume, and her face is vacant for a second. I don't like the straw figures, she says, her voice flat. The admission takes me by surprise.

I don't like them, she says again. I've been here quite a lot of years now and there they are every summer and I have never helped make them. When I look out my window and see people stuffing straw into old sacks and giving these things their clothes to wear, it's like, I don't know, like I am remembering something that never happened.

Then she snaps back into herself and looks at me and says again: You could've drowned, though, Thomasin.

I want to be angry at Nance for being angry at me. She knew about these underwater currents, knew people had drowned because of them, and she watched me swim out and out and out and then shouted at me for it. But I can't be angry at Nance because Nance's intentions were to make me happy, not kill me, and we are sitting pressed together even though Nina has got up so, if she wanted to, there would be space to move away from me. Nance hasn't moved away from me, though, even though I stink of my own vomit. She presses in even closer.

We don't have to say anything more about it, OK. Things happen and then they are over.

I'm OK. It's all just, like, whatever.

She asks if I want a sandwich or a coffee or something, tells me she can even do an iced one, or something stronger, or nothing at all. I am hungry, hungrier than I have ever felt, I think, so I say yes to it all. I realise I have no idea what time it is now. When we got in, we shut the curtains to block out the late-afternoon sun.

I go to bed in Nance's spare room and wake in the middle of the night in Leo's flat, in his firm double bed. He snores softly, tries to put his arm around me but cannot because my stomach is so big. I huff and haul myself up, stumble through to the bathroom. I bang myself against the door frame as I leave and then do it again, harder, but still he doesn't wake. His bathroom sink is a concrete square, the mirror above it small and frameless. I observe my pregnancy in the glass. I wonder how many months along I am and realise I do not know. I will ask Leo in the morning, I think.

I turn on the tap and hold my lips to it, drinking in big gulps. The water tastes metallic and has filled my throat – I splutter, pull away, wretch over the side of the bathtub and watch water splattering into the plughole where my own dark hair coils like a fist. I realise I cannot go back to bed until I have undone myself and stepped right out of my skin. To be myself successfully, I reason, I will have to be someone else entirely. I decide to start with my distended stomach, pushing the smooth hard skin until it softens under the warmth of my hands, until I can grab pieces of it and pull. The skin comes off painlessly, like a casing of dough. I need to get to the meat of myself and so I dig my fingers in further. My insides are rough when I reach them, and they crunch and smell like damp undergrowth when I take them out. I start to panic at the unfamiliar texture, feel my breaths coming faster, my movements more erratic. I pull and pull until I am empty and there is a pile of wet straw on the bathroom floor. When it is done, I kick the straw under the bath and go back to the bedroom. I don't want Leo to see me without the bump, so I slip under the bed instead. Finally, I am small enough to fit in the spaces between things.

The next morning, Nance has a shift at the hotel beside the hill and on her way she drops Nina off at a summer day camp run by the school. Nina in her white socks and denim shorts, patterned jumper looped into the strap of her JanSport. At school, I carried a handbag and I wore stretchy cotton tube skirts and shoes with cardboard soles and tights that would sag between my legs, the laddered nylon dipping below the hem of my skirt, and we would all wear denim jackets or faux leather that would soak up rainwater and stink of damp. Supermarket beauty-aisle make-up and acrylics and me feeling beautiful and electric and lonely. I think this old self of mine might have bullied the person I am now. I might have bullied Nina. I would have been so happy.

The weather has turned and it is grey and I am quite glad, honestly, because I can wear my sweater and my jogging bottoms and not look like a complete freak. Not that I plan on looking like anything, actually, because I do not plan on going outside.

I wander into the kitchen. Wooden counters and yellow wallpaper with little blue birds, but the paper has been pasted on upside down so the beaks are pointed towards the floor. I rifle through the fridge and take out a square of cheese. I remove the entire block from its packaging and cut it into bite-size cubes and then put all the cubes onto a plate and eat the entire thing. There is a heel amidst the crumbs in the bread bin and I scrape the mould off and stick it in the toaster. There is a jar of instant coffee on the side and I make myself a cup and it is silty and comforting.

Cup in hand, through to the bedroom, staring at the piles of books. They remind me of university and everything I should be doing so I take a sip of coffee and go across the hall into Nina's room instead. Dark pink walls like a sugary migraine and posters everywhere – animated films about anthropomorphic animals and girl groups with slick hair and serious faces, little ballerina music box and a gold-framed picture of Finn, a collection of Hello Kitty figurines clustered around him in reverence. Door obscured by different little beaded bags and purses on shiny chains. Plastic moons and stars on the ceiling around the paper lampshade, but no planets. I am sure I had planets when I was younger. Saturn, with a neon orange ring. She has a single bed with a massive pink quilt. There are fairies on the quilt clutching thorny sheaves of brambles and roses, acorn hats atop heads of flowing hair. Some of the other squares are floral or plain or intricately embroidered with the letter N, again and again and again.

Stopping at Nance's door now, but feeling like going in would be breaking some sort of sacred promise, invading her space even more. I push the door open a little and inside it is pitch-black and it smells of stale smoke and I close it again.

In the living room, I leaf through Nance's record collection. I am surprised she has one, because records are things that young people put in their university rooms and never touch. I have this great first pressing, I remember a boy telling me just before I met Leo. Really, really great. You should come and hang out at mine and we'll listen to it, I think he said. We'll have a really, really great time.

There is already a record on the turntable and I fumble with the dials on the amp and the buttons on the actual record player for a bit before it starts to spin. I drop the needle at a random point, and noise comes out and it sounds like an accomplishment. If this is all I will have done today then at least I will have done this. Made some noise. Heard something. Well done, me.

Well done, Thomasin, I think I hear Leo saying from somewhere very far away. Well done, my poor, crazy Thomasin.

Setting my half-empty cup on the sideboard, lying down on my back on a soft rug, muted light dancing through the orange, digging my fingers into the fibres. Fade away and radiate.

For a second, I think, at the reservoir, I saw something that wasn't made of straw and fabric. Something living and terrifying and determined to attach itself to me. I see that colourless teenage face, those wide dead eyes.

The record stops and I jump up. The thought of silence scares me now. I take my phone off charge and there are no messages from anyone but my dad: Hope you are settling in, Thomasin. From, Dad.

He sends two texts in a row which is a very rare thing for him to do. The second text says: And hope you have a great summer! as though we won't be speaking again until September.

Thanks Dad, I reply. I really really love you. XXX.

He replies with a thumbs up, but it makes me smile because he has actually replied.

I take my phone with me to the bathroom, find the song from the record on my phone and stick the album on. I peel off my rancid clothes and leave them in a pile by the toilet, thinking that I will maybe just get back into them when I am out.

Naked in the mirror and my breasts without their too-small bra look pointed and big and awkward. I feel as though I am looking at someone else's breasts. When I touch them it is like I am touching someone else's body. I remember my dream, where I was able to just pull everything out. I travel down down pulling at the flesh. The mirror cuts off just below my stomach. None of this is mine, I say, hating every part of her, and then: You make me want to throw up. You make me want to throw up, again.

It feels as though something is scratching my left side, the side the straw woman grabbed me from, just below my breast where I can first feel my ribs. Just a tickling, a stroking, even, but when I get closer to take a look – left leg up on the sink, hands pressed against the mirror – there is only the tiniest red mark. I touch it with my finger for a moment and, when I push down, I think I feel something pushing back.

I draw my focus back to myself, out of my head. I have always had a vivid imagination, but recently there has been no room for it because I have been so sad. In the mirror, I smile. This is technically a holiday, I think. I should stop trying to kill myself, or whatever it is I am doing.

OK. OK. I repeat this to myself out loud and I can see Leo rolling his eyes and saying: Pull yourself together, Thomasin. You are not being normal.

Stepping up and into the bath and being swallowed by the hot water. White tiles patterned with blue flowers. No moths to spray with shower heads. Clear plastic mat beneath my feet. Mud still under the toenails. Fade away and radiate.

I wash the jam and the toast and the reservoir and the straw girl from my hair and my body.

In a dream, Kate McNiven puts her fingers in a girl's side and drags her from the water. The water in her time is a river running into a loch, but in the dream it is bigger and flatter. Sun beats down on the surface and Kate sees the girl as though she is seeing her from a great distance and then they are close enough for their noses to touch and Kate has a feeling of great uncanniness because she knows she is dreaming and yet she is here too, in the water, and she feels herself in these two places at once and she does not wish to help the girl, the girl who is tall and strange and does not belong, but to grasp her, to float with her to the shore because with that uncanniness is a terrible foreboding, an assuredness that bad things are coming and she has to hang on tight. Kate reaches out, then, and she grabs the girl, and she doesn't let go.

Kate shifts in her sleep, then wakes. She hears the clattering of the kitchen, the movement of other women around her. She wonders how she could have slept so deeply and yet be so tired.

Kate has been working at The Big House for the Laird and his family for a short time and it is a lovely castle-like building, really, with views of the Knock hill and the water and the town too, if she looks long enough. But she does not often have the time to look long enough. Kate steels herself, slips out of bed. She gets to wear nicer things than she would if she had stayed at home with her mother and become something of a farm girl or a medicine woman or a wife to one of the town boys and then a mother herself and then a wet nurse for other, better-off mothers. Kate makes tea for the Laird and brings it to his chambers where he sits at an oak desk trimmed with gold. He breaks his fast here because, so the maids and the younger kitchen hands say, he cannot bear to watch his wife as she eats. She wants to talk about God, always, Maggie the kitchen girl, whom Kate has come to know, told her. She wants to talk about God, which I suppose is fine, but she wants to talk about Him while she eats. With her mouth open. Food gets everywhere, so the Lady's maid tells me.

Sometimes Kate has peculiar dreams. These, her mother tells her, are just another little thing that make you special. Kate does feel special sometimes, yes, but sometimes she just feels overwhelmed. When the Laird and his wife are too much for her, which they so often have been since she took up her position in the spring, and when she'd rather gouge her own eyes out than look upon his old face, and when she is angry at God too, for not always giving her the things that she wants, Kate closes her eyes and tries to dream. Sometimes her dreams are evil fantasies where she slowly flays the boys who have been mean to her with a blunt kitchen knife. Sometimes her dreams are lovely and she wears soft clothes and is in a white marble city and the ground is wildflowers and as she gets closer to the buildings she realises they are not white marble at all but soft dark pink velvet roped with gold and she likes, she loves, to touch anything and everything she can. Her dreams recently, though, have been in a place that is quite like the town but also unlike it in every way. It is not just the water that looks different – everything is shinier there and more colourful, as though The Big House has retched and vomited its garish interior onto the surrounding area. Straw effigies line the street but they do nothing to scare off the birds that flock to eat discarded food and carrion at the roadside. It was in this strange place, last night in her bed in The Big House but not there at all, either, that she first saw the girl.

Awake in the evening on the cold stone floor, Kate kneels and prays for a good long while and she always tries to stay down there longer than the other girls because she wants to be the most pious as well as the most pretty. Amen! she says in her sing-song voice, the voice she lets loose when she is among friends. Amen! And then she slips between the covers and she continues her prayers and she hears the voice of God in her head and He is chanting and encouraging her to chant too, and she is saying: Amen! And then she is saying: Thomasin!

Part II

Take the Wildness Off

1715

you will have sugar in your tea whether you like it or not
I say to my Laird, new in his employ
and bold and flush with country ideas
sugar, to take the wildness off the tea
drink too much and you'll rot your teeth
my head silky smooth, my scalp soft and sweet
clothes pressed and good shoes too
I am a perfect specimen for The Big House, which is a castle
I am a sprite that gets away with spritely things
I am bad at polishing the silverware
and this, the Laird tells me, means I am destined for so much
    more
for silks spun into the latest styles (by real worms, he says)
for powder-blue paintings on gilded walls (they are called
    frescoes, he says)
for a golden carriage with white horses (you'll never need to
    walk again, he says)
for a hot press for my long hair (we'll make a woman of you
    yet, he says)
and although he does not know my name
and I hear him say the same to other girls
I rather like the sound of golden hair spun by worms
and powder-blue horses
in dreams they encircle the cottage and
my mother runs out
her skirts bunched in a fist

and there is Archie as he was when he had only two years
hands like a bruised peach reaching up to golden reins,
    somewhere
and atop each horse is a girl like me
The Big House maids I see in glimpses along dark corridors
against wallpaper that is in, I have been told, the French fashion
their hair goes out behind them
the girls all laugh
and I am not in this scene, my dream
I watch it as though from above
and now, measuring out the sweet stuff by the teaspoonful
more, more, my sweet thing, the Laird says
I, skittish with the tea set, shuddering yes sir, yes sir
his hands drifting a little too low (all in good fun, all in good
    fun)
when I pour the tea, I whisper my name like a curse into the
    cup: Kate, Kate, Kate.

Four

I am at the bathroom mirror again. I think it is my favourite place in the flat. The thing in front of me is massive and panting, flesh heaving on a strange quivering frame, and it is pink and glistening and everything looks textured and sore as though it has been scraped red and smothered in cream. My body is the wrong shape for the sorts of things I want to wear. It is a new body, so I am not used to it yet. I don't think I will ever be used to it, to the way it makes me feel. Something that is meant to be beautifully oversized in that sort of cosy nostalgic way, hanging on bones, is just too big and exaggerates my breasts so they look long and matronly. A T-shirt that is meant to fit cropped and tight and tiny just looks too small, so I am like sausage meat crammed in skin.

I take one of Nance's moisturisers, a rose-smelling ointment in a pretty glass bottle, and smear it on my face. I rub and rub and it gets stuck in my fringe, which I've just washed over the sink with the hand soap, and plasters it to my greasy forehead all over again. There is already a streak of toothpaste on the semi-sheer black blouse I have borrowed from Nance.

Is this top, like, professional? I asked her, and she shrugged and said: Who knows, who cares, it's what I've got.

Now I hear her from the other side of the bathroom door, rapping on the wood with her long nails.

The soap is a smooth yellow egg and I press my thumb into it.

I am not looking at my face now but the mark on my left side, which has darkened so it is very slightly visible through my shirt. I lift the shiny black fabric and there it is and I swear it is pulsing slightly. It is a deep purple like a bruise, about the size of a fifty-pence piece, and outlined in vivid red which tapers off into a sort of yellowish green. I tap it lightly and pain rushes across my ribs, up to my chest. Here, I don't get the sensation that I am touching someone else's body – in fact, this tiny mark, this thing that the straw woman left behind that day, sort of feels like the only bit of me that is really me. Not that I want it to be – a few days ago I tried again to rub it off with one of Nina's flannels. The day before I smeared it with concealer from Nance's make-up bag so I could at least pretend it had faded. But when I lifted my top up over my head at night in the bedroom with the lights off, I could feel it, throbbing. You can't get rid of me that easily, it said, and I replied: Well, no, because I don't even know what you are, and then crawled naked and shivering under the covers.

Thomasin, honey, what the hell are you doing in there?

Pulling the top back down, unlocking the door, realising the whole reason I went into the bathroom in the first place was to put on deodorant and I didn't even manage to do that.

I open the door to Nance and collapse into her arms and she holds me tight around my shoulders and I nestle into her hair again.

Ach, Thomasin, you'll be OK. She is stroking the back of my head. It's just a job interview, my love, it's nothing really, and if they don't think you're the right fit, fuck them. She is quiet for a moment and then she says: Come to think of it, I'll fuck them too. Been looking for an excuse to leave for years.

She laughs and I do too, into her body, but I know that she won't really fuck the hotel beside the hill – it is a place she talks about daily.

Your dad said maybe a summer job would be a good thing, Nance says now. And: Not that I speak to your dad much. Just a text here and there, you know. If that. And: I'm not your mum but, you know. And: You'll be able to take some cash back with you to the city. That is good. And: It's also good to be busy when you're sad, you know, nice and busy. And: I really am not trying to be your mum.

Nance works as a receptionist. She wears a black skirt suit and a fitted white shirt and kitten heels and scrapes her hair back in a plastic claw. She puts on red lipstick and she looks like a flight attendant.

She tried to get me a waiting position at the brasserie, and when that fell through she went to the hotel with the intention of putting me in reception, with her, instead. I thought that maybe I could just be silent and go through the motions while Nance spoke for me, but that fell through too, and so Nance came home from work that next night with her arms in the air in surrender and said: If you can come in and prove to the old bat in charge that you have full use of your limbs, she'll let you be a cleaner. It's all hands on deck this summer, apparently.

The night Nance tells me about the job, I phone Leo because he hasn't replied to any of my texts. I tell him about the hotel beside the hill and he says: Don't you think that's a bit below you? And then: Then again, you are studying English.

I don't say anything and I can hear a woman's voice in the background but it isn't his mum's strong posh city accent it is someone else and then he is saying: Hey, that was a joke, babe.

But I have already moved the phone from my ear, I am already hanging up.

I allow myself to believe I will never return to him, even if he came crawling and crying and laid himself down at my feet.

In bed, I touch myself and my skin is rough like straw. When I wake up, my face is wet.

Now we are in the car. The hotel is less than a five-minute drive but I don't ask why we don't just walk instead. I sit alone in the back in case the door flies open again. The black blouse has tight cuffs and a big scratchy bow at the neck. I sit and itch until my skin is hot and flushed and then we are there and I fall out into air fresher and less stagnant than the previous days.

In the car park there are family cars, bikes left leaning against railings marking the start of a forest trail leading upwards. Quad bikes, a man in cargo shorts and a lanyard leaning against one, smoking. Nance nods at him on the way in and he nods back.

The entrance is glass double doors beneath a white wood pergola. Above it rises a reddish stone tower, which splits off into two smaller towers that taper to lead-roofed points. Behind them, I can see the tips of other pointed stone towers and chimneys and tiled outcrops. Rising from the highest tower is a flagpole, worn saltire flickering in the breeze, more pale grey than blue. The hotel beside the hill is more like its own town nestled between trees than a hotel.

Nance kisses my forehead and goes to work. I thought she might wait with me, but as soon as we enter, people come up to Nance and they are greeting her and asking her questions and a girl needs help with the computer behind the desk and she looks like she is crying, almost, and my aunt is gone.

The old bat comes to collect me from reception and she isn't really an old bat at all, she is just a large old lady with a little pinched face and half-moon glasses and white hair toned with some sort of purple shampoo so it takes on a strange but not at all unpleasant luminescent quality. She doesn't smile but she doesn't frown either, just ushers me in to a bare room off the reception and stares at me with a sort of blank impassivity.

We get a lot of tourists wanting to know things. How well do you know the town?

I know the town like the back of my hand, is what I say.

It'll be antisocial hours a lot of the time. Very early, very late.

I love antisocial hours. They are my favourite kind of hours.

Would you say you are a clean person, Thomasin?

A clean person?

A clean person.

Cleanliness is important, yes.

Sometimes guests leave the rooms in a state. Sick, blood, piss. Cum. Shit. How well do you deal with bodily fluids?

I don't mind dealing with them, I don't think.

Itching at my collar, fingers drifting towards the purple spot, stopping myself, coughing, pulling at the too-tight sleeves, trying to undo one of the tiny fabric-covered buttons and release my swollen hands.

And you're here for the long run? The whole summer? We get a lot of people joining our team and leaving straight away. I don't know why. It's bad for staff morale.

I am in it for the long run, yes. I want to be part of the hotel family.

The family? God, girl, you stink of the city.

Cleanliness is really important to me. I don't want to stink of anything.

The job is yours, then, the old bat says. Congratulations to you.

That night, Nance cooks dinner to celebrate. She fries prawns from frozen and douses them in cocktail sauce and lays them on a bed of soggy lettuce and we even sit at the table to eat. When Nina and I are sat and Finn is at our feet already begging for scraps, Nance appears in the door frame with a bottle of white wine and two glasses.

Surprise! she says. The best Sauvignon Blanc Co-op has to offer.

She pours us each a glass and we clink them together and drink and it takes like chemicals and sweetness and she gives Nina a sip and she scrunches up her nose and returns to her Coke which tastes like chemicals and sweetness too, and we all eat our prawns and talk about nothing in particular.

In bed, I rub the purple mark with the tip of my finger and it hurts a little. I check my phone in the darkness and Leo has texted: Fuck are you doing hanging up? Weird behaviour considering you were the one who called.

Light-headed and exhausted, I continue to press the mark, to test its limits and my threshold, I am pushing and tapping and rubbing and feeling and, when I eventually sleep, I dream of the straw woman, of the girl with her arms around me.

Kate's dreams were not her own last night, and she is tired. She wakes before dawn, the women around her shuffling under covers, bodies wakening as minds try to cling on to the last of their dreams. Some work during the night because there must always be servants on call. Those beds are empty, neatly made, cold. Soon morning light will start to creep in from the tiny window cut deep into the wall. For now Kate cannot even see the window, never mind the sky behind it, the moon like a circle of yellow paper stuck there in the blackness of it all. They say travellers use the moon to navigate the countryside at night, but Kate does not see how this is possible because to her the moon illuminates only the clouds around it. Kate slides out of bed, dresses loudly, heads for the door. She doesn't try to keep her footsteps quiet because she does not care about the women around her in the slightest.

She only met them in the spring and she thinks she will never be comfortable in such close quarters with people who are not family.

They're always snorting and snoring in their sleep, is what Kate thinks now, so they can put up with my wandering. The door is old and heavy and it creaks, and from beneath a big bundle of blankets an old voice thick with sleep croaks: Hush, Kate. Hush yourself, you old cow, Kate responds. She feels guilty as soon as she says it – this woman, who prepares food in the kitchens and tends the vegetable gardens, looks to be of an age with her mother. Still, Kate pushes the door.

Kate, not as light as air but as fast as it now, running through the corridors of The Big House. She goes up a small curling staircase two steps at a time. This is a servants' passage, she knows, and it is proper for her to be here, but she does not feel like a servant. Everywhere Kate treads indoors that is not the house where she grew up, she feels an interloper, her stomach bundled with nervous excitement.

Out through another door she can just push with her body because this door is the sort she would often go through with a tray of tea. She is in a dark red corridor lit with candles, flames catching on golden frames. The paintings on the walls are unfamiliar men. They are not beautiful but the way they have been captured is, all pretty rich colours all plump rosy cheeks the way you usually see babies painted. Even the stern old ones clutching swords and swathed in tartan have those cheeks. Kate would like to know their names and she can see writing at the base of the frames but she cannot read. Before coming to The Big House, this was not something that bothered her. Now she is surrounded by things she feels she cannot really see.

She enters a large room where the Laird's lady keeps her jewels. Most of them are old and dusty and it is a room nobody goes into, Kate doesn't think, because the Lady no longer adorns herself in the way Kate supposes she would have when she was young. Kate cannot imagine the Lady as young in the same way she cannot imagine herself as old. What she can imagine is herself in these fine things before the household wakes. There is a mirror in this room too, so she does not really have to imagine. Looking in a mirror, seeing herself in shiny silver glass, still feels like a novelty. Kate drapes herself in pearls, and when she looks in the mirror her hair is shorter and darker and her face bigger and she is the girl she pulled from the water. This doesn't scare Kate, really. She wants to reach out to her, in fact, is excited at the prospect.

The pearls wash the girl out. Kate finds some deep blue gems instead and fastens them around her neck. She stares, she scrunches her nose, raises her eyebrows, sticks out her tongue. The girl's face moves with hers. She says Ahh and the girl says Ahh and it is like when she was younger and the animals she grew up around – cows, dogs, chickens who had belonged to someone once but were now communal and uncared for, which Kate took to mean as wild, pecking at the grass – spoke to her in clucks and barks and blinks of eyes, which should have been an impossible thing too.

Then Kate feels this other self start to split, to rise up up back towards somewhere else. I don't want you to go, she says. And now Kate sees herself again in the mirror, and she sees Thomasin too, who looks as though she is far away, but has the recognition of something other glinting in her eyes.

Thomasin, Kate says. Thomasin.

Stay with me.

Kate is alone in the room again and suddenly she is very aware she is doing something she shouldn't. She takes off the necklace, sets it carefully back in its box, puts that box in a bigger box and that into a drawer and slides the drawer shut.

A dull part of her feels she has gone too far. She sets everything back as she found it and leaves the room as the household wakes and the silence of predawn is killed by the clattering and cooking and cleaning and dressing and eating and shouting and slurping and neighing and stirring and pissing and sighing of the rising sun.

Kate. I wake up and for the first few moments the name is all I know. The air in the room is freezing and the small window is wide open. I can hear cars on the high street, and people chatting and music spilling out from the pub across the road. I untangle myself from the covers. The door is ajar and Finn comes in, nose to the ground, stopping every few steps to lick the carpet, to nuzzle and scratch his face against it.

Baby, I say, and open my arms to him. He climbs up onto the bed and I stroke his face as he mouths my wrist. Mouthing is like biting, Nance told me, but instead of hurting you he is trying to show you love.

My phone is face down on the floor by the bed and it is vibrating and I wonder what time it is and I wonder, too, if it is Leo. If it is Leo, I shouldn't answer. I shouldn't answer, but I will. I flip the phone over and on the screen is a picture of Elaine, smiling at our dinner table, waifish in her blue high-waisted jeans. Big fluffy socks because the hardwood floors in the flat make everything so cold. I let her ring out.

My first shift at the hotel isn't for a few days and Nance is at work and Nina is at camp. I get up and pad through to the kitchen and Finn stays in my stinking bed and I take my phone with me.

Elaine leaves me a voice note. I listen as I spoon low-fat yogurt into a mug, add a spoonful of thick honey and then another. Add cereal from the cluttered kitchen cabinet, chopped and slightly mushy pear. More honey.

Hey, girl, she says. I tried calling. I mean, you probably know that. Haven't heard from you for a wee bit. You know that too, obviously. OK sorry I am just talking at you. That is what this is, I guess, but I am doing it more than I should. OK anyway. Anyway anyway anyway. Things are weird in the flat without you and Claud. The flat misses you already. The shower just leaks and leaks like it's crying. I wish I could drive and I wish I wasn't working full-time and all those things. I would come and see you. You are lucky that you are able to just do stuff. OK sorry that was annoying of me. I am being really annoying, I know. This is going to be a pain for you to listen to. I'm sorry. Sorry sorry. Anyway, what I also want to say is I hope you are OK. I think it is good for friends to check in with each other. Like, we should definitely check in with each other more. OK, I love you, friend. I love you, bye. Bye. And sorry. And bye.

I reply to Elaine in a text: Yeah hi thanks for your message it was nice to hear your voice. Sorry the flat is crying but can you not? I still love you, I just don't want to keep hearing about things that just don't really matter to me at the moment.

I am standing in the hall now with my yogurt and my phone that was once Elaine, and I slide down onto the floor and press my mouth right up to the screen and start to sob and I let myself sob so loudly and I flip onto my back retching and heaving and stare up at the yellowing paint on the ceiling and the many colourful lampshades. Then I get up and I eat my yogurt, all of it, just standing there swaying. Bad things will happen if I don't leave the flat today, I realise.

I don't shower because I don't want to see the mark on my side. I think that it is maybe getting worse, darkening. Maybe I got some sort of infection from the reservoir water. I smile wide in the mirror. I manage to brush my teeth and I wash my face and steal Nance's moisturiser again. In Nina's room, I find colourful hair clips and take two to pin back my greasy fringe. I put on the only pair of jeans I brought with me. They used to be baggy but now they are tight. I leave the top button undone and fold the waistband down so it doesn't rub on the mark. I wear a top I think belongs to Claudia. In the flat, I am always taking her things partly because they are nicer than mine but mostly because I like to see her searching through the dirty laundry pile and under her bed and behind the door in the bathroom and I like to see her get angry. The top is a long-sleeve mesh patterned with moons and stars and the moons have wise androgynous faces and long noses. Something about tarot cards in cursive. Scratchy fast-fashion label. On her it looks sort of mystical and beautiful. On me, my boobs look massive and ugly.

Do you think I look cheap, Finn, baby? I ask. Do I look like a piece of cheap shit? Am I monstrous and grotesque? Do I deserve to have no skin, or something?

Sometimes I think I am not sad but just frustrated. Like, if I could just crawl out of myself and into someone else I'd be really happy.

I think about going on a woodland walk because that is what I came here for, right, to clear my mind? Something about that path up the hill, though, the Knock hill, sets me on edge. I think of the small glittering high street instead, tattered little shops and cafés letting out good smells. I think of the pub across the road, even, and how funny it would be to go in there in my strange going-out top with my city stink and order a pint and sit at the bar with all the locals.

Finn wags his tail at the door expectantly. Not taking him is not even an option. I want to be with a sweet beast, one of my hands always on him, raking through coarse fur to hot soft skin. I think that I might never leave here just so I don't have to leave him. I clip his lead onto his leather collar. I haven't seen Nance walk him yet. He seems like the sort of dog that might just walk himself. I run my fingers from the top of his domed head down between his eyes all the way to the tip of his snout.

Down the stairs, paws thudding on the carpets. The wooden double doors have frosted glass panels set into them and through the blur I can see a figure, orange and glowing.

What is that? I say to my dog. I feel like he really is mine, and I put on a baby voice for him but he doesn't look impressed at all.

There are envelopes by the door and I skim the names on them. I don't expect to find any addressed to me. I think I am just stalling, some part of me worried the orange apparition is some other incarnation of the straw girl.

I do open the door, though, obviously. My hands shake when I do it.

Oh, I say.

Standing there in the grey with her hair in braids and sunburn from those hot days peeling across her nose is the ginger girl.

You are the one who nearly drowned at the reservoir.

Finn presses his snout into the back of my knee and the lead pulls taught but he doesn't bark, doesn't try to retreat upstairs.

You were wearing a pink swimming costume and denim shorts, I say. And then: I think I was going to go to the pub across the road.

She says: You think, do you?

I say: I do.

Five

We hold our drinks as though they are hot, hands cupped around the glass, heads bent low. I think she blows on it, even, and the beer shudders.

When we ordered, the bartender looked the girl up and down and said: What are you doing here?

She laughed and rolled her eyes and said, Ach, come off it, but the ach didn't sound quite right because her accent is so posh she almost sounds English.

I'm twenty now, David, and I have an ID somewhere to prove it.

Hoisting her leather satchel onto a stool, rummaging through the contents. She sets books onto the bar, making sure to avoid the sticky patches. I take out my own book and place it on the table as if to say: Look, I read too. Then I think: Why am I wanting to say look, I read too to her? What am I actually trying to say? Picking the book back up, sliding it into Nance's canvas shopping bag, the back cover with some sweet-smelling beer or a strange cocktail or something.

The bartender is saying: Look just leave it, it doesn't matter, and at the same time the girl is saying: Maybe I don't have it. Maybe I never had it.

They share a weird look that I can't really interpret and then we sit down. Finn takes himself off to his own corner at the feet of an old man who scratches him between the ears and murmurs something into his newspaper.

Now the girl says: I am Evan. And then: I know, I know, it's a bit of an odd one.

Evelyn?

I wish. Or maybe I don't. That is kind of a granny name. No, Evan, like a boy.

I am Thomasin.

I know. Like, everyone knows.

Evan, the girl, the strange way she talks, the way she looks directly into the eyes of the person she is talking to. I notice that the bartender has flushed red, he who seemed older and so unbothered. I feel my own face getting warm, I don't know why. Maybe it is just because she reminds me of that day, the blazing sun, hot dirt beneath our bare feet.

Like, everyone knows?

I don't want to fit the town into this stereotypy little box, Evan says. Like those crime shows and things, because it definitely isn't. Like, nothing goes on but everyone does know everyone's business so everyone knew when you came to stay with Agnes and everyone knew that a girl nearly drowned at the reservoir and if it wasn't for one of those straw things being thrown into the water the night before she would've actually drowned. But everyone doesn't necessarily know that you are both the new girl and the nearly dead girl, you know?

I don't know what to say. The straw woman being mentioned by another person feels so strange, so deeply personal, that I am almost embarrassed. The actual event at the reservoir already feels so long ago, some hazy yellow thing, but still the straw woman permeates everything. It feels like she is at the table with us now.

I don't know what to say so I don't say anything. Evan keeps talking, unfazed by my awkwardness. Part of me wants to reach out and hold her hand.

And, um, my dad kind of dragged you out the water and my parents sort of wanted me to go round and, I don't know. Like, I don't know what they expected me to say. Oh, that's good you haven't drowned or something, I guess. I was sort of working up to it all week and then eventually I got myself round to Agnes's and I was just standing out there for ages and I was about to leave cos it all felt a bit silly and pointless but then you opened the door.

There is something sort of childlike about her, but not in the way that makes her vulnerable. Instead, it makes her brazen.

My aunt said they are – like, the straw figures are – a weird tradition. They're creepy and it's weird they saved me.

This isn't what I want to say, this non-thing that I'm worried will bore her, but it just comes out my mouth. I take a large gulp of my drink after speaking so I don't have to elaborate. She is silent still, so I take another.

Eventually: Your aunt? Agnes? Nance on the high street? Your aunt? That is what you call her? But she looks so cool. Evan laughs.

Well, no. I obviously call her Nance.

I think we are over the straw person now, but then: They've been around for as long as I can remember. A weird thing older than my parents even, I reckon. People dress them up in literally the worst things. Not a good look for tourists, which is good I guess cos I don't like tourists. No offence. You have family ties so it's fine for you.

Do you find them unnerving? I ask. Just because, you know, Nance told me she finds them unnerving.

Evan looks as though she is really thinking about it. She takes a sip of her beer, swills it around in her mouth, scrunches her nose. No, I don't know but, like, I don't think so. They have always just been here and I have always just been here.

My younger siblings really love them, you know. They keep their hats and scarves out from winter and save their old socks and stuff just to dress them up. I used to think it was cute. And then: That one was meant to be a witch, you know.

I say: Oh. Right.

High-school boys and guys our age with time on their hands mess with them sometimes, but what's the point really? Just a bit embarrassing, you know, chucking a scarecrow in the water because you just left sixth year and have nothing to do with yourself. It's really weird.

Yeah, absolutely, I say. It's really weird.

Evan looks at me in a sort of quizzical way. I think that, with her, I might not get away with just parroting back her words. This scares me a little.

What are you doing here, Thomasin? she asks.

I came here to escape the big city, I reply. This surprises me and I like how it sounds, as though I am a character from an old book I would've read in first year, when we were doing the classics and I had an attention span so could read them just the same as everyone else.

Very dramatic.

Also, I'm going to work at the hotel now, apparently. Really, though, I've just moved from one apartment to another and I haven't really seen any of the town yet, you know, haven't breathed in that country air or anything. I laugh and it comes out as more of a splutter.

Apartment. I've never heard anyone call a flat on the high street an apartment. Evan laughs. I just like that so much.

I take another gulp of my drink. I realise that Evan is the first person my age I've spoken to since Elaine. My first real, in person twenty-something since Leo dropped me off. Leo. I have become adept at pushing thoughts of him from my head. I try to find the energy to care.

Evan waves her hands in front of my face.

Sorry, she says, that was kind of rude of me. I don't know what to do when people zone out other than just, like, bring them back to Earth.

She is wearing a pink T-shirt like her pink bikini that day, tight and smattered with rhinestones. Her jeans are low-waisted and a few sizes too big, ragged cuffs trailing on the ground, hiding her shoes. She looks the same as a lot of girls at university, ones I hated or wanted to be. Every bit of bare skin is covered in freckles. Her wrist with the nice silver watch, the flash of her ankle I glimpse when she reaches down to scratch it. The lobes of her ears, even.

Evan orders us another round and I ask about her books and I ask all the boring questions I can think of too, like: What are you doing at uni?

Uni? She says it like it's a word she has never heard. And then: Oh, I see what you mean. No, I don't go there. Anywhere. Haven't moved out or away or anything like that. The concept is strange to me.

This surprises me. I ask her what she does, then, just the same as Nina asked me.

Oh, stuff and things. I read a lot and I've got a studio at the bottom of the garden so I just, like, make things and one day I'll sell them. And I've got all these wee brothers and sisters and they're all at school still so I just spend my time trying to avoid them and I go stay with friends down south and stuff when I get bored. Oh, and when it's hot I like to sunbathe by the water. Covered by a towel. Wearing factor fifty.

She laughs. You've kind of ruined that for me now, mind you. And then she says: Also, I sort of have an online presence.

Evan is loud when she speaks and louder when she laughs and she asks me about university as though it is something that disgusts her slightly and I start to tell her things about myself.

Dump him, she says when I, tipsy, tell her about my call with Leo the other day. Don't even give him the courtesy of a text. Just dump him in your head and be done with it. She leans in and gives me a white-toothed smile. She smells sort of expensive. Cut all contact.

Cut. All. Contact. I say this really slow and, actually, I believe it. This is what I will do. Maybe this is what I have already done.

Then Evan says: I know we've just met and everything, but do you want to go do something fun?

I ask Evan to wait outside when I drop Finn back at the flat because I am worried about the state of the flat, the smell of Nance's smoke on everything. Also because it isn't my flat and inviting a random girl up feels sort of wrong. If it was just you and me, Finny, it would be different.

He leaps up onto the sofa. If it was just our little place. And then: I'm sorry for ditching you, baby boy. The sofa shudders as he shifts himself into a comfortable position and looks at me with dark tired eyes.

I lock the door behind me – a city habit I'm not sure anyone even does here – and run back down as fast as I can. I grab the shearling jacket from the hook as I go and I know it's too hot but it's the sort of jacket that I think Evan might appreciate.

Nice shearling jacket, she says when I come out.

Evan tells me there's nothing really to do in the town except drown and suggests we get the bus into her version of the big city, which is really just a slightly bigger town. Suggests is putting it lightly, actually. She says: Fuck your boyfriend, we are going to the city. By bus because I'm slightly drunk, sorry.

I like the idea of a bus ride through the country. I also like the idea of knowing someone who can drive who isn't Leo, and I like how easy she makes things seem.

By bus it is, I reply, and we go.

The bus takes forty minutes and stops at every little town between here and the bigger town. In the fields in between there are groups of sheep, fleece yellowing as they lounge in the grass, or horses, eyes covered by mesh masks to keep away the flies.

I could drive us all the way to your city in almost forty minutes, Evan says, if I was speeding. Not that I would ever speed because I'm not an idiot and Mummy would kill me. Then: Oh god, did I just say Mummy to you out loud? Pretend I didn't just say Mummy. Don't let me embarrass myself, Thomasin. She reaches for my hand and we are both giddy.

We pass the cemetery outside the town. This place gave Leo the creeps, I say. But maybe he didn't say that. Maybe he said I gave him the creeps.

Well, Leo sort of seems like an arse. Evan hiccoughs.

A good-looking arse. People are always surprised we are together. They never used to be, when we were first a thing, but now they are.

Ew. She looks me up and down with her pale eyes and paler lashes and says: You don't care about good looks, Thomasin, no offence. Not as in you're ugly. You just seem like the sort of person that would want to try and transcend good looks, you know.

I think if I met Evan in the city, I would hate her.

All I really think about is how I look, I reply.

Oh god, don't listen to me. I'm chatting shit. Also, do listen to me. I like you.

And on and on the bus drives.

We talk more about university – me in the city moving out of the house but not out of the city because for some reason I couldn't yet. Just when I feel I am too confessional, about to reveal so much more than I care to, she brings the discussion back round to herself. I wonder if she senses my emerging discomfort and does this to be kind. I wonder if this is just how a conversation is meant to play out.

My parents were literally raging when I decided not to go, says Evan. They wanted me down in England and out of their hair, I think, and believe me, I wanted an adventure too. But more than an adventure, more than most things really, I just want to have fun on my own terms and sit around and read and eat and watch films all day, you know.

I tell her I know because I do and I also tell her she can come work at the hotel anytime she fancies because the screening process wasn't exactly intense or existent and she scrunches her little nose. Oh yeah, sure, *me* making sandwiches and tidying rooms and stuff, as though I know her well enough to know this would never happen.

We pull into the bus station.

Evan, you said that that straw thing in the reservoir was, like, a witch?

This is not what I intend to say. I don't intend to say anything at all but the words are there now between us and I can't take them back and I feel like a bit of a freak.

Ohhh, Evan says, and her face is surprisingly gleeful. There are some mad stories from my illustrious hometown, I can assure you. This be a place of witches and hags and fae and all sorts of things, apparently.

Oh?

My dad always used to bang on about preserving our folklore, that sort of stuff. He reads a lot of history, or at least he did when I was younger, and up here the local history is so interspersed with myth it kind of feels like one and the same.

That's cool.

When I was younger, like, before my siblings were born, he used to really freak me out talking about poltergeists and murders and witches and things like that. Made me think the town was cursed. My mum would get really mad.

Maybe the town is cursed.

Oh, yeah, no, totally. I mean, it completely is.

And the straw people? They're, like, I don't know.

What don't you know? says Evan.

I think that maybe she is just winding me up.

Of course it's all just hatred of women, right, I say, trying to rein the conversation in. I don't want to be talking about witches because it makes me feel like the straw woman could be listening. This is why the mythos of the witch exists.

They can have a little agency, though, says Evan. I mean, give them at least a little magic, Thomasin. Wouldn't you rather be a witch than a victim?

I didn't realise those were my only options. Also, I don't think they were really given the choice.

Evan decides she wants to go to the cinema, so we go to the cinema. We buy cans of gin and tonic in the supermarket first and she pays. She pays for the tickets too.

At the cinema, I get that sensation that I am in a film of my own and that film is set here, with the patterned carpets and the yellow popcorn behind glass and the big colourful signs with Coca-Cola logos and the Fanta orange and the pick-and-mix shelves like boxes of gems, sugar dust on the floor, and the people, more people than I have seen in once place or at all since leaving the city. Cinemas in the actual city are always these empty liminal spaces because people there have better things to do. They are showing new films and old films and the screens flicker slightly and Evan points at *Return to Oz*.

This is really fucked up, she says. In, like, a vintage way.

OK, I say. Cool.

Indeed there is Dorothy, mad as a box of frogs, so they say, and some strange machine approaching that little white-frocked girl tick tick ticking getting ever closer men with needles and suchlike and some evil older person of course and all the while that tick tick ticking and the frustration of knowing there is something more and nobody else knowing there is something more so you are mad, obviously. Dorothy in a witch's castle and this witch has a removable head that she can twist off just like that and swap for younger prettier heads and Dorothy's head is next, of course, because she is the youngest and the prettiest. I look at Evan beside me and her gaze is fixed on the screen and she looks so serious like it might be her red head next and I watch her for at least a minute but she doesn't blink.

When I look back at the screen I am not in the witch's castle any more. It is just a sort of flickering grey nothingness. At first I think I am just staring at the blank screen with no projection. I am about to lean over and whisper something in Evan's ear. Something like: Is this part of the film or what? Has the projector broken? Should we go? But then I remember that I don't know her well enough, or at all. I sit and stare.

In the centre of the screen is a dark blotch and it seems like it is moving closer. It is a static thing and it seems to push out, to struggle, even. I look at Evan again and she is smiling and laughing and I think: This is a funny part of the film, then? This is when it gets so fucked up it becomes hilarious?

The black mark on the grey screen is a woman. I see her now, the lines of her dark hair, limbs bent at weird angles. Her skin is dirty and her head hangs so I can't make out her face.

Her whole body hangs too, kept upright only by the bonds that secure her to a post. This post takes up everything now, the branches and logs piled high around it. It is only this woman on the screen but I feel as though there are so many people around her, pressing in on her, straining their necks for a look. A great thrumming audience threatening to suffocate. No, not suffocate – suffocate seems too obvious. This unseen audience longs to pinch and poke and cut and pull and bruise and peel the skin from her and then do things with that skin and with her naked bony body too, and this audience wants to see her face. Something leaks from a wound somewhere and it trickles down her neck down her chest drip drip dripping into the pyre and because this image is black and white I am not sure if it is blood or pus or spit or semen. A bit of flesh hangs half off a thigh, the skin blacking and the fat underneath white and shiny and stretched thin over muscle and bone. A bone sticks out of her lower calf, the shin split clean in two like some ripe fruit I assume to be red, and that bone, the broken middle of it, is smeared with mud. I have never seen a mangled body like this never seen someone so utterly inhuman so brutalised to the point that they are physically terrifying and I feel sick looking at her, at the holes bored into her, puckered and broken around the edges, at pale hands worn down to jagged knuckles and blunt nail-less fingers. She is breathing quickly her whole body shaking and I know that the audience all want to see her face.

    She lifts her head slightly but her hair hangs in her face still, and she is looking off into the distance towards the projector room seeing something that isn't here but is there but I don't know where there is and I stand up because this isn't the film any more and I start to shuffle along the row towards the aisle because I know one thing only now and that is that I need to leave. The cinema is busy and the people I am pushing past are looking around my big frame, taking in the screen in a sort of absent-minded way, peering round my body to get back to the picture and they are all smiling and some are even laughing and they all look really quite pleased with the way the story is going and I look back at the screen and the girl on it is the girl from the reservoir, and she is looking at me.

I make it to the aisle, feet crunching on popcorn so it is like I am walking on twigs in that place on the screen, and this is a silent film but I can hear people chanting, men's voices and women's voices all chanting or some are just chatting quite excitedly and more figures approach around the straw woman and she is still staring out, gaze fixed on me and then moving off, back towards the something I can't see, and her face is terrified and livid but also neither of those things, or any human emotion, because it is contorted in a way that makes her seem as though she really is just bundles of straw stuffed into an old pair of stockings at odd, wrong angles, spiky bits pushing through rips in the nylon.

I am at the doors when a nicely dressed man advances towards her holding a flame on a stick and drops it on her pyre. It is strange to watch a person burn in silence. There is nothing now, nothing to hear or see but that flickering white flame consuming her and the screen and everything. When that bright whiteness becomes the cinema, I double over. The pain in my side is immense. Not that constant ache, or even a sudden sharpness. This is the pain of flesh being wrenched and coming undone. There is a redness spreading on Claudia's top. It is a redness large enough and bright enough to push through fabric, illuminated by that white screen which, as I grab my ribs and whimper and scrabble for the door handle with my free hand, goes dark.

Running along the hall now and I don't know where to go and there is the sign for a bathroom and I throw myself against the doors and I stumble into a cubicle and I sink down onto the tiles and push the lock closed, clutching my body tightly, making the pain worse, maybe, but needing to know I am still there.

I peel Claudia's top from my side slowly. I smell my own sweat, and something acidic and strange that could be me or could be the toilets. I am dark red at the ribs.

The purple mark is now broken skin, raised and angry and held by tender threads like it could pull back further at any time. I want to push my finger in and find out how deep down it goes.

I actually feel sort of drunk. I touch the skin around the hole and it hurts so much it makes me laugh.

Six

Evan and I are on the bus back to the town. She came and found me in the bathroom but by that point I was standing by the big mirrors smiling and I had tried my best to dab the stains from my top.

Ketchup, I thought I would say to her if she asked. Someone brushed past me with a hotdog. I am delirious, so this seems a plausible explanation. Even now on the bus I keep it on the tip of my tongue.

Evan doesn't ask about the blood, though. Instead, she looks directly at me and she is in the window seat so she is framed so nicely by the dusky green outside and she says: What was that, like, a panic attack, or whatever?

Well, I don't know. Maybe. Yeah, it could've been.

You give me the vibe that you are, like, extremely mentally ill.

I nod. Her directness is odd to me. The way she talks to people – the way she exists around people – is the way I want to be. I imagine saying how I feel and asking for what I want and then I realise that I don't know how I feel or what I want.

Then Evan says: So, are you?

And then: Wait, no, ignore that. This is my one question: when you nearly drowned at the reservoir, did anything about you change? Like, did nearly dying give you a new lease of life, or something? I know that's a weird and probably wildly insensitive thing to ask but, like, do you feel as though you were once living on borrowed time and now that time is spent so the time you have now is just your own? Does that make sense?

Her orange hair, flashes of green, sun setting over distant hills, motorway gone now and we are going up country roads to this place I want to call home. She says: I am often wildly lonely so I think a lot about death.

Her eyes are hazel, which means they are made up of flecks of brown and green.

I think that when I went under I didn't really register I was dying. Or maybe I did but I couldn't really find the energy to care. And then I did care, after a while, but I cared in the way that an onlooker might. Everything was, like, maybe passive is the word, you know?

I feel drunk, still, but not from anything I have consumed. From that girl in the film burning burning, like my insides are oozing out.

I was an onlooker and I didn't feel passive. I mean I didn't scream or anything or swim out to help you because I'm not useless and I'm not an idiot. But I did see you.

She leans in really close. Green brown green brown and she says: I see you now too.

You know the worst thing about that day wasn't even the drowning. It was when I was getting changed afterwards and this old guy said he wished he could have seen me naked. Actually, he said he maybe wanted to see me naked, as though he was, like, still making up his mind. That was the worst bit.

I want Evan to say this: Fucking old pervert creep I want to slit his stomach in the street so all his guts just fall out into the trash or onto the kerb, or whatever. Let me do that for you, Thomasin. Let me avenge you.

What she does say is just: I hate old guys. And I hate that he was assessing you, like he wasn't sure you were worth a thing.

Evan's eyes are hazel.

* * *

When I stumble into the flat it is the early evening and Nance and Nina and Finn are in and they are watching something with the door closed. I hear their hushed voices over the television, Finn's barking as soon as I push down on the door handle.

Standing in the hall, I still feel kind of delirious. I type into my group chat with Claudia and Elaine: Guys I have made a friend. Haha. We went out. XXX.

I think about going to my room but I don't want to be alone so I knock on the living-room door. I think of Evan jumping off the stop before the main town one, still in the green. I live in the countryside, Thomasin, like the *countryside* countryside. Kiss kiss and off she goes.

Nance wraps me into a hug and I wince but I lean into that pain as I lean into her.

I got ketchup on my top, Nance.

Oh baby, sweet baby, and at first I think she is talking to me but she is talking to Finn. Don't you think my Finny looks the best when he's all wrapped up like this. She taps his leathery nose and the massive bundle that is him groans contentedly. Oh, he's just everything, don't you girls think?

I do. He is grey and sweet and kind and I didn't even realise dogs could be kind. I look him in his dark eyes and think: You would probably keep all my secrets if I asked.

Then Nance says: Leo called.

I ask Nance to repeat this several times and she does. Eventually she says: I think you heard me the first time, honey.

He said he was thinking of coming up for a wee while. I wasn't sure what's going on with you two so I just pretended the line was bad and hung up. I know that was a silly thing to do.

It was an immature thing to do, Mum, says Nina.

Is he quite good-looking? asks Nance. His voice sounded very good-looking.

I don't say anything for some time, but now she has me thinking about his golden face, his hard body, how odd he'd look in these surroundings.

Yes, Nance, he is actually really good-looking. I don't know how I ended up with him. We are not together any more, though, I don't think.

Ach you'll find out soon enough, won't you? If he comes, he wants you. If he doesn't, you can do whatever you want.

I am sort of uneasy about the fact that the decision is his. If he comes to me then I go to him. If he doesn't, he has decided that I am free, and worthless. I am caught between this constant need to be nothing, nothing at all, and this new desperation to see him. It's a gross way to exist. I want to be in private now so I can finally stab my finger into my ribs, prise apart the flesh and get leverage beneath the bone. Push push pop and out I come.

I want to text Evan so she can give me renewed resolve. I realise I never got her number, even though I gave her mine. Everything is in her hands and his and everyone's but my own.

Kate first met Maggie the kitchen girl on a grey day. She was down in the kitchen because the Laird had requested fresh scones with cream – he was always requesting fresh scones with cream, ever since he had tried them while on business in the city. Kate would pour him tea and the Laird would say: Girl, never has there been a better treat than a scone with fresh cream, you must try them if ever you get the chance, and he would say this with a smile, cream around his jowls, devouring the scone before her eyes while her stomach rumbled. Sometimes he would even lick the plate, and his tongue was cut with deep cracks and his teeth were dark yellow because anything with sugar was sure to be his favourite thing.

But Maggie – oh Maggie. There she had been as the cook spooned clotted cream into a glass bowl. She was at the wooden table where they prepared the bread. Sitting on it, swinging her legs off the side. When the cook set the cream down on Kate's tray, left to begin preparation for lunch, Maggie jumped up and pretended to stick her finger in, pretended to lick cream off her littlest nail. Mmm, she said. Kate was appalled at first and then delighted. Maggie turned to put the scones on the plate and the back of her dress was dusted with flour. When she turned back to face Kate, Kate stuck her finger in the cream and licked it from her littlest nail just as Maggie had pretended to do. This was a bold act, a terrible act, but the kitchen girl made Kate brave, and Kate knew instantly she wanted to befriend her, and that this was how she would do it.

Maggie feigned shock then let out a snort and the cook turned round from the hearth and the girls straightened their skirts and set their faces into placid smiles, knowing that from then on that was it and they were friends.

Kate takes the scones to the Laird with his tea, then she sets out silverware for the Lady and her grandchild, the boy. The Lady and the boy break their fast in the big dining room, away from each other at opposite ends of the long wooden table. It is strange, she thinks, that they do not speak. Kate does not remember her grandmother but she remembers hanging on her own mother's every word and hanging on her skirts too, and asking her questions about anything and everything like God and the flowers outside their cottage which were God too, and those cows with long eyelashes that Kate would swear spoke to her with slow, deep voices and it is called lowing, Kate, her mother would say, the cattle low, and Kate would laugh into her hot tea or her mother's beer watered down, the drinks of her childhood, and say no no no the cows speak to me and only me.

In the dining room, the curtains are drawn and the room is lit by sweet-smelling beeswax pillar candles. The candles are creamy yellow and emit the most glorious glowing light and no smoke or meaty smell. They are not like the candles in her quarters, or the candles in her home, which her mother would blow out right after dinner so they would have to sit talking round the hearth, close to the embers so they could still see each other's faces. Kate imagines keeping a bee as a pet, a whole hive of bees, each one on a fine length of string, and have them all around her tied to her fingers and her toes and each strand of her long hair. Kate counts out the cutlery as the serving girl sets bright green grapes and sliced apples at the little master's seat. When the serving girl came in, Kate told her hello and the serving girl stared at Kate with a blank face as though she had never seen her before, as though they do not stay in the same quarters and have done for several months.

I was just thinking about these candles. Do you not wish you could have a whole army of bees to make you candles like these? Kate laughs because the sentence rolls nicely off her tongue. She looks to see if the serving girl is laughing too. She isn't.

Kate puts a knife down and the serving girl, who is actually a woman, lets out a huff, picks it up and sets it back down.

What? says Kate.

Nothing, says the serving woman.

Kate sets down the spoons – big bright shiny things and she looks at her reflection upside down in each one first – and the serving woman picks them up and sets them down again.

What?

The serving woman just huffs again and Kate throws the rest of the silverware into the centre of the table. The beeswax flames shudder. Do it yourself then, Kate says. It does not matter to me.

Kate storms from the room. She has not been working here long enough to know she will be spoken about later, in hushed voices over the silverware and the polishing cloth. In the town there is gossip, yes, but Kate's world is her house and her brother and her mother and between them they storm and they stamp and they shout and they laugh and they tell wild stories and they fight, sometimes physically but always in jest, and then they forget and wild jests become quiet laughs and everything is perfect and normal and balanced. Kate believes that everything she does at The Big House will be forgiven in the same way. She does not understand, later as she strips down to her shift for bed, why nobody will meet her eye.

Now, though, to calm herself, Kate tries to count how many days there are until Sunday. This is something she has done from the first week at The Big House but now she is distracted by a large black fly that hums beside her face. She hits it away and feels the weight of it, its furriness against her palm, and it spins away in the air before returning to her face where it hums again. She tries to listen carefully between the days she tries to count, in case the fly has anything to tell her. But the fly is no cow and it has a million eyes instead of two dark ones, and she cannot read its face.

I wake in a strangely good mood. It feels almost uncomfortable, like I am wearing someone else's skin. I jump out of bed and the air in the room is thick and stale and my blind can't keep out the sun at all and Nance is in the doorway telling me that the heatwave is back. Just in time for your first shift too, you lucky girl.

In the mirror I am only momentarily disappointed to see myself instead of the witch-girl straw-woman thing that is called Kate. Then I say oh well and I take off my hot damp layers and laugh at my reflection. The hole is still small but also black and pulsating where the skin has split, as though I was burnt a very long time ago and that burn has become infected and been left to fester. I am leaving myself to fester, I say out loud, ha ha ha. Life feels like a farce today. It doesn't seem to matter. I'm living on time that is my own, or something.

I have a nice long shower and the water runs pinkish. I wash my body with something strawberry scented from the very back of Nance's cluttered shower tray. It looks as though it hasn't been used for a while because there is a line of dark brown grime around the lid, and a dark brown oval left on the tray where I picked it up. Thick soap lathers around the hole and drips in and I feel nothing even though I see pale pink suds dip beneath my flesh. I think about her sweet long face in the mirror. Obviously it is hard to reconcile her with the woman burnt alive on the screen and the thing that grabbed me from the reservoir. Obviously nothing makes sense. That sweet feeling of losing control, madness taking grip and me, blissfully, doing nothing. Oh well oh well oh well oh well oh well oh well oh well.

I walk the long way to the hotel. Down the high street, past the takeaways which will be closed until five, the pub which is open now and always, charity shops with lone old people pulling apart rails kept stocked by donations from other old people, or things they donated themselves, just to forget and repurchase. And then past the houses, which get bigger and nicer as I make my way up to the top of the town. I hear the creak of children jumping on a big round trampoline, their cries of delight. Watch this, one of them screams. No, wait, watch this. The houses near the hotel on the hill are big old Victorian ones instead of roadside cottages, three floors with bay windows and turrets and neat gardens at the front and the back. I walk past Range Rovers and Land Rovers, and a tractor drives past me, honking its horn because apparently I am walking in the middle of the road. The young driver leans out as he chugs past and asks me if I am OK. I think I stare at him blankly because he says nothing else and continues off up the winding road. I wonder if the tractor is going to the hotel too. I wonder if it is going up the Knock.

At the hotel I trade my grey sweater for a navy polo neck. No starched white shirt for the cleaners, thank god. I am allowed to keep my own black slacks, though, and wearing them again is a strange sensation. My going-out trousers, souvenirs from weird nights in the pockets. A fluorescent green plastic straw, tip chewed white and flat, a pair of small chunky hoops, once plated, with the faux gold wearing off in brassy patches. Strange, different, person that I was. Were those earrings mine or Claudia's or Elaine's? Did my mouth suck and bite that straw or was it someone else's?

Nance's old bat gives me a trolley of cleaning supplies and ushers me into the lift. You know how to clean? she asks as though she hasn't asked before, and I give that same sordid answer: Yes, yes, actually I love it.

She reaches one shrivelled hand around the metal. Try to avoid the guests. Pieces of work, the lot of them. Her spittle flecks my face as the doors between us close.

There are little traces of these guests in their rooms once they leave, though. I wash the pus from popped pimples from the bathroom mirrors. The duvets stripped of bleached sheets are spotted with yellow patches. Also, there are nice things. A velvet scrunchie under a pillow. A single AirPod. Balled-up socks behind a radiator, bright red. A thank-you note to the staff in an old person's curly writing. I think about the sort of old person that might leave a thank-you note to hotel staff, but I don't pocket it like I do the other things.

I am assigned to some top-floor rooms and I lug round my big trolley with stuff to spray and clean and I reach my hand down toilets and jump from hall to room when I hear the ring of the lift, those big metal doors starting to slide open. I manage not to run into any guests. I knock on every door and when there is no response I go in and do a bit of a half-arsed job and sometimes other women push their trolleys past me and I know I am rubbish and lazy and probably meet their exhausted smiles with some dumb stare that makes them want to dig their nails into my eyeballs.

In a bathroom mirror I see the sweat pooling under my arms, making the navy darker. A line of damp on my back too, and a spot on my side. Coarse fabric clings to the hole. My gross wet body is letting me down. I wonder what I am doing. Bleach tickles the back of my throat and I think I feel it on my hands, even through the gloves.

I allow myself to pool away into nothing on the bedspreads. Near the end of this first shift, I strip the covers and lie under the naked duvet and look out the window, where heatwaves warp the green trees. Beyond that is the brackeny mass of the Knock, looking in. It is just a hill but I feel like it is watching me.

Someone bangs on the door and asks me what the hell I am doing, says there are guests in the lobby waiting to head up, a schedule we have to keep to, and I open up and say sorry, sorry, sorry, and I push my trolley out wondering what I am doing, really, and the hours go by so so slowly and I finish in the early evening as the guests trickle back to their rooms before dinner and I check the rota and I see other women's names against the five in the morning start but not mine and I wonder if this is Nance's doing and for some reason I can't look the other cleaners in the eye as I leave because I am not one of them at all and I walk home smelling of chemicals and the sky is still as blue and bright as it was hours ago and I feel exhausted.

* * *

When Kate brings the Laird his evening tea, he hands her a thick blue beaded necklace and asks her to put it around her neck. It is the blue necklace, in fact, the one she tried on that feverish morning. It is heavy and freezing and, Kate thinks, in the light of these brighter candles, the beads are too bright and smooth.

This is the most beautiful thing I have ever seen, she says.

She pours the tea, adds his sugar, stands. The Laird looks at her over his cup. Somewhere in a nearby corridor, Kate hears a child running. She stands still, imagining the beads burrowing into her skin, becoming a part of her so she can't remove them. She does not meet the Laird's eyes, of course, but she can feel them on her.

Eventually he tells her thank you, Kate, that will be all, and holds out his hand, and she does not fumble with the clasp but returns the necklace to him with composure. She curtsies deeply and looks back at him from between the hairs that have fallen from her cap.

Before she sleeps, Kate pays particular attention to her neck as she scrubs herself. She scrubs so hard she glows red, and the soft skin comes up in rough, angry patches.

When she wakes she feels sweaty and uncomfortable. Her shift clings to her and she knows she has had a bad dream, but she can't remember what happened in it.

Part III
The Offal

1715

my girlhood was one of rough walls and hands
the stream at the back of the house trickling long into the forest
that green man's gaping maw
where Archie and the young boys would poke around with
    sticks
untouchable boys, daring the shadows to touch them
and my mother:
if I got another chance at life I would plant many things
and have the whole earth
become my verdant sprawl
and I would relax a bit
drink more tea
let us heat some water
says my kitchen girl now
my Maggie, my curious friend
smiling, peering at her feet
eyes darting to invisible doors
we are crouched on the clay tiles picking up broken glass and
it is like we are holding hands
my name is really Katherine, I tell her
although I hate it
I want her to know the truth of me, the first name given when I
    was born
Katherine and then McNiven
which came from my father who was a good man
God-fearing

or so my mother says after an evening out with friends
something hot and spiced on her mouth
Kaaaaaaatherine cried out into echoey kitchen abyss
we are eating scraps
the offal and the bones playing with this name
and other offcuts and broken bits
we feel briefly like more than just
small things called from long distances:
Maggie come, Kate come
and when it is dark I do dishes just to be near her
her at the hearth or her cracking eggs
for him in the morning
he eats about seven she says with gross glee and
I say, yes, I smell them on his breath
later still I think I dream she crawls into my bed
all the women sleeping around us
and her hot wet breath on my bare neck.

Seven

The Laird's wife is hunched so when she walks she just stares at the ground and the pretty shoes on her little feet. Little, yes, but wide as well and one big nail half off. It hangs by a pink fleshy tendril because she once tried to squish herself into a pair of too-narrow leather shoes.

The Lady's maid, a sharp-tongued gossip Kate saw something of herself in, has taken ill and been banished from service. A red rash spread across her face and neck and chest that the Lady took to be the touch of the Devil. The Lady's maid no longer works in The Big House, no longer lives in the town, even, which means it is Kate who must rub salve in the creases of the old woman's skin because in summer it chafes and gets chapped. The old woman refuses to rub herself. Kate lifts up a part of her that has drooped far down and underneath is a red line where the skin has broken. Kate thinks this is a disgusting job but she takes pleasure in it too. The Laird's wife sitting half naked before her, Kate with her hands in all these different sweet-smelling ointments. She feels as though she is caring for an elderly horse. Not in the way a stablehand would, but in the way the owner of a steed that was once very fine might. An owner in her own big house, with a fleet of better horses, but this one she likes the best. This allows Kate to be kind to the old woman. She takes her time with each bloody crevice and although she does not talk – she is not that brave, this woman is strange after all – she keeps what she believes to be a sweet smile on her face.

Strong sweet steed, more an old mare put to pasture than anything now.

Her milky eyes stare out vacantly. The Laird's wife does not acknowledge Kate, maybe she does not believe her to be here. Kate smears salve under her long breasts and powders the area after, then dresses her for the Kirk. She laces the old woman into a black gown with beautiful embroidery on the stomacher. It takes a long time to assemble the different pieces and layers of the dark dress and although the fashion is no longer of the time, Kate wishes she could wear something as complicated.

When the old woman is a dark bride again, Kate dips her head and prepares to take her leave.

Before she can, the Laird's wife says: You will come to the Kirk with us, will you not?

Kate is startled. She does not mean to look the old lady in the eyes, but she does.

When the Laird's wife talks, her words are clipped, but in the Kirk she gets so animated that she drools.

My Lady, I shall be at the Kirk as I always am.

And then the Laird's wife grabs her wrist with one manicured claw and the words she says are not her own, but those whitish dead eyes glow and her sermon is this: It will be no easy thing to go to Hell in a throng, child. Everyone there will kindle another's Fire, and make it hotter.

Kate smiles at the Lady of the house. It is what she has been taught to do. That's a nice image, she says, detaching the hand from her wrist. Everyone together kindling each other's flames.

Kate is shivering as she exits the Lady's chambers. She forces herself to walk slowly and calmly but her wrist is red and looks as though it might blossom into a bruise.

* * *

I wake up to blood on the sheets. My breasts feel heavy and sore and I am bloated but I like bleeding too. I like pulling down my pants and seeing thick red streaks and dark clots at the bottom of the toilet bowl and I like having my blood on my fingers but this time it is different because I am bleeding from two holes now. Could I give birth from that hole organically, parthenogenetically, like a seahorse, or would I first have to be penetrated by something other than Kate's finger?

Nance is still in bed, and I pour milk into the last scraps of cereal for Nina. I want Nance to be the sort of person who says: Girl, you need to get a life, let me take you shopping and we can get our hair and our nails done and leave the salon with matching turquoise gels and blowouts. But she has been tired these last few days and comes back from the hotel and falls right onto the sofa or even her bed with her cigarettes and big baby Finn curls up beside her, inhaling her smoke and her human smell. Mostly, I make food for just me and Nina and try not to unload my adult problems onto her even though I am self-obsessed and irresponsible.

I think my boyfriend is going to show up at some point, Nina, and I don't know what I am supposed to tell him when he does. Also, I am being haunted by a witch girl and I'm not sure if it is because of this town or because of me or, like, what it is really.

The witch-girl bit is not what she chooses to respond to. Nina asks instead what my boyfriend is like.

He is like the sort of person you might see on a TV show, if you know what I mean.

Not really, she says. Sorry, Thomasin.

Nina's friends buzz the door and she runs down to walk with them to her summer-school club. I sit at the kitchen table picking at the yellowing linoleum coating and eating her soggy scraps and I think about Leo and his phone call to Nance. The fact he is most likely seeing someone else. The fact that I am not fussed at all and, actually, the idea of him cheating on me makes me feel sort of good. Maybe because it doesn't even really feel like cheating – I am not that person now, he is cheating on someone who doesn't exist – but also more likely because it is a proper reason to feel like shit. I want bad things to happen to me and I want people to be cruel to me, because wallowing in sadness is fun if there is a reason to do it. I want someone to walk up to me and punch me in the face and when I cry it will just be because of that and it will make sense to everyone.

At work I drift from room to room and bed to bed, fingers raw with bleach and eyes stinging in the chemical air. I scrub shit from toilets and puff pillows into lumpy clouds and when I crouch to scoop up all the things left behind by guests, the hole in my side pulses. Before my shift, I cut an old T-shirt into strips and tied them round me like bandages. This is the sort of thing that people in the pictures do when they are injured. Men barefoot in smashed-glass-ridden skyscraper halls with a length of white cloth to stop their guts from dropping out.

I trudge through reception with an armful of dirty towels just so I can get a look at Nance. We are not meant to walk around anywhere we please, heaving our trolleys in our sweaty polo shirts, but I just want one little look to remind me that I live here, with her. She is at her desk, reapplying cakey lipstick, and she is talking to a large man with rucksacks on his front and back and little packs strapped to his side, too, and I wouldn't be surprised if he had even smaller bags wrapped round his meaty thighs under his shorts.

No, honey, I don't think you're getting it, she is saying. The Knock isn't the sort of place you go to climb, yeah. It's, like, a place for wandering. Or you can hire a bike. Whatever takes your fancy as long as it doesn't involve scaling a rock face.

I paid to come here, he is saying, English accent. I paid good money to come up here to climb.

And I can't turn a hill into a mountain, can I, honey? The receptionist at the desk next to her is listening, eyes narrowed, and I wonder how Nance hasn't been fired yet.

I mean this is ridiculous. The service here is awful. You are awful. And don't call me honey like I am a little boy.

He looks around the room for support but there are no other guests in the lobby.

I am just standing listening now and eventually Nance catches my eye but she doesn't smile, just shoos me with a flick of her long hand and this hurts, badly, and I limp away pulling my big trolley like an injured creature dragging some sort of carcass; again and again, my mind circles back round to rot.

You need to calm down, honey, I hear Nance saying as the lift doors close on me.

In a big master suite under the stand-by glare of an old television set, I slump onto the carpet and hug my knees to my chest. The hole hurts and I am tired. I wonder if this is the sort of situation I wanted to be in when I left the city. I think about how mean I can be to my friends. It isn't that I don't like them, I don't think, but I don't know. The fact that I am twenty-one and I feel like a child. I think about my dad palming me off onto his sister because a woman could handle me, surely, but not him. Over mashed potatoes and a lump of meat he said: How about you stay with Agnes this month?

Am I too much for you? was my response.

The meat was seeping blood, turning the mash pink. All I wanted was his attention but my words made him get up from the table and leave the room.

The self-pity feels good. I think about switching the television on to keep me company as I scrape limescale from around the tap. Something banal and mesmerising, like an older woman's face and body being cut up. I am scared, though, that on the operating table, with the presenters standing by, she might start to turn into the witch. Kate, on display on the screen. There is promise of her everywhere now.

Later, when I take my clothes off for bed, I realise I have bled all over everything. The bandage, my sanitary towel, the room. My body smells of hot blood.

Kate is in the Kirk with her best dress on. It is pale lace-trimmed linen with flower embroidery down the middle of the skirt. She did the embroidery herself and she thinks it looks a bit French. Most of the other ladies have tartan skirts and stiff jackets and she thinks that is dull. She doesn't want to look like an old maid, or a Highland girl. Kate is unmarried but she is young too. She wants to find a man above her station who is better-looking than the Laird. But the Laird is the best man in the parish, and when she enters the Kirk with him and his weird wife and their chubby little grandson and the rest of the household, she does feel quite special.

Working at The Big House is the most desirable job in the area for a girl of her age. She knows this because she has been told it many times, and even as a young girl she would stare at that glinting manor in the distance and see it as some sort of goal. That was when the Laird was a younger man who a younger Kate, from the furthest pew, still saw as ancient. She would fidget and fumble after each service because they had to wait for the Laird and his family and his household to file out before they could. Silence yourself, Kate, her mother would hiss, but at the time Kate could not understand why the rules were as they were, why the Laird's pregnant daughter-in-law, his odd wife, his son, why these people meant more than her own mother, her brother who at the time was a tiny child, robust and red-faced, clutching her tightly by the hand.

Now she stands behind the Laird in case his wife needs assistance. Her wrist is still bruised from the Lady's assault, but Kate is in another world. If there is a travelling gentleman attending the service, he might think me to be one of their children, she thinks. A noble girl. Then she thinks: Maybe the Laird's son will return and fall in love with me. He is the heir and maybe he will ask me to marry him and be a mother to his son. The Laird's daughter-in-law died only weeks after childbirth, so Kate has heard in the kitchens. Men are not made into widows the same way women are, she knows. They simply become eligible again. Being a mother to a child like that, though, Kate thinks, could very well be a fate worse than death. The child howls at night sometimes, gets his greasy paws on all the things Kate has just polished too. Sometimes she has to serve him and he looks at her with dead glassy eyes like a doll bloated with stuffing. He is kept scrubbed clean and glowing yet there is always a trail of snot from one nostril, a crumb of food at the corner of his little mouth. It is cruel to leave a child in that state, Kate supposes, and yet she does not want to help him.

This is what Kate is thinking while the sermon goes on. She doesn't hear a word from the minister's mouth. He says a prayer and she snaps back into herself in time to say: Amen. Her mother's voice is gruffer than the other women, and from far at the back of the Kirk she can hear that one hoarse voice above the others. She wants to be in her mother's arms a lot of the time. She wants to take her brother in her arms too, even though Archie is bigger than she is now. She wonders if her mother has washed his Sunday best, if he is wearing his hat. All his clothes are so tatty from the fields. She isn't embarrassed of him but she is glad she is standing here, at the front, while they are at the back. I love my family but look at me, her position might be suggesting. I will hold them in private but here, before God where it matters, I am a lady. Kate pokes a finger under her cap to itch her scalp. The precentor starts a psalm and the congregation follows. Kate tries to pick out the sound of the kitchen girl a few pews behind her. She cannot. She wonders if Maggie even made it to the Kirk, because sometimes she doesn't. Maggie can be bad and strange and Kate wonders how she can feel so comfortable and yet so uncomfortable in her presence.

When the service finishes, the Laird and his family leave first. The Laird shakes the hand of the minister and his wife presses something into his cupped palms. They take a horse-drawn carriage back to The Big House and Kate is allowed to spend a few hours at home. This is her favourite part of the week. She can breathe so much easier when she is not within those tall walls.

This Sunday, there is meat – the offcuts, the offal. Her mother has made a stew. Kate takes a spoonful while it is still on the hearth and tells her it needs more salt.

What are you now, her mother asks, a cook?

I spend a lot of time in the kitchen, says Kate.

Kate's week has passed in a haze of the Laird's increasing demands for her company, whispers from the other girls. Sugar to take the wildness off is something she has stopped saying, because sugar is everywhere in The Big House, in every pot on every side so there is no wildness anywhere at all.

There is also, though: the kitchen girl laughing, exhausting work that takes the skin from her elbows, counting down the days until her mother and her brother, and Thomasin, the girl, the strange excitement of her dreams. Kate has been having more and more of these dreams recently, where she is in a different body and in a different place. Or a place that looks different but feels the same.

Mother, Kate is saying, do you think that my dreams mean something? Can God talk to you in dreams?

I'm sure He can, Kate. Most likely He can.

I think He is talking to me then. I think He is talking to me through a girl.

She stares into her bowl, the brown translucent liquid. A piece of white intestine floats to the top, like thin skin. Kate picks it out, rolls it between her fingers, bites down.

Kate can hear the neighbour now, calling for her mother over the low garden fence.

What? her mother shouts back.

The front door is open and there are leaves and dirt on the stone step, which they call the porch. Kate worries that, now she is at The Big House, her own home will fall to rack and ruin. Her mother is clever and sensible and Godly but she does not care much about sweeping the porch.

What? she shouts again, voice gruff.

Mother, says Kate. Hush.

Archie laughs into his bread. He works on land leased by the Laird to a neighbour of theirs and gets Sunday afternoons off too, and Kate finds herself carried through the week by his sweet face, his confidence and his humour. He is four years her junior and even at his fifteen years he has started to look like a man. Because Kate no longer sees him every day, she is struck every Sunday by how much he is changed. On a weekly basis, even, he becomes less and less her baby brother and more and more a man she does not know how to converse with.

Eventually the neighbour shouts: You haven't seen Madam anywhere, have you?

Madam? says Kate.

Their dog, if you'll believe it. They've got some aspirations. Her mother shouts: No, I haven't seen Madam. I haven't seen her since the last time she got out. You should keep Madam on a length of string.

The neighbour shouts: I don't have a length of string.

Go and close the door, Kate, will you? her mother asks.

I am comfortable. You go and close the door, Archie.

Archie does as he is told and that makes Kate happy. The little house is dark whether the door is open or closed because the walls are so thick, the tiny windows deeply recessed. This is good in winter because it is warm and cosy and good in summer because it is cool and safe.

I love our sweet house, says Kate.

Do they treat you well at The Big House? says her mother.

Yes. They love me like I am their own. I hardly have to work or, at least, the work I do does not feel like work because I like it so much.

She does not know why she says this, exactly.

Madam! Madam, girl! Madam.

Kate's mother slaps her hands on the rough wood table, gets up. I am going to give that harridan a good talking-to.

Kate and Archie listen to their mother and the neighbour bickering outside. The door is open again and a big moth flies in, beating its wings against the whitewash.

Archie watches the moth flapping, chews on his lip and inclines his head towards the window. The Big House is out there somewhere although they cannot see it. Be careful up there, Kate, he says.

Kate says: I know. And then she smiles and she adds: But you should see the rooms, Archie. And the jewels and the paintings and, let me tell you, his lady's body is just repulsive but, oh, in glittering gems and the smoothest, shiniest silks, it just looks beautiful and everything is lace and softness and I dream it is us living up there all the time.

She laughs to fill the space because Archie has not said a thing. She thinks maybe it is because she mentioned the Lady's body, but she knows too that when she first secured her position, they would spend hours discussing what might go on within the walls of The Big House, and they would discuss this in great detail, down to the colour of the old lady's shift, whether the Laird's hair was his own or a powdered wig.

And then Archie says: You could leave, Kate.

Kate laughs. I could not. And then: Leave and do what? Something in her leaps and she thinks that this thing in her is the girl from her dreams, because never before has the notion of leaving entered her head, and even if it had, it could never ever have made her feel anything but dread.

Do what?

I don't know, Katey.

Holding this, Kate says, this position, it is respectable. It supports us well. There are other girls who wanted it in the town, but it is mine. Every mother wants their daughter at The Big House.

Oh, of course, says Archie. Every mother wants their daughter under the Laird's thumb. I'll bet it's nice and comfortable under there. His face twists, briefly, into a bitter smile. Mothers don't always know best, Kate.

Kate does not like to be talked down to by her younger brother. She does not like to be cruel to him either, but she is confused, can feel tears welling, swears to herself she won't let them spill.

Oh, and what would you have me be instead then, Archie? And, after a moment: A farm hand like you? Kate forces herself to laugh and it comes out more like a high-pitched cackle.

Archie looks as though he will speak but just then their mother walks in, dry dirt on her skirts.

Madam has been found, she announces. In the bushes, with bramble juice on her chops.

It is too early for brambles, Kate says. She keeps her voice steady, does not look at her brother. Are you sure there was not a small creature twisted in the dog's mouth? She envisions a white rabbit, blood or red juice matted in its hair. She would not blame Madam, of course, for her need to eat, for the hunting instinct in her.

Kate looks to Archie, eventually. She expects to see anger, or that same mocking smile, but the boy looks vacant and upset and he cannot meet her eye.

He gets up, tells them he isn't hungry any more and that, in fact, he needs to go out. He is already lacing his boots and heading for the door.

This is the first time since Kate left home that they have fallen out like this.

The siblings do not bid each other farewell. A precious Sunday wasted, thinks Kate.

What was that all about then? Kate's mother asks her over the rest of the stew. The old woman sets her spoon down, brings the deep wooden bowl to her lips, slurps happily.

Archie is filled with envy, says Kate. He does not like me working. Perhaps he feels he should be the one to support us instead.

Ach the boy loves you, Kate, looks up to you. His hours are long and he's lonely in this house with just me.

Kate remembers when Archie was little and everything she did was amazing to him. Let him be lonely, she says.

Although. Kate's mother chuckles into her bowl, tells her Archie is seeing a local girl. In fact, that might be the reason for his little strop, Kate. There is a waywardness to him as of late. Do not worry yourself.

Seeing? Kate asks.

Seeing, yes. I am yet to meet her but the family is good.

Kate doesn't like the sound of this. In fact, she is indignant. I bet the local girl is ugly, she tells her mother.

You're a real fishwife, says her mother, but she means it nicely.

Kate asks her mother if she is thinking of getting a dog, if Archie is out so much.

A dog or a second husband, her mother responds. And then she says: God bless his soul.

Kate doesn't remember her father, has never felt the need to try to recall those years when she was a baby and he was there. She'd much rather think about dogs.

It could be a big dog, in case there is any trouble.

The second husband could be a big man, not like your father wasn't, of course. And then, again: God rest his soul.

While Kate is home she tidies her corner of the room she shares with Archie. She supposes she no longer shares the room with Archie, really, because she lives at The Big House now. The next room I share with one man will be when I have a husband, Kate thinks. She sets her trinkets in order on the dresser and puts fresh flowers in a glass bottle. She wishes she had new candles to liven up the space, maybe even a little fold-out looking glass to reflect their light.

She slips a nice polished stone off Archie's bedside table into her pocket. They are tie-on pockets that her mother sewed before Kate got her job. To stash all your pretty things in, she had said. Kate plans to show the stone to Maggie when she gets back. We will talk about how pretty and potentially powerful it is, Kate thinks. She also thinks that it could ward off bad dreams. In stealing it, she hopes she is cursing her brother sleepless nights forever. I really am turning strange, she thinks, and then: Oh no, I am turning strange at the age where I should be turning beautiful.

She repeats this sentiment to her mother, who says: You are a special girl, Katherine.

Kate does not like when her mother calls her Katherine, because Katherine is not her name. I don't just want to be special, Kate says. I want to be beautiful.

Her mother says: I think it's time for my own Madam to be on her way now.

Before I go, Mother, could you please fix my hair?

It is only a simple braid her mother does for her, because a simple braid is all her mother can do, but Kate loves the feeling of those rough hands in her long hair.

Before Kate leaves, she lingers in the doorway of her old room, imagines her little brother tossing at night amidst the rough sheets, lying awake as the crack of dawn creeps in across the whitewash and the next day of work begins.

She throws the stone back into the room and it lands with a muffled thud on the mattress.

The walk back to The Big House is a long one and on the way Kate passes the Knock. The Knock hill sits beside the town, and from her house it looms bright green in spring and yellow green in summer and brown in autumn and white in winter. It is not a tall hill, really, and from The Big House it is an inconsequential bump in the landscape. Still, Kate feels as though it occupies space, blocks out light. She wonders why, in all her life, she has never walked up to look at the view, and then she continues past because she has work to return to and, while the Laird won't wait forever, the Knock will.

At night she has a dream that the hole in Thomasin is a hole in her. She reaches in to feel the girl but instead there is the offal, and Kate starts to pull the pieces of dark liver out, then the strings of washed white intestines that come to lie in a pile, bloodless on her pillow.

Eight

Leo is leaning against the bonnet of his shiny car. He is smoking a menthol cigarette and wearing a grey marl sweater, the fine knit stretched across his broad chest. The sweater looks like something his mum might have bought him many years ago and I wonder what made him want to put it on for me today. It is hot, still, but his skin looks smooth and dry.

I want my feet to stop walking towards him and turn in the other direction and take me away. He is looking right at me though, and even if he wasn't I would probably continue to go to him. I am in my hotel polo shirt, stomach bloated from the couple of sandwiches I scoffed with a juice in the brasserie after my shift. Underneath, I can feel the makeshift bandage chafing. I keep walking, yes, but at the same time I ruffle my fringe so it sits better and I undo the buttons of my top so I can pull the collar over the embroidered hotel logo.

When I stop just before him, he is smiling, not the sort of half smirk I was expecting, but a true smile like the ones he used to give me when we first started going out. All those glittering pearly whites.

I've missed you so much, my girl, he says.

My girl, like I am an old pet. Him an adult child returning to the family home and the decrepit dog.

You look so good, he says next. So much healthier.

There is no way in hell what you are saying is true, Leo.

No, no, I mean it, baby. This country air is doing something for you, I swear. Makes me think I need to get out the city too, you know.

I have kept my distance from him but he pushes himself off the car and walks towards me. Maybe I need to come out here and spend some proper time with you, Thomasin.

You can't be serious, Leo. The thought of Leo in the bed with me in Nance's flat, Leo and Nina at the dining table, Leo tugging Finn's lead just a little too tight on a walk, is horrifying. It reminds me that in so many ways I am not past caring, not past wanting and not wanting.

Deadly serious, Thomasin. I just think we should be spending more time together. And I'm sorry, you know, I really am, if I came off strangely on that call. I just don't know what to do with you when you're acting all weird, you know, it's weird for me too. But I'm here now and I want to be with you and I've said sorry for whatever it is you think I've done, so just let me, you know, let me be here.

His expressive actor's hands, his minty fresh scent, new little gold stud in one ear.

This is enough to keep me interested for longer than I should be.

And then he says: I love you.

I reply: I bet you say that to all your girls.

What the fuck did you just say? He runs a hand through his hair and he steps back and sighs and looks up at the sky, playing exasperated, and he says it again: What the fuck did you just say?

I said: I bet you say that to all your girls, Leo. And then, because I realise I should maybe minimise the damage a bit: Mostly, Leo, I was joking, but I did hear someone else in the room when I called you.

So I can't have friends now, Thomasin, is that it? Jesus fucking Christ that's a bit controlling, no?

I didn't say you couldn't have friends, Leo. I don't care who you're friends with or who you fuck, like it really doesn't bother me now and I try to let it worry me and make me sad but it doesn't, it just doesn't.

You're being a fucking freak, he says, and you're fucking delusional in general. Like, come on, I've done a fair bit for you, haven't I, so why the fuck would I fuck someone? Just tell me one reason why the fuck I would do that.

He is speaking quite calmly, actually. Once he has finished he tries to take a long drag of his cigarette, splutters, drops the half-smoked thing to the pavement and crushes it under his shiny white trainer.

Look, I don't care, I say. Just go.

Ach get to fuck, Thomasin. I've come all the way here so I'm fucking staying and we'll work through this later, OK.

Whatever, I say.

I am exhausted from the hotel. Maybe me in the city would have pushed his buttons a bit more. Maybe me in the city would have licked his trainers and begged for his love.

Leo pushes his car keys into a tight jeans pocket and heads for the front door. I fumble undoing the lock but eventually I get it and as he is walking up the stairs, he says, silently so no one in the flats can hear: Sometimes you have no fucking self-respect, Thomasin, none at all.

Nance makes apricot chicken from a greasy recipe book. She has all the ingredients laid out on the counter when we get in, which makes me feel betrayed. Did you know he was coming today? I ask when we are alone in the kitchen, her fumbling with an onion and me with a corkscrew.

She rolls her eyes. His hair is so blond, Thomasin. Like, blonder than mine but I think his is natural. Is his natural, do you know?

I think about just dropping the bottle so the red wine goes everywhere. Into the gaps between the laminate, the cracks in the wooden counters. I don't want Leo to drink or eat anything from this house.

Finn doesn't like Leo so he is in Nina's bedroom with the door closed. He howled when Leo entered and Nance tried the treat routine but Leo didn't want to touch the treats so he kept howling and now he is shut out. Nina is in there with him because she feels bad for her little brother and I'm not sure she likes Leo either. What is that, he asked when he met her, like a costume or something? She pulled at the neck of her leotard, took two steps back.

Nance, smiling and saying: This is good, that the kids are in their room. This will be an adult dinner party. And, laughing, looking at the intruder with my boyfriend's face: I should've dressed up.

I am just about to let the bottle drop when Leo appears in the doorway. He gives me a warning look. Let me take that off your hands, babe. And then: Agnes, is there anything I can do to help?

Oh, says Nance and she is flustered. Oh, just yourself just yourself. Just do something with yourself. Also, call me Nance, please.

I set the table and they talk. The chicken is in a ceramic dish in the centre. I put three big flat plates around it, give us each a fork and a spoon for the gelatinous orange sauce. I pour the wine into glasses and I give myself the least and Leo the most.

Leo watches me as I take my first bite. Aren't you going to cut that into smaller pieces?

Yes, honey, says Nance. I wouldn't want to be responsible for your death or anything.

Death by chicken bone, says Leo and they both laugh. That would be a grim way to go for you, baby.

Why are you calling me baby? I ask, and the table falls silent. We sip our wine. Nance tops herself up and then Leo, even though his glass is full. The wine goes right to the brim. Leo stares at me and I can't read his face.

Nance coughs. So, Leo, what are you up to at the moment then? Apart from being here, with us, in this moment, of course. She laughs.

Leo talks about his dad's company. Mostly, though, he talks about waking up before the sun rises and getting into health and fitness and cold showers and getting a nice suit to wear for work and how much better things are now he isn't in education, now he is really living. My mum still worries about me though, he says. And it's like, Mum, look at me. You don't need to worry any more, you know? I've made it, or I'm making it. The money is good. And I have this, to keep me young. I think at first he is talking about me, but then he fingers his new earring.

So the money is good, isn't that great? Nance looks at me and gives an exaggerated wink. You hear that, Thomasin. Lucky girl.

The truth is that I don't know what Leo does. When he talks about work I zone out and when I talk about myself I get angry that he does not listen. I think that at times we are as bad as each other. I start to wonder whether Kate and Leo would get on, then remember that Kate is not a real person.

Later, Nance and Leo move through to the living room and I load the dishes into the dishwasher. I scrape the leftover sauce into the bin. I drink Leo's untouched wine, rinse the red rim from Nance's empty glass.

We were just talking about you, says Leo, when I go through. I was spilling all your dirty secrets.

I force a laugh and sit down. I want to say something funny but I can't think of anything. I think that innately I am not a funny person and this makes me stick out in social settings.

So many dirty secrets. Like, the time you thought you wanted to kill yourself and you didn't and I had to scrape you off the floor and you were all damp and red like a weird newborn and how in that moment it was like you really were reborn and we talked about how poetic it was, after, and also how awkward it was for you, you know, starting something and then not being able to go through with it.

Oh, I don't know how I feel about that, Leo. I don't even really remember that happening.

Nance says: I think someone has had a bit too much of the old red, eh, Leo? Maybe you and Tom should get to bed.

He gets up and he tells me that he hasn't brought a toothbrush so he is going to have to use mine and when he is gone Nance looks at me with sad, wide eyes. I don't know what he was talking about just there, Thomasin. I'm sorry that he said that.

Leo gets carried away but he means well. Saying this is a reflex. I rush to defend him, still. I want Nance to marvel at how I managed to get a guy like him, even now when I don't think I want to have him at all.

Well, yes, I don't doubt he loves you. Men can be strange when they love you. I know that from experience.

Nance, I say, this isn't the kind of love I have been dreaming of, I don't think. I don't know if I dream of love at all, actually.

Let's get you to bed, sweet girl.

The camp bed is small and I say to Leo: I will set up on the floor as long as you let me have the duvet. He says: Why can't we just lie together?

I slip off my black work trousers and I pull my top down as I do so I am still covered. I don't think Leo would want to share the bed with me if he saw my side, which is pulsing as I stand there before him, but maybe this would not be a bad thing. When I am under the covers I take the top off but I keep my vest on, the old bandage underneath. When Leo lifts the blankets and gets in beside me and the bed creaks and dips, a sharp pain tears through the hole. Or rather, radiates out of the hole. Nothing goes into me and everything comes out, now. Kate was the last thing to enter.

We lie side by side on our backs like sardines.

This is almost like how things used to be, I say.

This is not at all how things used to be, says Leo.

He is naked and I touch his hard smooth chest and I trace my finger all the way up to his chin, where hints of blond stubble threaten to break the skin. I put my hand on his lips, which are soft, on the thin bit of skin under his eyes. I go up to his hairline and I put my fingers in his short hair. It is like I am taking stock of something, counting all the bits, seeing they are in order. My hand goes between his legs and he lies there and he pushes himself into me but I feel nothing so I stop. I feel deeply sad. I thought that maybe in his anger he would grab me and want to do things to me and I was ready to scream into a pillow and feel good and feel awful and feel worthless and special but I don't feel anything at all.

I think we are both just going through the motions, Leo, I say.

He mumbles something and I realise he is already half asleep. He turns into me, back pressed to the wall and I can't fall asleep with him like that because it is as though he is staring into my face. His breath is hot and slow on me. I wonder if he feels calm. A line of streetlamp light hits his face directly and for a while I lie and stare at him like that. He is peaceful and beautiful and here he really is like something from a film. I reach out to brush his eyebrow with my thumb, just to feel him again, and when I do he mumbles once more and he is saying: Go to sleep, baby, go to sleep.

He stretches his thick arms out and the bed is his.

I go into the living room and get onto the linen couch, wrap a throw around me, rest my head on a velvet pillow. Finn is in his big bed on one of the many carpets and he greets me with a silent lift of the head.

Sometimes, when I was in bed with Leo at the flat or his house, I would watch him sleep and hope he might just stop breathing.

Leo wakes me up with a cup of instant coffee. I hear Finn barking before I smell the coffee, but I think it is a dog in a dream so I don't open my eyes. Kate, Kate, I think I hear Leo saying but what he is really saying is: Thomasin, Thomasin.

Leo takes Finn by the collar and pulls him out of the room. Finn is strong, I know, but more than that he is gentle, so he doesn't resist. Leo closes the living-room door.

I pull myself up into a sitting position and wrap myself in the throw. My side hurts, but I am almost used to the continuous pulsing. I think that maybe if it stopped I might really start to freak out. I feel self-conscious in just my pants and my blood-smattered vest top. I reach out for the coffee but Leo moves the mug from my grasp, perfect clean face even in the early mornings. Oh, yeah, I just helped myself. Hope that is OK. There is enough water in the kettle if you want one.

He sits down beside me, almost on my feet, so I have to bring my legs further into myself. He takes a sip and it is more like a slurp and he says: I was hoping we could talk.

And then he starts to talk. Leo tells me he is willing to wait, to stay with me and compromise his own happiness while I try and improve my mental health. He is willing to move in together, even. He can help me as long as I am willing to help myself and when he thinks of his future, he says, he really does think he can see me in it. Even the physical stuff, he says, can get better.

Like, when you are feeling better mentally you will probably start to look better physically too. He tells me he wants to help me invest more time into my appearance, and he is clasping my two bitten hands as he says this. I respect you too much to just let you go, Thomasin. I see children. Like, little children and stuff. That is how much I want to make this work.

Yes, OK, Leo. The thought sort of makes me feel like I am falling to pieces.

Yes? he says and I say: Yes, yes.

Great. Well, I'm glad that's sorted. Things won't be normal straight away but we can make them normal again soon, eh?

Eh, I say, but it is just a call and response. I am not really thinking about a new normal with this man.

Leo packs his things and I notice that he packs my toothbrush too. I don't say anything, just watch, swaying on my bare feet with my top still pulled down mid-thigh.

I want Nance to wake up, Nina not to have gone to school club already, Finn to burst out of my room. I don't want to have to say goodbye to Leo alone.

Me, first year, just turned eighteen, and Leo, already in his father's good job, looking me up and down at a university club night and asking me what school I went to. Zoning out that night as I have sex for the second time, the same methodical thrusting into me again and again and me wondering if it will ever get better, if anything will ever be more exciting. Leo and my dad in the kitchen, skirting around awkward silence by talking about boy things that neither of them really likes: football and beer and me. Leo on my birthday, collaring me with a gold necklace even though I like silver: You're an adult now, baby, you're a proper adult. Later, Leo cornering Claudia and Elaine at the restaurant while I go to the toilet. Elaine saying: He seemed kind of pissed you weren't wearing that necklace, girl. I don't know. It was weird. Claudia saying: He looks good tonight, though, eh. You both look really good tonight. Me feeling ugly, pretty, less like myself than I ever have. Me, rosy-cheeked, calling Leo my love in public. Friends flush with jealousy, me relishing that. Asking him to pick me up in his car after class. Hoping the few high-school friends I still have see us online and resent me for it. Leo, two years down the line, grabbing fistfuls of my hair and shoving me face down into his freshly laundered pillows, thrusting and pushing and bringing me right back to eighteen and me knowing I should be happy but also knowing that something deep in me is wondering how I let it get to this point.

From the living-room window, I watch Leo drive away. I need to watch to make sure he is really leaving. I wait half an hour. The drive back to the city takes longer than that but I know he can't do a U-turn on the motorway.

I text my boyfriend, my Leo: I don't want to be with you any more. It is over now. Please don't contact me again.

I trim my fringe in the bathroom mirror. I trim it really short, so it doesn't even reach the middle of my forehead. I lose about an inch of hair. I think that maybe I should bleach my eyebrows too. I ask Nance if I can use her peroxide and she tells me she gets it done professionally. It only looks home-done because the hairdresser here is shit, she says. Also, why would you want to do that to yourself?

I tell her I want to do it because I think it might look good, mostly, and also because Leo and I are officially over and I want to become someone entirely different from who I was when we were officially together. You know, Nance? He kind of just hates weird women or maybe all women and definitely me, now, so what does it matter what I look like or who I become?

It isn't just Leo who would hate my new choppy hair, the line that cuts my forehead in two, a look that turns me into a little boy or, as Nina says with a shy laugh when she gets home: Sort of a monkish look. Somewhere inside me or around me or down the road on the high street, I know Kate is cringing. I'm not sure how I know this but I do. This is my body, I am telling her. If Nance did have peroxide maybe I would squirt it directly into the hole.

Well, I don't have bleach, Nance says. How about you just go and read a book instead? I haven't got your sort of stuff, but I've got ones about vampires that'll make Leo seem like a lamb.

Instead, I want to watch the sort of reality television that is as far away from reality as possible, but Nance isn't in the mood. She is in a fluffy dressing gown and her hair is in plaits, which give her a sort of girlish look.

She says: I am going to go and sit in my room and have a smoke. That is what I want to do on my day off. She giggles and she hugs me again but it isn't that long tight embrace that I crave and she whistles for Finn to come and snuggle up with her and I think that she is killing him.

I spend the next few hours checking my phone. I refresh my emails, even, as though Leo might think to contact me there. There is nothing and I think: He is giving me exactly what I asked for.

I text Claudia and Elaine too, but I don't tell them anything important. Sorry, is what I say instead. I think I've been a bit of a bitch lately.

They don't reply but I do get a text from an unknown number: You can come round mine if you fancy? XXX

Evan. For some reason, against every wish I have, I text back: No thanks but hopefully see you soon. XXX.

She replies: Go and just come round. She sends me a pin of her address, a million heart-eyes emojis, two hands clasped in prayer.

OK fine. You have convinced me. Fine fine fine.

I then send my dad a picture of Finn, a close-up of his wet snout, his big grey eyes. Your nephew, is the caption. He reacts to the picture with a thumbs-up again and I tell myself that, for someone his age, this is an appropriate response.

Then, my phone dies and I don't reach for the charger.

Nine

I have only slept with one other person besides Leo. Marcus came up to me shyly in the bathroom queue at a flat party in my first year of university. Later, in the stairwell of his student accommodation – him drunk and me drunker – we got talking and I thought that he was sweet. A little shy, maybe, which at the time I was sort of into. It turned out we were both taking a poetry class – which he liked and I hated – and I felt bad for not recognising him from that. Afterwards, I became embarrassed when he made eye contact with me in the hallways, or read his work out in the class. His poems were usually about women. They said things like: She is a goddess with stars for eyes. I knew they weren't written about me but they made me go red anyway. I think I just felt sorry for him because he was such a bad writer. One day after our seminar, he stopped me in the stairwell and asked me if he could come home with me.

We are, like, he said to start the conversation, always meeting in stairwells.

We just sat together for an hour, I said. Your poem was about a girl with cherry lips and dark circles under her eyes.

Bluish purple dark circles, he said. Like the glow from the moon. And then he said: So, can I? Can I come to your room?

Everyone else had filed out of the class and away. I chose to break things off.

Why? he asked and I said: I'm just not feeling anything. We will still see each other at parties and stuff, though.

You're cold, he said. You're really stone cold. I mean, am I not nice? I think I've been nothing but nice. I don't really understand.

That weekend I looked at Marcus over someone's sticky kitchen table. I was with Claudia and Elaine and a girl that none of us talk to any more. Marcus was clutching a plastic bottle of juice half filled up with spirits and he was trying to make conversation with a girl in leopard-print flares. She was with friends too, and when she turned to talk to them he would tap her on the back or gently tug at her arm. He whispered something in her ear and she rolled her eyes and left the room and he stared listlessly after her and because she had refused to entertain him I decided that she was definitely much better than me.

Even though he made me feel sort of sick, I waited all night for Marcus to come up to me. I thought: Maybe this time, when he asks to come back to mine, I will pretend to seriously consider it before saying no. Always, but especially when I had been drinking, I wanted to feel desired. I have always seen myself from the perspective of others, even when I am alone. In everything I do, I am doing the thing and also picturing myself doing it. In that way, even before Kate, I was already split in two.

That night I ditched my friends and wandered to my house in the dark. I cut through the meadows. I crawled into my childhood bed fully clothed and I woke up in the morning to a handwritten note on the kitchen island: Remember to double lock the door when you leave. Dad.

The next night, we all went out again and it was then that I met Leo.

Later I go to Evan's. I walk because I don't want to ask her or Nance for a lift. The walk takes me half an hour along country roads with no pavements and by the time I get to the big isolated house I have picked what little nails I do have from my fingers. I am excited and nervous and feel the need to prove myself to her after the cinema. I see you now too, she said to me then. I think about what it is I want her to see in me and imagine myself being hit by a car as I round the corner.

I don't have any traditional aspirations, Evan is saying now. Work wise, I mean. I just feel like we shouldn't have to do anything we don't want to, you know.

Yeah, you said that before, I reply, and she says: Look, dude, I don't know what you're like with your friends in the city but go and just not be like that with me, OK?

We are eating smoked salmon on toast. Evan says she bought it specially for me.

The bread is sourdough but I didn't make it or anything. M&S and stuff. There isn't even one in town so I had to drive. Just to let you know.

She puts hot sauce on top of the cream cheese, lays an orange sheet of slimy salmon on top, puts on more hot sauce. We are in the studio at the bottom of her long sloping garden. Her house is big, but in a different way to the hotel, which is a collection of smaller buildings sewn together with mortar. This is a block, a large square with four turreted wings. Small windows cut into thick walls. Older than the hotel, I think, less inviting. The garden room is double-glazing sliding doors and polished wood. Inside there is a big fold-out desk and fabric scissors and a sewing machine and clothing rails cluttered with charity-shop tops and wicker laundry baskets of yarn. Posters adorn every white wall, but they are artfully placed.

It is very aesthetically pleasing, I say.

Yes. I like posting pictures of my space. Organised chaos is sort of what I go for.

Beside the desk is another basket filled with scraps.

My discard pile. I haven't been too good at sticking to one project, like, ever.

Her bookshelves are here too, a whole big wall of new hardbacks, bookshop stickers never peeled off. She has all the new releases. Or at least the releases that were new a few months ago, when I knew how to read.

My babies are safe in here, she says. In the house, damp sometimes creeps in.

She is sitting on a very white bouclé chair, coffee stain on one curving arm. I am on the hardwood floor. I am glad we are in this beautiful room, because it is away from her dad, who is in the house.

He would probably want to have a conversation with you. He's like that. And then: Dads are tricky. Mine embarrasses me but he funds me too. And then: Wait, maybe that is the embarrassing part.

Your dad dragged me half dead from a reservoir, so I am also a bit embarrassed around him too.

Yes, well, that absolutely makes sense.

Two children appear at the big glass doors. They are red in the face and panting and laughing. They are wearing matching corduroy trousers and the same chunky knitted jumper, bright red flecked with blue. They press their faces to the doors and when they step back the faces are still there, round and immortalised in grease on glass.

Ignore them, says Evan. They have just come to ogle at you because I never have people round. Most of my friends are online. Mum probably sent them out here on a recon mission.

Should we, like, let them in?

Absolutely not. This is my sacred space. You are an honoured guest. You do realise that, right?

The children get bored of us eventually, disappearing back up the garden and round the side of the house. They emerge again later with another, slightly older child in tow. The two younger ones are clutching a tablet now, engrossed in something on the screen, but they point the older one in our direction, even giving her a little shove. She approaches the garden house shyly.

How many of those do you have? I ask and Evan shrugs. There's one more but he won't show. There was a time when I was, like, a teenager, and Mum and Dad just kept churning them out. I don't know, those were weird times.

The girl is at the glass and I go to get up to let her in. Don't you dare, Evan says. Seriously, Thomasin. She takes my clothes and all my stuff. She'll probably try to steal you, too, when I'm not looking. Charm you with her, I don't know, her childish charm?

The girl is still just standing there at the door. I feel awkward, exposed. There are no walls to hide behind. I start to laugh.

Go and piss off, Ada, Evan shouts. Go and look at your iPad or eat some sweets or something.

Ada wants to be an influencer, Evan tells me. I told her she would need a nose job first and my mum didn't let me eat dinner with them all for like a week.

What did you do? I ask. For some reason I think she is going to tell me that she just didn't eat dinner. For some people, I think, food is so optional.

Instead, Evan says: I can't relate to them. The age gap is so big and I just can't relate.

My cousin is probably the same age as her, I say, and Evan asks if Nina goes to the Academy. If your cousin goes to the Academy, Evan says, then they might be friends.

No, no, I think she just goes to the regular school in town.

Oh, Evan says, and she takes another bite of her toast, chews slowly, staring into her sister's eyes all the while. Ada looks back, mouth set in a determined line.

I think she really wants to come in.

Yeah, she can want all she likes. This is my space. Like I already said.

When Ada leaves, I consider telling Evan about the hole in my side.

Let me see, I imagine Evan saying. Lift up your top and let me see. She traces the perimeter of the hole idly, places cool small freckled fingers around the entrance, presses down just enough for it to hurt. I gasp, feel my face flush.

What? says Evan now. From across the room, she looks at me with an unreadable face.

What? I reply.

Later, Evan drives me part the way home. I count seven bits of roadkill. One is a pheasant, its neck flattened by a tyre.

I just don't want to go into town today, which is why I'm not taking you all the way, she says.

I find this offensive, wonder if I have failed some sort of test and this is the last time we will hang out.

OK, Evan. Sure, whatever is easiest for you.

She tells me to connect my phone and put on some music if I want and I pretend not to hear her because I don't want to be responsible for choosing anything.

At the side of the country road, the town hidden twenty minutes' walk away, Evan stops the engine and reaches into the canvas bag at her feet. This is really awkward, but I made this thing and, like, if you don't like it or whatever you have to let me know so I can just take it home and sell it. She pulls out a mohair jumper, baby blue and light as air. She passes it to me, and when I touch it, it is like I am touching nothing.

It isn't like I made it for you. I mean, I did make it, but it's been in a drawer for ages.

It has a wide neck and a wide body and long wide arms but it is so light it is almost sheer, each intricate yarn loop making up some sort of net or fluffy mesh like a single soft blue sky. Kind of powdery, almost. I realise how hard it is to describe nice things. I want to eat the jumper, or for it to eat me. I am scared that I will rip it, or get a sudden compulsion to tear it apart.

Thank you, I say, and Evan says: OK, sweet.

It is dusky and the air is colder, small spatters of rain turning the tarmac black. There is no pavement so I have to walk on the grassy verge by the roadside.

Put it in your bag so it doesn't get wet. Also, try not to drown on the way home.

I start walking, still holding the jumper. I stumble in the undergrowth and am conscious of her headlights, the fact she is still there, and most likely she is on her phone but she could also be watching me as I go. I see myself from her perspective, or at least some imagined version of myself, vanishing between trees.

Evan turns her car around and she goes and that is when the muffled air of the countryside at night, the haunting eeriness of stretches of field and forest, becomes apparent. The ground is uneven and the road is unlit. Every so often, a car going towards the town or away from it speeds by and takes the wind from my lungs. Birds and the sound of rain on leaves and, as the night settles, I see the silhouettes of bats darting across the sky.

I walk in darkness with my phone torch and I curse Evan. What sort of person ditches their friend in the middle of nowhere when they could have just as easily driven her into town? I say this out loud because no cars have passed me for a while and the silence is scary. I see lights from the visitor centre flickering out and, before that, the neon-blue glow of a petrol station. I will get there in just a little while. I rationalise the walk – one foot in front of the other and I will get to where I need to be.

And then I shine my torch off the path and into the forest and there is Kate, standing a little way off in the trees.

She is a solid thing. Still with her pale brown hair and her translucent face but she doesn't flicker in the way I think a ghost might.

Sleeves on slender arms and the hem of her white dress skimming a ground where ferns sprout, obscuring her feet. She is captured in my single round white beam of light and she is looking right at me and she smiles a sort of absent smile and she reaches out a hand to me. It is a hand so real I forget she isn't. I think of the girl who is her, burning on the screen. Decomposing straw in the lake. A creature, grabbing my side and latching on. I want to tell her to fuck off and leave me alone but I don't, I just stand there. My torch is still on her in her white and I am not sure whether I feel hunted or like a hunter.

I say: Are you real?

Or at least, I think I say it. When I speak those words, I see Kate's mouth moving in place of my own, but it is my voice I hear coming out, too loud, bending itself between trees to reach me.

I try to speak again but it is Kate's mouth moving. I am immobile, her mouth steals my words and yet I hear myself, coming from her.

Kate, we say. And then we say: Thomasin.

Kate starts to move towards me and I realise that I want to run and I focus on moving just my little finger, that old trick to wake up from a paralysing nightmare, and I find that I can and I take a few steps back so I am on the road. I stand there seeking solace in the tarmac as the witch girl advances slowly closer and closer and I will myself to run but I can't because running would mean turning my back on her.

A car approaches. I am standing by a turn in the road and it skids round and screeches on its brakes and I throw myself out of its path but in doing that I am throwing myself into Kate. Headlights blare and someone shouts something out the window. I grip my phone, the torch illuminating my hands and her hands. Kate reaches out for me but instead she grabs the blue jumper and I see slender fingers dig into the knit and her skin is grey, practically, and the jumper even in the darkness looks joyous and wrong against her. I drop my phone and the torch lands facing up, a beam of light into the canopy that renders everything else into nothing. I reach down for the phone and I am winded by a great force, a horrible ripping that has no source in this complete black and when I manage to stand up again she is gone.

There is blood on my hands but it is not hers because it comes from me. I press my hand to my side to staunch the hole but the pressure pushes more blood out and I feel it trickling warm and wet into the waistband of my trousers and down my legs.

I throw up in my mouth, swallow back down the lumps of everything Evan served me earlier, keep my torch pointed ahead. I back out onto the grassy mound and walk by the roadside, as fast as I can. The jumper is gone. I tell myself that I probably just dropped it, but I know, really, that she took it, that she is reaching out of her world and into this one through more than dreams and screens.

What it would be like to feel the touch of those grey hands? I wonder. Would they mark my skin and cause it to tear? Would I be splitting not just at the side but everywhere, a thousand holes in my skin filled by little Kate-sized seeds?

Are you real? I think I asked her. Are you real, as if that matters at all.

I stop at the petrol station, relieved under the bright lights and the neon of the shop sign. I go up the ramp into the shop and stand there at the entrance. I am not sure why I am here. The man behind the counter looks like a boy, really, but I think that he is maybe about my age. You all right? he asks but he barely looks up. He is flicking through a magazine from a stack on the counter, licking his finger every so often so he can turn the page.

I go to the coffee machine in the corner and take a paper cup from the stack. The screen offers me a latte and I say yes, sure, and I even add all the syrups so it is entirely disgusting and undrinkable. The machine whirs and an unsteady stream of milk spurts out.

The man shouts over: Oh, we are out of coffee beans. Like, you can have the milk or whatever free of charge.

Generous, I want to reply but my voice is inaudible, too high-pitched and raw. Instead, I give him a smile. I can smile even in the worst situations. He goes back to his magazine.

I don't see the syrups going in but I can smell them, cloying in the air above my cup. The drink is hot, though, and I am cold. I clasp my fingers around it as I wander about the shop. Racks of magazines, some commercial fiction books from a few years back. Protein bars and vitamin waters. Coke and crisps and slimy packet sandwiches behind steamed-up plastic sheets. Sharing bags of chocolate and a crate of soft apples and brown bananas. Who buys fruit from a petrol station?

I pick up an apple and a packet of crisps and I take them and my milk to the counter.

Are you real? I ask the man behind the till.

Um, yes, I think so.

He only charges me for the crisps.

I eat them in the shop because I don't want to go back outside again. I have to walk into the town, I tell the man between salty bites. Like, how long do you think it would take me to walk into the town?

Probably ten minutes, something like that.

A girl made me something and then a different girl stole that thing, all in the same night. My lips and my fingers are greasy. I roll up the empty packet and hand it to the man to put in the bin behind the till. I start on the apple between sips of milk. It is so soft that I barely have to chew.

Oh, really? the man says.

Yes, really, I reply. The girl, the one that stole the thing, it was a jumper, she won't leave me alone.

Really? says the man again.

Yes, really. The soft brown apple slides down my throat.

Maybe you could just, I don't know, talk it out? He is still flicking through his magazine, eyes occasionally scanning the petrol pumps, the few cars that go past.

Well, the thing is – big drink of sweet milk, layer of milky film on the top and then thick, thick warmth – she stabbed me and now the wound is infected and that is how I met her, actually, but anyway she stabbed me and the pus and blood goes everywhere on all my clothes and things, you know, so I think we're past the point of really being friends.

Hmm, that's weird. And then: Look, are you OK getting home? You're not driving, are you? You've got somewhere to go and all that, yes?

Yes, I say. Well, I mean, yes.

I give him the paper cup with the apple core in it to put in the bin. I am still hungry.

A van pulls up to one of the pumps and an old man gets out and the man behind the counter says: Oh, oh, so I'd better go make sure that guy is OK and everything. You have a good night, OK?

OK, I reply.

I stand under the fluorescent lights for a minute and then follow him outside into brighter, bluer light, the darkness beyond it.

Eventually, I phone Nance and ask her to come and pick me up. It is the middle of the night, I tell her. And I am scared that someone is following me home.

It isn't the middle of the night, says Nance. It is just after twelve.

Please. I am on the road leading into town. At the petrol station.

OK, fine, she says.

Nance arrives in the beaten-up old car with Finn and Nina in the back.

Mum said I had to go back to bed but I didn't want to, Nina tells me when I get in. I wanted to stay up. I wanted to come and collect you with her. She is smiling proudly, wearing her pyjamas, eyes small and red with sleep. Finn sits upright on his seat like a human. I get into the back with them and push my face into the flat wiry top of Finn's head.

And then I say: Thank you. I sort of thought I was going to die.

You smell of cheese and onion, says Nina.

Nina has her school club tomorrow morning, says Nance, and I am working.

I know, I say. I know.

This is our second rescue mission. You're a liability.

I am relieved, slightly, because I think that maybe this time she isn't angry. She is talking, and she smiles distantly as she does.

I know. I'm totally unhinged. I think I mean it in a joking way but it comes out flat and Nance just says: Yes, well.

I press my face to the window and the dark outside. The heating is broken and my breath steams up the cold glass. We are in the town now, sparse street lights illuminating drawn lace curtains and figures hunched over the ground. Through trails of condensation I think I see Kate again, in blue, and I want to rip that jumper from her tiny frame and kick her into the ground until she is pink mush in dirt and until she is out of my mind and my body.

Kate wakes up in her bed in The Big House. Her bare feet are muddy and it has rubbed off on the covers. At first she thinks Maggie is tucked in next to her, breathing loudly, a fine trail of drool running down the side of her mouth. But she is not there, of course. There is only faint light outside.

In the middle of the night she was in the forest and the forest was in her head and Thomasin looked at her through the trees and Kate felt as though the girl was really truly seeing her for the first time. Kate stands, and under her the bed creaks. On top of her shift, she is wearing the blue jersey, the warmth of its wool an embrace. She cannot contain her gasp. In her dream she had never seen such a wonderful piece of clothing, and she reached out for just a touch and then realised it had to be hers, even just for the night. Now the night has bled through to the very early morning and the jersey is here, with her, and Kate knows that she is closer to whatever else there is, beyond her world, than she has ever been before. Her strange dreams have physical shapes and she used to wonder if they were God or the Devil or someone else. But those figures feel so distant now, the girl in the forest so real, so close. Kate isn't tired and she doesn't feel like praying or working, but the Laird's wife will want dressing soon, the Laird his tea. Kate realises now that she hates the Laird and will always hate the Laird. She is angry at herself for not having hated him sooner.

Kate does not have a mirror but she knows the jersey looks so good on her. I will give it back to Thomasin next time I see her, Kate decides, because I will see her again and it will be soon.

Later a very large grey dog sniffs around in the dirt by the stables. The horses whinny and stamp into their straw, but the stablehands do not seem to notice the dog, who continues his sniffing then trots away past the servants' quarters, where Kate sees it out the corner of her eye, and back towards town.

Kate re-enters The Big House through the scullery, where the cook looms over a new maid, fingers already raw from the hot water. Look at what you have missed, the cook says. I cannot prepare food when my tools are as dirty as you have left them.

In the kitchen, Kate hears her name. Kate, Kate, it comes in whispers from the pantry and her heart skips. She assumes it is the girl, she goes down the stone stairs to the coldest room in the house. When September comes around, the boys will shake down apples from the orchard and the kitchen staff will wash and line them up, not touching, on the pantry shelves so they will last the winter. The apples that are marked will be sliced and cooked down with sugar, then encased in pastry. The Laird will lick the crumbs from his lips.

Kate, Kate, says the voice again.

Thomasin? says Kate. She pulls at the blue knit sleeves, feels exposed and unready to return what she has taken.

In the pantry, there is Maggie. She is perched on the shelf where the apples will sit. Beside her, also perched, is Archie, and with them is a tall girl who stands awkwardly by his side.

Kate stops, opens her mouth. He shouldn't be here and she doesn't know how to feel. Her brother and Maggie both jump down and hush her at the same time.

Don't hush me, says Kate. I was not going to speak. And then, to Archie: You've come to see me, then. With him looking at her in this setting she feels embarrassed, almost. The forbidden mixing of her work and home life disturbs her.

Yes. I am sorry for leaving you on Sunday. I am sorry for how I left you. He looks at the floor when he says it, pulls at his frayed cuffs.

Well, you should get out. You'll be in trouble if you're found.

I let them in, says Maggie, and she looks proud. But it is true they shouldn't be here, cannot stay long.

Mother told me off when I got home on Sunday. He coughs, flushes, looks at the tall girl beside him. I didn't come here because Mother told me to, though, of course. In fact, she advised me against it.

How is our mother?

Quick to anger, quick to laugh, her brother replies. She is well as always but, Kate, please. I am sorry. I spoke out of turn and I shouldn't have just left after I did that.

Kate gives in. She should be apologising too, most likely, but, instead: Hmm, you're sorry, are you? How sorry?

The siblings laugh, relief seeps into them both. There will be no grudges held between them.

This is Elizabeth.

Kate says: All right.

Archie's local girl is neatly put together. Elizabeth has mousy hair tucked neatly into a cap and she laughs shyly, always with her eyes on Archie. When there is a noise somewhere else in The Big House, the thud of footsteps or the clattering of cutlery or the splashing of dirty dishwater, the cook's cries at the scullery maid, Elizabeth flinches.

Elizabeth isn't supposed to be out with me, Archie says, and Kate wants to dislike her but, despite herself, she won't, and so she tries to find ways to impress the younger girl. She becomes proud of her position in The Big House again, starts to feel as though everything around her is hers.

Look, Kate says, relaxing now. Look at this nice brass brooch. And: I have a little cake the Laird didn't eat at breakfast. Share it with me, sister.

Restrained Elizabeth just smiles and looks to Archie and Archie says: Kate has some aspirations. She is a lady now, really, but he seems sad, almost.

Share this with me, sister, she says again, reaching out to Elizabeth with crumbs in her hand.

Maggie then says she might spit in the pot next time she prepares the Laird's stew, and Kate laughs and so does Archie, and Elizabeth looks appalled as if she doesn't realise it is all just a big joke. She adjusts her cap.

Kate says: I have been having visions of a girl from another time.

You and your stories, Katey. You have always told such wonderful stories.

Yes, brother, except this is real. I have been visiting her in her dreams just as she visits me in mine. We are close, so close. I think God is bringing us together.

What she does not admit is that she is scared, can feel the girl pulling away or trying to, could feel her hatred between the trees last night, feels now as though Thomasin is black loch water between her fingers.

Archie's gaze is on her and Kate knows his eyes will be wide and cross but she doesn't look because she is looking at Elizabeth.

Or maybe it is not God bringing us together. Kate leans towards Elizabeth, eyes as wide as her brother's. She smiles sweetly and to Elizabeth she looks crazed. Maybe, says Kate, maybe it is sorcery.

Elizabeth adjusts her cap again and a few stray mousy hairs escape.

I really could just spit in the pot and nobody would know but us, says Maggie.

Archie, says Elizabeth, let us go now.

Kate grasps the pale girl's hands. It was wonderful to meet you, sister. It is wonderful to have another sister. I have two now, if you must know. And then, removing the jersey, knowing she should not be wearing it in The Big House, knowing it will be taken from her if she does not protect it: Archie, my dear, take this home with you. Hide it under the bed. Don't show Mother for she will only have questions I cannot answer. I'll visit you and her and it on Sunday.

Archie takes the jumper with reverence and confusion. Kate. Her name in his mouth sounds like a question.

The cook comes in then, red-faced. She is aghast. Get out, she yells like they are rats, and they scurry. Later, Kate will feel angry at Archie again, this time for not staying, for not defending her, and she will be angry at Maggie too, for causing this trouble and then running, but she will suppose that she is the older sister, and she will suppose that she is a trouble-maker, too, so it is not just her brother and Maggie who are at fault. Now the cook looks at Kate with a pinched mouth. Her eyes have hatred in them and she says: You are a trouble-maker, girl, and she will ask for Kate's name and Kate will give it, looking the cook right in her eye and telling herself not to shake, and not shaking, and saying: My name is Kate McNiven. And the cook will say: I have heard about you, heard how you threw the cutlery down upon the table, and she says this no longer seething, but with the strange satisfaction of someone who has absolutely been proven right.

The cook leaves Kate in the empty apple room and she stands there looking at the bare shelves wondering what September might bring, whether the fruit will be dark red or pale red streaked with yellow or a bright poison green. She imagines the people she loves as apples on that shelf, but there is nothing she can do, really, to move her mind from the face of the cook, from her anger, her smile. She thinks of her mother preparing her for The Big House, telling Kate to be her sweet, good self, and wonders if her reputation might be something worth trying to preserve, wonders how she might even go about it, what parts of herself she would have to change, or kill.

Later, as she leaves the little master's grand bedroom – the nursemaids had flocked around her with suspicious eyes as she delivered sweets and hot salted porridge with cream – Kate brushes past a serving girl. The girl stops when she registers Kate's presence, stops so close that Kate can see her smooth greasy skin, the flecks of green in her brown eyes, even. The serving girl laughs under her breath: You are Kate, surely.

What is it to you? Kate replies.

I heard the Lady's maid is gone, the one with the rashes all over her. The Lady thought it was the Devil's hands on her, those red rashes.

I heard she is well again, says Kate, who did not know the woman and does not care either way.

Her face is marked with pocks now, though, because the rashes became wounds which made holes in her skin. And then: I heard the Laird will be asking for you now, instead. She looks Kate up and down, laughs again, says: I can't think why.

The girl has mean eyes, Kate thinks. Mean, ugly eyes. She is laughing in Kate's face and Kate is thinking: Be good, be sweet, but the girl is saying: I thought it might be me, you know, but it is you. Someone will come to fetch you this evening if you do not go on your own, and Kate feels an anger in herself that might be Thomasin's, might be her own, and she plants her two small hands on the girl and she says: Enjoy yourself while you can because you won't be laughing long.

The girl, wide-eyed, pushes past her, her walk down the corridor near breaking into a run. Kate wants to feel pleased but she cannot. Instead, she feels the spite of these thick old walls pressing down on her. Here, she realises, she has but one ally. She thought people might love her as they have always loved her in everything else she has done, but now, as she stares at the blankness of the corridor until the plaster blurs and the walls take on the look of scales or chapped skin, she realises she has never felt more alone in her entire life. She feels, too, the weight of those blue beads around her neck, and it is as though she has never taken the necklace off.

Kate does not want to go to the Laird that night, but of course she will. She is happy her brother has found a girl who likes him, who could be a woman who loves him, and this is what she thinks of when the Laird is on top of her. This, and Thomasin, who might be somewhere with someone on top of her too. His thrusts are arrhythmic and the sweat from his exertion drips from his forehead into her mouth. Then he flips her round, throws her skirts up over her head so she is encased in a scratchy darkness. The assault takes but a few minutes but those minutes warp, stretch themselves on into the night, take the form of shiny-backed insects that cut Kate's skin and slide in, burrow deep. Kate wants to leave her body, hover above it until she is ready to return, but she can't.

The Laird sliding out of her is a wet, muffled sound. The air in his vast, ornate quarters is thick and hot and smells like salt. She gathers her skirts around her, feels her way out as already he starts to snore contentedly, feels something warm and unfamiliar sliding down her inner thigh.

Kate returns to the dormitory and washes herself with her hands and a basin of freezing water until she is red raw, skin lined with scratches from her own nails. She is trying to claw something of herself off. She envies the pockmarked woman, realises it is the first time she has envied someone for their ugliness. When she dresses for bed, Kate slips a piece of cloth into her undergarments to staunch the bleeding between her legs.

Part IV

Face in a Spoon

1715

and then, again: waking
the gloom of dawn here is always the same
the shift into morning a boring dance
I used to love the country and felt it loved me back
when I was a girl and my mother would lift me up
onto the counter and
press a warm damp cloth to my temples
where mud was somehow streaked
or else it was hands plunged into an icy bowl and:
always dirt under your fingernails, Katherine, Katey, Kate
where is it you go when I let you out to play?
Mother I am alone on a wandering upper floor
touching old wood
I am thinking of taking you out in silks
what might have been
his stinking hot breath
what will still be because all is well, all is well
silks and fresh pressed linen and crushed velvet ribbons and
    golden reins and
his hands which are not soft or rough but slippery, sort of
a creature I don't know and have never seen
I, quiet, nervous, then quick-tongued
was this was he
not what I wanted?
this is not what I want
his stinking hot breath

all that good food curdled in a concave stomach
clean white skin polished like a pearl and stretched
over a bag of bones
thinking of home still, pallid light eases in, the women shift
his hands
and I want to go home or curl into myself
but I don't exist any more he has killed me and
in my mind I go out into the blank fields
screaming for my brother
to the unfamiliar trees with weeping fingers
and then home
I used to love the country and felt it loved me back
but now: disorientated from the forest, the scents and sounds of
    a damp place
my mother's still strong arms holding me
I am lifted up
the women wake while I am still between places
in tepid water dreaming of
copper goblets and silver swords mounted on solid stone
and fair maidens who look like the kitchen girl
holding stale bread out to me
as though it is big-game meat from a hunt, and all the other
    things I have not tasted.

Ten

The storm arrives in early August. Rain comes down in sheets, bursting pipes and overflowing drains. The tarmac cracks and old cars float down the hill and collect at the grassy bottom of the town. People dismantle their scarecrows, or else strip the old clothes off to use next year. Naked clumps of straw clog grates. School starts back and then is cancelled and children put on waterproofs and paddle in the high street. Nina folds printer paper into a boat and takes it out with her friends, returning moments later with white mush on her hands and a group of girls in tow. There is lightning out there, she says. The girls drip on the carpets and disappear into Nina's room. I hear music and see lightning flashing from between the orange curtains and, moments later, thunder shakes the flat. At night the street is silent because the pub is closed. No people shout drunkenly but the rain beats down incessantly and Nance says she feels like everything is being cleaned. Some of the girls stay over because their parents can't get into town to pick them up. It feels like an apocalypse, says one, clutching her Nokia to her like a life raft, pixelated texts from MUM flashing up to reassure her daughter. Nance kisses Nina and shuts herself in her bedroom for hours. When she opens the door, smoke pours out and the smell is suffocating. I put a film on for the girls and sit on the sofa with Finn. When I stand up there is a red stain where my side was pressing into the linen. I cover it with a cushion, excuse myself and tell the girls not to pause the film.

The girls are still in the living room in the morning. The storm has not abated and we sit in front of the TV as it flickers grey and white. One of them is homesick and starts to cry. Nina sighs, moves to sit next to me on the carpet, little legs outstretched. I manage to put on another film and I watch it with them until their parents wade up the high street to pick them up.

The storm blurs the days so I barely feel them passing. The hotel stays open and Nance walks to work in old wellies with her skirt hiked up around her thighs. I rarely have shifts because so many guests have cancelled their stays, but when I do, I go with her. Going uphill is walking against a current. We cling to railings and bushes and each other when we can. I bring my uniform and plimsoles tied up in a bin liner. Worst storm in years, warns the local radio station. The town doesn't have the infrastructure for this.

When I am not working I sit in the house and pick at the hole and think about Kate. I don't want to think about her but there she is, always. You probably brought this storm on, you bitch, I say in the mirror to her. Instantly, I feel awkward and also terrified. Just to clarify, I didn't mean that. And then: Sure you didn't mean it. I stick my finger into the hole and bring the mouldy juices to my lips. It is not salty like I expect but rancid, like rotting berries.

The storm is as good an excuse as any to isolate myself. Our Wi-Fi stops working and I decide not to text. Evan doesn't get in touch and neither does Elaine or Claudia or my dad. Probably it is because they can't, I tell myself.

The night before the worst of the storm hits, Leo phones, though, and calls me a fucking dirty little slut. I thought you were different, he says, you know, one of the good ones. And I fucking looked after you, I sacrificed so much for you but you're fucking crazy you're a fucking psycho you make me sick. He pants into the phone like an excited dog and I wonder if he is touching himself and then he hangs up.

After, I wonder why I didn't hang up. I could have listened to him talking like that for longer, is what I think next. I remember being younger and asking him to hit me and him saying: I respect you too much, my baby. You torture yourself enough already.

Pay it no mind, says Nance when she gets home the next night, drenched, red fingers wrapped around a cigarette. She is shaking slightly.

No, I know. It's just I think he is sort of harassing me.

An overflowing pipe above the kitchen window means a constant cascade of water obscures our view of the outside. I am drowning, again.

My aunt is staring vacantly at the peeling kitchen cabinets, at the window to the row of cups inside, the greasy fingerprints on the glass. This storm is a big one. Nobody will be able to get you.

Because I am certain that Nance isn't listening to a word I am saying, I tell her that there is a witch haunting me and she has been since I got here and also my insides are falling out the side of my body, just at the rib, and it feels like one day soon the bone will start to poke through. It feels like I am being turned inside out or ripped open and I hate her but I love her and death is scary but also just seems kind of fine, you know?

Tapping ash onto the table, a little grey pile. She stubs the cigarette out on the linoleum and starts to draw in the ash with her little finger. The nail polish has chipped off a bit and I wonder if I am infecting everyone in this house with my slovenliness. After a while she calls for Finn and, dutifully, he nuzzles his leathery nose into her ashy palm.

Good little boy. My good baby boy. And then: You know, Thomasin, the storm doesn't scare him one bit. Some dogs hate thunder so much they have to be swaddled but not our Finn. It's like nothing is happening in his little life at all.

Brave baby, brave baby.

Later, Leo texts me, gets to me still despite everything: I am so sorry Thomasin I don't know what the fuck came over me. I just feel like you wound me up a bit but I know you're not really serious. If you're ready to talk about it then I am. I don't want to give up on us.

He even puts an: XXX.

Nance is working a 5 a.m. shift right through to the late afternoon. I go into her room and try on her clothes. The room is still hazy, unmade bed with yellowing sheets, book left splayed open face down on the bedside table, phone charger still turned on at the plug and snaking under the duvet. The wardrobe is a big old one and it looks like it has been in this space longer than the flat has. I open it and at the bottom is a big open plastic box with work clothes and yoga pants and jeans and colourful knitwear and the things that Nance wears all the time. Little velour hoodies and stretchy capri pants. Lace-trim vests and fitted blouses. A denim maxi skirt she wore a few times at the start of summer until I told her that she looked a bit frumpy and kind of weird. It was one of my bad days.

You're one to talk in your full grey suit, she said, but it sounded less like an insult and more like she was just a bit hurt.

Hanging up are all her nice things. A sheer lace slip, black, crawls below my calf. I can see the hole through the black fabric, which strains around my breasts and stomach. I take it off and it tears a bit and I feel guilty so I hang it back up and then I see a big thing with puffed sleeves and a puffed skirt and a sweetheart neckline in shiny pink crinkly chiffon and I think that it could have been Nance's prom dress or something and it is ugly and that makes it good, for some reason. But then I pull out this silvery blue cowl-neck silk dress and I think: No, Nance, I bet this was your prom dress, and I try to get it over my head but it won't go and it probably won't fit Nance now either which of course makes me think it would be perfect for Kate, Kate who likes blue so much and Kate who likes to steal other people's things, and in my struggle with the dress it becomes smeared with my blood and the effect is something like blood on ice, a piece of roadkill in winter.

I reach for the big pink thing instead and this slides on like a glove. I twirl in it. It weighs me down and that weight is a comfort. I look like a big fluffy cake. I want to eat myself and I take out all her clothes now, just to see if there is something I like better, and I am throwing things about the room, these big lovely flashes of colour and light, and I am wondering who this person is that uses Nance's wardrobe and I am forcing her small rings onto my fingers and hanging her earrings from my ears and my nose and my lips and I am smoking and I throw open the blinds and the window so the rain comes in. It is the first time fresh air has hit this room for a long, long time, I think. The wet will do it good, wash away the blood I leave in trails as I go. Nance said it herself: Everything is being cleaned.

I open her make-up bag and pull things out. She has shimmery eye shadow and lip gloss and it looks like the sort of make-up bag a child would have. Things she has got free from magazines, supermarket mascara. I take out a frosted-pink lipstick worn down to just a sticky nub and I throw myself onto her bed and I hoist the skirt of the dress up and I am looking at the hole in my side, the witch's hole. I press the lipstick into the gross mass of myself and feel this rush of euphoria and I draw all around the hole and into it and I press the lipstick down and because the skin is so soft and squishy like it is rotten it doesn't hurt at all the stick just slides right down to the bone. I am putting make-up on Kate's face so she can feel good wherever she is. Or maybe I am doing this for me, making myself feel good by fucking Kate who would wear these nice decadent clothes, who would fit them all and look modern and beautiful. I reach for another cigarette and my ring-laden hands catch in the wire of the bedside lamp and it comes crashing down. Glass smashes but it sounds like it is happening somewhere else. I reach one arm back and grip the rattan headboard. I start to touch myself. I think that maybe everything will feel better soon. Feel the best, even. I look up at the damp creeping in on the ceiling and the walls and see all kinds of lovely shapes. Rain pours in around me. Kate, I say, and it is really just a moan escaping me and I arch my back off the bed and I feel all the skirts of my ugly pink dress creaking and it is like an old house I am living in, this dress, and I say her name again because now it feels good, so good, like I am getting closer to something I never knew I wanted. Kate.

Thomasin. Nance is in the doorway and I am on her bed, dress pulled up to my waist. I have smoked many of her cigarettes and left the ends on the carpet and the ash on the pillow. I have ripped her charger from the wall and thrown it and my phone from the room. I am breathless.

What? she says. What? She takes a step back out of the door. This is not my space any more, is what I think I hear her say but actually she just keeps saying: What?

I come back to myself. What the fuck. I pull the skirt down to cover myself. I jump from the bed and my feet touch the glass of the broken lamp. I recoil, drag myself to the other side of the bed but I can't see my grey clothes anywhere because all I see are Nance's things and they are everywhere and everything is broken.

No no no. What is this, Thomasin?

Nance. Oh my god. It isn't – I didn't mean it.

You come here and think that everything is yours.

I don't.

Don't you?

This is all yours, Nance.

I find my jumper and my jogging bottoms. I fumble with the zip on the bodice of my dress.

It doesn't feel like mine. Look at what you've done to yourself. Nance is crying and laughing. Is this a cry for attention, Thomasin?

Nance, I say again.

You're here, always, and I get home and I just want to relax but it's you, always, I can smell you and see your hair in my sink and my clothes smell like you and the door to my daughter's room is always slightly ajar even though I know she likes it closed when she goes to school and you've brought everything from the city here, Thomasin.

I know, I know, I know.

You're unbelievable, Nance says. I can't talk to you right now. I can't even look at you. You're self-indulgent and you're self-pitying and I do pity you, I do, but I have to think of Nina, Finn. They're the ones I signed up to parent. I have to parent them, Thomasin.

And she quietens, seems almost sad, but then her rage returns. It's attention-seeking behaviour. That's it. I'm sorry, but that's what it is.

She is still in the doorway like she can't cross the threshold. She reaches her hands over and tries to pick up some jewellery but she is shaking and she can't quite reach unless she fully enters the room. All my nice things, look what's happened to all my nice things.

I am bleeding, Nance, and I am scared.

I know, says Nance, and it looks as though she is going to calm down but then she starts to blink profusely and wring her hands together. No, actually, I don't know. What are you talking about? You can't do this sort of thing to people, Thomasin. You can't go into people's spaces, you can't impose yourself on me and then do this, whatever this is, because what sort of situation does that put me in? These are my things. This is me and you've just taken it all apart. Nance flaps her hands a bit. She looks at the floor beside her bedside table and says: Oh, my light, my lamp, I kind of loved that, and it comes out as a little sob.

Please. I really need to talk to you. Since I have come here, I don't know, a lot has happened, and there are so many things I need to talk to you about.

Nance says: You really pick your moments. There is just no way I can talk to you right now.

This isn't me, doing all this. There is this witch.

Nance lets out a loud sharp laugh. Witch, she says. Oh my god, that really is something. She takes a deep breath and she cannot look at me. You'll find a way to blame anyone but yourself, Thomasin, do you know that?

It doesn't start with silverware, like those at The Big House will claim. First, The Big House itself will seem to contract, to withdraw into itself. It was her that made the house shudder, the servants will say later. But the house moved of its own accord, seeking to keep the girl within its walls.

For now, there is Kate, in her head and outside her body at last, designing for herself so many nice things. Dresses that would be scandalous in the Kirk, a tongue as long as a serpent's body, a tree she can coil that tongue around, a tree which bears solid silver fruit, and water which turns to liquid gold and Thomasin Thomasin Thomasin. She imagines herself mounting the dais in a few smooth and sultry steps and standing before the congregation clad half in silk and half in lace and dripping in pearls below the carving of Christ on his cross. Christ is wooden but in this imagining he is gold too, and shining as though from within, and Kate tips her head back and her long hair is loose and she lets out a laugh louder than anything that has ever come from her before and the congregation gasps. The Laird looks up at her and there is terror in his face, but awe too, and he sees her power, now, and she starts to glow and it is her instead of Christ who is golden and she is rising so high her feet aren't even touching the ground and she floats up so she is level with the highest arch of the highest plain-glass window and she touches it and it bursts into colour and she turns to the stone next and paints it in great swoops, powder blue and red, with just her fingertips, and she is no longer wearing a dress but Thomasin's jumper, which spills out like a cloud around her, and she kills the Laird with a flick of her wrist and it is Thomasin in the pews now, looking up.

Kate's eyes are glazed and a small smile traces her lips, and then the young boy throws his glass of milk across the room. The cup shatters, the milk, which is thick and yellowish, a layer of cream on top, crawls out across the wood. The Laird coughs and the nursemaid scoops the boy up and rushes from the room with him. Kate watches milk seep between the floorboards.

The Laird has been demanding her presence more often now. That night was the start of something Kate cannot turn back time on. Sometimes he takes her to his bed, sometimes it is just to serve him tea. Sometimes the worst part is not knowing which one it will be. She is thankful when his snotty-nosed grandson is with him because it means serving him tea will be all she is required for. This will all be yours, she heard the Laird say to his grandson once. This will all be your father's and then everything as far as your eyes can see will be yours. She hates seeing the snotty-nosed grandson too, though, precisely because he is so snotty, and sometimes she wants to slap that vacant needy look from his face. Kate has never spoken to the boy directly but she has started to hate him so much. He is never satisfied, always hungry, always ripping his nice clothes and pulling hair and leaving trails of drool and destruction in his wake. Sometimes, when the nursemaid is not standing guard with a cloth, the Laird's grandson will wipe the lard from his face on the furniture. Kate spent an hour just days ago gently sponging greasy food marks from a new silk seat.

Kate realises she is still holding the teacup. She stands behind the Laird, and he cranes his neck to see her. Their eyes lock. He raises his eyebrows, motions towards the small table where she should set down the cup. Then she will clean up the milk and the broken glass on her hands and knees and he will sit and sip and watch her. There on that table is a small pot of sugar, a tiny silver spoon. Sugar, to take the wildness off.

The Laird reaches round and grabs Kate's wrist. It is the wrist his wife grabbed too, and there is still a bruise.

What has gotten into you, girl? he says.

When the Laird's skin makes contact with hers, Kate feels a revulsion worse than she felt even on that first night. It is a revulsion akin to when she put that blue necklace on and realised that maybe she could never take it off.

The tea, girl. Now.

Kate, standing over the Laird, tips the cup into his lap.

* * *

I run into Nance in the hall later that evening. She is going for a shower and she is in her dressing gown, hair in a scrunchie on top of her head. I look at her bare feet and am surprised to see them unpainted, the start of an ingrown nail reddening one of her big toes.

Thomasin, she says. I texted your dad. I think you should pack up your stuff and I think you should think about heading, OK?

Nance, I say.

I can text him again. Or you can text him – maybe you should, it might be better – and you can ask him to come and get you, or Leo maybe. My car's a good girl but she won't make it to the city.

Not Leo, I say.

It would be fine if it was just me here, Thomasin. You know, I could do this. She signals to me, the space around me. But I have Nina to think about too and, you know, you're OK with her, she likes you loads, I just worry that she might think, I don't know, that everyone your age is meant to be like you. Do you know what I mean? You feel like a bit of a risk?

You smoke around her, I want to say. It is you who is selfish and a bit dangerous. I don't know how much I really believe this though.

It was a cruel thing you did in my bedroom, Thomasin. It's not just my things that are broken but the flat itself, you know? You let the storm in.

Nance, I say again. Agnes, Nance.

I don't want it to be like this, obviously. But I'm going to need to see your case in the hall and my office stripped when I'm out the shower, OK?

I wish I could bury my face into Nance's hair again, breathe in her scent. I wish Nance was my mum and not my aunt because if she was my mum then everything would be forgiven and there would be nowhere for me to be but here. Motherhood might be like that, I think, it might be unconditional.

The pipes gurgle when the shower is on and I sit on the camp bed listening. I feel a bit embarrassed but mostly I feel numb. I don't pack my things because I hope that by the time Nance is out she will have changed her mind. I sort of feel like I have nowhere to go.

It doesn't start with silverware, but silverware is how it ends. First, there is Kate pouring tea into the Laird's lap. She scalds him through his layers of finery but for that, even, he is willing to forgive her. The Laird has come to like Kate McNiven from the town, even though he has just learnt her name, even though she was previously just the serving girl with the long brown hair, the one that is not pretty exactly – not like his wife's maid was pretty until her face was ruined – but the one that will do.

The Laird jumps up. At first he is livid, but his need to have everything, to take what he wants, burns hotter than tea. He is an aged man who feels he is in the prime of his life, and Kate could be a body without a face and it would not matter because in that moment he would still want to take her.

It does not matter, says the Laird, and he starts to strip down to his tea-soaked undergarments.

Kate watches him. She is shaking, still in shock that she doused him with tea, still fearing reprimand, a firing even, that has not yet come. She wonders if, when his trousers are off and he beckons her to him, she will go.

And then she thinks: But I did douse him with tea. And she realises she can scald the Laird, if she likes, and although he is the one with the power, it has been her, always, who has been able to scald him.

Kate tells the Laird he disgusts her, says she will never lie with him willingly, tells him he is a lecherous old fool, and all this, still, the Laird could set aside, and then Kate says: And I will tell your wife. I'll tell your wife, and I'll tell your grandson, and this, even, does not give the Laird pause because his wife and grandson are like limbs attached to the big body that is him – limbs that can think what they will of the heart and the head but cannot detach themselves and live independently.

The Laird has never not had exactly what he wants. He moves towards the girl.

If you touch me again you will not live to see the morning.

She is not sure why she says it but she does, and it stops the Laird in his tracks.

In that split second, Kate steps over broken glass.

I've heard what they say about you, says the Laird. Don't think I haven't heard them call you strange.

Kate runs for the door as the nursemaid returns, holding the little boy by the hand.

The Laird says: If you leave this room, girl, you will not go unpunished. I can promise you that.

And usually Kate would be scared but she is not scared and the little boy is in the doorway looking at his grandfather standing there and she pushes past him, pushes him hard, and in this moment she does not know her own strength because the child goes flying back into the hall into the big wooden chest where the silverware is kept, silverware Kate has polished again and again and again until her fingers seize up and no longer look like they belong to her, and the glinting silver knives and spoons rain down upon the boy who lies there screaming but unhurt.

Candles flicker as she runs away down the corridor.

Back in the sitting room, the nursemaid rushes out to the little boy and the Laird is left standing, half naked and red in the face. First he shouts: Kate, and then, because he has maybe never felt as angry, as humiliated, as disgusted with himself and with her and with everything, he shouts: WITCH.

Hot tea and cold milk run into each other, curdle, and seep between the floorboards, dripping down on the heads of those working in the kitchens.

Eleven

The storm goes on through the night and into the next day. I watch Nance smoking at the window. She doesn't look at me but she says: I am watching for a break in the clouds.

I join her at the window. I can't see a break but I can't really see clouds either, just the amorphous mass of grey.

I like this weather, I say to Nance. When I was a child I would always press my face to the glass when it rained.

Press your face to the glass now, Nance says.

I look at her and her face is serious. She is looking at me intently. I wonder if she hates me. I press my face to the glass. The rain is so torrential I feel the vibration of it on my cheeks.

Nance stubs her cigarette out and brushes down her dressing gown and leaves me there. She does not mention my continuing presence, the unpacked bag. I want to move, but I feel stuck. I think I see a straw figure outside the pub across the road, but when I unpeel myself from the glass and take a proper look, it is just an old man huddled under the awning and staring into space.

The Laird tells the story of Kate McNiven. How it all started when she was caught stealing the silverware. The servants had noticed there were some fine spoons missing, and it was Kate who had last been seen with the spoons, pretending to polish them but really just looking at herself. She threw them down on the table in anger when I caught her trying to slip one into those strange pockets of hers, one of the maids will testify.

When the Laird confronted her, she tried to seduce him with her devilish powers but luckily he was strong, stronger than most, and was able to keep his wits about him. It was then, in frustration and rage, that the witch Kate McNiven threatened to kill him, said she would see to it that he would not survive the night, in fact, and then, perhaps realising the Laird was too strong a foe for her to face, she turned on his grandson, only a boy, and sent him flying with nothing but a flick of the wrist. He only just managed to survive the attack, the poor child. Thankfully he is robust, says the Laird, thankfully he is of good stock.

The Laird will not mention he was found standing in his undergarments by this boy and his nursemaid, that at first the boy thought it was all a game, pointed at his grandfather, laughing. The Laird slapped him then across his fat face, slapped him again and again until he started to cry, and then slapped the nursemaid, too, for her complicity. And the boy and the nursemaid will not mention any of it, ever, because it is easier to corroborate a story than oppose it, and they are told this tale and tell it time and time again until it becomes real for them in every way, until both young boy and old woman wake up screaming, convinced a demonic apparition of Kate has appeared at the end of their beds.

The Laird will tell his wife this tale, and then the local court officials and the city magistrates and the town he owns. With each telling, any shame, that brief loss of his sense of self, seeps away and he adds more detail, becomes more emotive. He starts to look forward especially to the part in the tale where he says: She tried to seduce me, she tried, and I fought her off. He will tell them that she must be a powerful witch and a devious whore. The Devil must have commanded her to kill my family and end our great lineage, he says, and he is scared and excited.

He summons a young kitchen girl known to be close to Kate, forces her to corroborate everything. You will be fired if you refuse, he tells her, or arrested as the witch's known conspirator.

His wife sleeps in her own dark chambers and, later, when the Laird is alone in his great bed, he clutches his silken sheets and sees the Devil fucking Kate above him in the four-poster canopy. He masturbates and an unsteady spurt seeps into the fabric. He wants her now more than he ever had when she was just one of his many servants – now she has a face, a devious one, and a deep pink forked tongue.

Even later, he goes to the chapel in his nightclothes and kneels before Christ. It is a wooden one, like in the Kirk. The exact same Christ, in fact, because it was the Laird who commissioned them both. He has two servants light the chamber because suddenly he finds himself afraid of the dark.

The Laird has never had to question whether or not God is listening to him. He is a fan of old sermons and he enjoys making donations to the Kirk. He appointed the Kirk's minister, even, so sometimes when he walks into that building he feels like it belongs to him just like the chapel does.

The Laird rises and the servants trail their light behind him and he knows he is protected under God's great wing and nothing can touch him because he is on a righteous path and so he sleeps soundly that night.

I wake up and someone is holding me. My mind jumps to Evan, for some reason, her hair encasing me like a blanket, her warm breath on my neck. I lie still for a second, imagine her sliding out from beside me, telling me she is just going to make breakfast. Coffee, sweet ripe fruit cut into perfect slices, pulling covers around us, our cold bare feet. But this frame is so small, smaller than her, even, and clammy and it holds on too tight. I try to control my breathing, keep it in that slow heavy sleep state because if I stop, it will realise and it might react, might pull in closer, but I feel slender fingers on me and in me and I can't help it, I jerk away.

Throwing off the covers, standing. I am naked and alone in the room. I scramble to cover myself.

Kate, I say, when I am wrapped in a blanket and she is long gone.

I text my dad. I don't tell him what happened with Nance. I type: Thinking of heading home soon, what do you think? XXX.

He replies after a few hours: Hi Thomasin. You should probably ask the girls you live with. Dad.

I think that maybe Nance never got in contact with him after all, or maybe he just never read her message. Maybe he doesn't care. The possibilities are endless.

There is another voice note from Elaine. Ten minutes. I leave it unopened because as long as it is there, waiting to be listened to, there is someone. I will open it at the right time, is how I rationalise my ignoring her.

I have a text from Claudia too: Hey. Hope you are well. Elaine keeps trying to get in touch, keeps asking me to check on you too. Here I am, checking on you. What are you getting up to in the town? How is your aunty? Elaine is exhausted from the café, poor thing. Do you have a summer job? Rent is due, by the way. XXX.

I don't have many things and they are all strewn around the room. I decide that if Nance does kick me out I will just leave everything I have behind. I know that in leaving the town I would be leaving Kate, too, and I know that this should be an incentive to go. Still I do nothing. I do strip the bed, though, because the sheets are stained with pink lipstick and fresh blood. I even bundle them up and put them in the washing machine. I am good I am good, I say to myself.

After, I make myself jam on toast and sit with it for a while, looking down at the uneaten red slice and realising I can never eat a breakfast like this again after seeing it regurgitated on the surface of the reservoir.

I have a shift that morning and when I come home in the early afternoon Nina is crying.

Why are you not at school? I ask her and she says: Everything hurts.

She has toothache and it turns out a strawberry seed has lodged itself between her back teeth, causing one of them to rot. She opens her mouth for Nance and I see it too, little pink gum receding from the brown. Nance asks me to take her to the dentist while she is at work. I am glad that she is trusting me with her daughter. I don't understand why, after everything, but I am glad.

Maybe I overreacted, Thomasin. You can always talk to me instead of, you know, acting out? And then she says: But please don't touch my stuff again.

Sure, Nance, I say. Thank you.

I've only been put on the hotel rota once this week. I wonder if it is because I am a bad worker. I am quiet and slobbish and other cleaners don't talk to me beyond greetings and goodbyes. I think that maybe I can just text my dad and ask him to pay the difference on my rent, the bit my student loan doesn't cover. I text Claudia back: I flit between working and not working.

How very holistic, she replies. XXX.

When I put my phone down, Nance is looking at me. She hates it there, at the dentist. Hold her hand when she screams.

I want someone to hold my hand, I think. Nina is a child, but I am just a baby really.

I take her and she does not cry, I don't think, and I sit in the waiting room instead of going in with her because being around the antiseptic and the chair with its plastic cover and the bright blue floors and the white walls and the cleanliness of it all feels wrong. On the way out, the receptionist takes my wrist. Her hand is soft and warm. At first, she eyes me warily and we just stand there but then she smiles and I suddenly feel a bit like I could cry. She says: Your Nina was very brave today. A whole tooth out and she didn't flinch. And then: Tell her mum she eats too much sugar. Way, way too much sugar.

We stop at a café on the high street and I buy Nina a brownie and myself a flapjack. The biggest, gummiest cakes are usually the ones I enjoy the most. I like things that taste like vanilla and glue my mouth shut. I ask for a coffee too, with lots of sweet syrup and milk. The woman behind the till gives us our cakes in brown paper bags and we wander back to the flat and it hurts to walk and chew and swallow.

Nina, between bites, says: I heard you and my mum having a fight, by the way. You both thought I was in my room, I reckon, but I wasn't.

Nina, you do realise that not everyone my age is like me?

What are you on about? Nina replies, and she says it as though she is an old woman, scolding me.

There are scraps of straw on the street still, lumps of yellowy brown collected in the drains. It is the first afternoon it hasn't rained in days and everything is muffled by the lingering damp. People come out of their houses unsure, blinking in the first new light.

The town looks like it is reborn, an uncanny version of itself, stripped clean by the constant torrent. I start to wonder if the curse has been lifted, but the straw is not contained to humanoid bags any more – it is everywhere, on every bit of ground and plastered against the worn old walls too, so it is like everything has been touched by Kate now, everything as well as me.

Nina offers me a bite of her brownie and I take it. I have already eaten all of my flapjack.

In the house, Nina takes her tooth out the cup and puts it on the mantelpiece. It is brown around the edges and in the centre it is black. She takes a can of juice out of the fridge and tells me she can drink these again now because she is all better now, Thomasin. I am all better and I am fixed.

Twelve

Kate runs home. She does not realise that because she is a witch now, she is no longer a person.

At first she says to her mother: I can stay, make them see I am not what they say I am.

Even as she says this, though, Kate knows that she does not want to stay. She knows she has wronged the most important man in the area, employer and landlord to everyone she knows, benefactor to the Kirk and God's representative in the town, and she knows, too, that she does not want to go back, that even if she had not heard WITCH screamed out behind her as she ran, she would not go back for anything in the entire world.

She knows that men will come looking for her. Some of these men will be boys she has known her whole life, or older men who are known in the town. It is when Kate thinks of these men that the last of her excitement seeps away and she starts to shake and cling to her mother. These boys and men, they know me, Kate thinks. But the Laird is a big man, not in stature but in every other way. He can kill her or have her killed if it is what he wants.

I could no longer take the place, Mother. I could no longer take him.

All is well, Katey, all is well. But Kate sees the shake in her mother's hands, the red flush that always spreads across her chest when she is on edge. Kate watches as she draws cloth over the windows.

Kate has never thought about the fact that she will one day die, or even have a proximity to death. Nobody she really loves has ever died – she has only the faintest memories of her father, only really knows him through her mother's words. In the Kirk she listens to stories about death in the same way she listens to Maggie's gossip. She gasps aloud, says to herself: That is awful, but that will never happen to me. She has a feeling she is special and so at some point, preferably while she is still young and beautiful, special things will happen to her. She doesn't know exactly what they will be, but she knows that everything up until that point – what was once the boring and which has now become the terrifying – is just an interim, a prelude. One day she wants to be wise and regal and say to some adoring person: Would you just look at where I came from? At night, when she closes her eyes and dreams herself into a different state of being, this too, she knows, is a sort of premonition, a strange possible future she has to try to hold on to.

Her mother packs some things for her into a cloth and ties the four corners of that cloth together to make a sack. Kate wants to bring her one nice Kirk dress, an empty vase or at least a nice bottle so she might have flowers in whatever place she'll live next, and the blue jersey of course. Instead, her mother gives her Archie's Sunday shirt, some coarse old trousers. She wears her good shoes because they are the only shoes she has and, as her mother used often to remind her, she is lucky to have even those. Now her mother braids Kate's hair tightly then knots those braids together and stuffs them under Archie's Sunday hat. It is the hat he bought with his first meagre wages, a hat that sent their mother into a rage because they needed those wages to pay the rent. It is the only hat he has ever owned, and until Kate takes it with her, it had never seen so much as a tiny fleck of mud.

After, her mother steps outside and Kate hears her muffled grunts, hears her stamping her feet against the stone of the porch. Kate stuffs her nice dress and her cap and Thomasin's jersey into the sack too. This is the sort of thing that makes sense to her. She doesn't want to be a boy.

When her mother steps back in she says: He said witch? You are sure he said witch?

I have already told you what he said, says Kate, but because her mother looks as though she has been crying, and Kate has never seen her mother cry, she also says: Yes, that is what he said.

You are a grown girl now and you have to get yourself away from here. There is so much more I would like to be able to do for you but I can't, girl, even as your mother. All I can do is point them away from where you are, from where you will go. And you do have to go.

At first, Kate takes this like a simple command: Go, be gone for a bit, come back to us soon. She takes a cup of hot tea while her mother fixes her pack to her and says how she wishes Archie were here and she and her mother laugh a bit even, about Archie and his girl, Elizabeth. Then, as Kate is at the door, the imaginary voices of angry men on the other side – voices her mother will hear for real so soon – she breaks down.

You have to do something, she screams at her mother. You have to do something to stop this it isn't fair I haven't done anything and I won't go I won't do this this is my life they can't just make it not my life. She takes a big heaving breath, she sobs, wipes snot from around her mouth. You have to tell them I'm not a witch they'll believe you you are respected surely or we can just lock the doors and windows and stay in here I can't go out alone all by myself that just isn't something I can do. She says again that it is not fair, because it isn't, and she wants so badly for her mother to make it all go away.

Hush, Kate. You don't have time and you have to go, my love.

Go where? Kate says.

Her mother tells her to take the path by the fields not the town, to get to the cover of the trees. To keep the Knock behind her, to know that if it is she is going the right way. Walk until you can no longer see the Knock, Katherine, she says. And then you can ask someone for directions. Go to the next town, to the city.

Who will I ask? Kate says.

No one you recognise, no one if you can still see the Knock. You are a Godly girl, Kate. There will be those who will see this in you and they will help you, sweet girl, I swear it.

Kate's mother feels the words stick her like a knife. She has never known herself to lie.

When will I come back? Kate says.

When all is well. When I tell you to.

How will you reach me? Kate says.

I am your mother, I will always be able to reach you. Do as you are told.

Archie, cries Kate. How will he go to the Kirk without his shirt and his hat?

Kate knows that things can't possibly end for her now, after only nineteen years – and how many of those years spent really living? – and it is this rising panic that makes her scream. She claws at her mother's arms, her mother slaps her quiet. Kate has never been properly slapped by her mother before. She takes it as an affront and this is the push that finally makes her leave.

I am in the butcher's with Nance. I think that, because Nina and I made it back from the dentist alive, I am completely forgiven. Maybe it was all a test.

I wish I could cure my skin. Make it hard and shiny. Make it so nothing could get in and nothing could come out. I like the idea of being a hard little shell. Not this big soft thing. I think as well, though, that if I have to spill my guts then this would be the place to do it. In the back of the shop, there is probably already blood on the floor. And surgeons and butchers used to be one and the same. Although maybe, I think then, that was surgeons and barbers. A butcher could take out the thing inside me, though, surely. Rip it out and stitch me up with the string used to tie legs of lamb and secure brown paper packages smeared in grease.

Nance wants to make something nice to celebrate Nina's tooth removal.

I'm thinking, like, pork, she says. You know how they do it at the Chinese. I mean, I won't be able to do that. But the general idea could be the same.

You have to be a really good cook for that, I reckon, I say.

Oh, is that right? You mean you don't think I'm a good cook?

I look at her and realise she is smiling.

We'll have a cheap cut, Nance says to the butcher. But, you know, something that is still good.

I'm hardly going to sell you sweepings off the floor, says the butcher.

What, you're going to give them to me for free?

He rolls his eyes, hands her a package of meat and says: You look after your girl, crazy lady.

He says that to me every time, says Nance when we are walking the few minutes back up the high street towards her home. Look after your girl. He doesn't know Nina's name, doesn't know anything about her, but he still says it every time.

I suppose he is just being nice.

Nance looks at me with narrowed eyes. Eventually she says: God, yeah, I suppose he is.

So, I say after a few minutes of silence. So, I am sorry. We are standing outside the front door. Nance has her keys in one hand and the meat in the other.

If only saying sorry could clean my sheets and walls and put everything back together again. Oh, whatever. Come here.

She hugs me tightly and the bag of cold meat presses into my back.

Thank you, I breathe into her shoulder. I am so relieved.

Finn greets us in the hallway, scraggly tail wagging back and forth. Nance drops the meat and buries her face into him and leads him to the living room. I follow.

You know his baby tail can bleed and even split? If the little guy gets too excited and wags it too much and it bashes against the walls like that, it can just burst.

Ew, I say, and Finn peers out at me from Nance. He looks bigger than her, a huge hulking body and long bony limbs sticking out from her cradling arms at odd angles.

Actually, he could never be gross. He is a perfect boy.

Isn't he just? About the only one, too.

Later that evening we find out that Nance is cooking with nice meat from the butcher's for a reason other than Nina's tooth removal.

Mum, says Nina, flushed from her walk home in the late-summer air. Mum, is he really coming?

Then Nina turns to me and she says: I am talking about my dad.

Oh, I say.

Nina's dad isn't the sort of man I expect him to be. What I expect is a man in a leather jacket, heroin chic and middle-aged but so young, dyed black hair maybe and the last smudges of eyeliner around bleary dark eyes. Some sort of washed-up rockstar type who was extremely attractive in the nineties and still believes himself to be just that gorgeous. I thought I would maybe make eyes at him over the dinner table, or something, and I thought his existence would explain all the wonderful things in Nance's closet. Because Nance is so unlike my dad, a man she chose to have sex with would also have to be so unlike my dad, too.

In fact, Nina's dad is really like my dad. Maybe a bit redder, a bit louder. He is balding but he hasn't committed to it and shaved the rest of his hair, so what remains circles a shining scalp like a little brown halo. He is average height and average build but the buttons around his middle strain slightly when he takes a seat. I find myself sort of disappointed.

He sits at the head of the table.

This is Matt, Nance says to me. Or, Matt, do you prefer Matthew now?

What? Matthew, because I'm old? Eh? He lets out a loud laugh. Is that it, Nancy?

No, I didn't mean, Nance says, and Matt interrupts her. I am just pulling your leg, Nancy. Come on, haven't I always just been pulling your leg?

Nance pours Matt a glass of red and she is still pouring when he takes the glass away and puts it to his lips, so some of the wine sloshes on the table. I realise I don't know where Finn is.

Where is Finn? I ask Nance. It is the first thing I have said since Nina's dad arrived.

He is just taking a little nap, Thomasin. She nods her head to her bedroom door and it is closed, so even if he wanted to get out he wouldn't be able to.

Finn hates all men, says Nina. Not just your boyfriend. She is sitting on the chair next to her dad, has pulled it even closer so her little shoulder is brushing the side of his stomach. She is smearing the wine splatters in circles on the tablecloth.

Finn even hates my dad, which is crazy cos, like, he's my dad. She laughs as if this is all so obvious.

Matt looks at me, then, as if he is seeing me for the first time, and his face breaks into a slightly crooked smile. You really are your father's daughter. Wow, the likeness.

Oh, well, I suppose so.

You're so grown-up, wow. You are a woman now.

Nance brings the meat to the table, tells Nina to give Matt some space.

God, Mum, he doesn't want space. Nina rolls her eyes and huffs, looks at her dad expectantly, looks away when her conspiratorial gaze is not met.

God, Matt says to me, I used to be so jealous of your dad. His face is even more flushed now from those first sips of wine. He takes another sip.

I say: Oh, really? I didn't know you really knew each other.

Oh yes, I wanted us to be like brothers for a time. He had this house and this job and this gorgeous newborn girl and his wife at the time, your mum, you know. He had it all.

Nance flinches. Matt, she says.

He looks at me. Have I put my foot in it? he asks, and then he says: Oh, Jesus, I bet I've put my foot in it, eh?

Thomasin's mum has a different family and lives in a different country, says Nina. Thomasin's mum isn't the same sort of mum as my mum is to me. That is what my mum told me.

Nance stares at her daughter but her daughter is staring at her dad glassy-eyed.

I mean, I knew that, says Matt. He looks at me and says again: I mean, I really did know that. What is our family like, eh? Ha ha ha.

Wow, Nance, this wine is, like, better than the usual stuff you buy, I say.

She flinches again and I think that I have maybe said the wrong thing.

No, Thomasin, I think this is just the same as the usual stuff I buy.

My pallet is so unrefined, I say, and Nina's dad says: Oh, Tom, I'm not so sure about that. Don't you be hard on yourself, now.

OK, yes, I'll try.

Nina leans in even closer to her dad. Thomasin can be quite strange, Dad.

Thanks, Nina, I say. Really, though, I feel betrayed.

I don't know what you're talking about, baby girl. And then he turns to me: I think you're ever the conversationalist.

Yes, Dad, you are totally right. She is ever the conservationist.

Nance is cutting her pork into tiny pieces but not eating any of them. The meat is grey and water comes out when she pushes down on it with her knife. She doesn't say anything but she looks up at Matt intermittently and the look on her face is one I can't read.

Matt doesn't notice because he is looking at me. My disappointment in his nondescriptness has turned into a sort of devastation. How could Nance have ever been with a man like him? How could Nina have come from a man like him? He is just fine, really, and in comparison I realise that they are exceptional.

What do you do, Thomasin? asks Matt.

She wants to be a famous author, says Nina.

Shush, baby girl, let the big girl talk. Nina sinks into her seat. Nance reaches over the table and squeezes her daughter's hand and a look passes between them that makes me jealous.

I am studying English literature. In my final year. I don't know what I'll do after that. I take a gulp of wine and splutter, spattering my meat with red. The hole in my side clenches and it is the first time I have really noticed it since this morning.

Instead of showing any interest, thankfully, he says: Hmm. Your dad still have that nice big house in the city, then?

It is a decent size. Quite big.

I remember it being huge, and real nice too.

Or maybe you were just small. I am not really sure what I mean but now it is his turn to splutter.

I'll have you know that I am average height for a man my age, young lady. He is laughing, redder than ever.

OK, I say, whatever, and he says: Have you got a boyfriend?

I am about to say no but Nance says: Oh, she does. A lovely boy named Leo. Very good-looking. In his father's business. Blond. Very handsome boy.

He's a lucky man, says Matt.

I have been chewing the same bit of meat for a while. I wonder if I should spit it out and stuff it into the hole instead. Feeding Kate might be a more effective way to consume, now.

Dad, how long are you staying for? You're going to stay, aren't you?

I'm not staying this time, baby girl. I know, I know, but I've got a little room in a B & B for the night and then I have to head to the city. Got a flight to catch down south early tomorrow.

He looks around the table and smiles like it is all his. Have to get back to it, girls, he says.

Get back to what, Dad? asks Nina, and her dad says: Get back to life, baby girl, and all that comes with it.

There is silence. Nance pours more wine into her glass. Matt picks his up and puts it down next to hers so she pours more into that too.

Thank you, baby, he says.

She coughs. Don't call me that, come on.

What? Matt holds his hands up, laughing, pretending to be appalled. What did I say?

Then he leans over to me. She's a crazy lady, my Nancy. Still wild in her old age. Still enjoys messing with me.

I don't know what to say. Saying anything would feel wrong. I don't want Nance to feel as though we are talking about her like she isn't there.

Eh, baby, Matt is saying. Isn't that right?

Nance looks at Nina and then at Matt and, like a switch has been flicked, she starts to laugh. She says: That is so right.

Nina takes the cue and starts to laugh but her little laugh is a real and blissful one and then they all turn and look at me so I start to laugh too, and I feel as though my laughter is letting Nance down but I keep going and going and going because it would be too awkward to stop.

What do you think of my dad? Nina asks when Matt gets up and stumbles down the hall to the toilet.

I look at Nance and she nods encouragingly, frantically, smile wide.

I think he is a really nice man, Nina.

When Matt leaves, he asks me to pass on his regards to my dad. Nina watches him get into his car and then she disappears into her bedroom. Nance tries to tempt her out with the promise of Diet Coke and ice cream, but she won't come. I hear music from her little speaker through the closed door.

Nance lets Finn out, makes us both a cup of milky tea, asks me to come and sit on the sofa with her. Finn bags the linen one as always so we sit on the cold leather. Nance turns the television on. Not to watch, she says. Sometimes I just like the overstimulation. I kick off my socks and press my feet into the fluffiness of the rug. Everything smells like meat.

Nina tries very hard with him, she says.

Yes, I can see that.

Last time we saw him was a year ago, you know?

Oh, I say.

He's got this wife. I mean, we were never married or anything even close, you know, but he is still my daughter's dad. And, anyway, he's got this wife and she's a bit younger than him and whatever, and they have a baby and they live down south and I sort of feel like he only comes back up here to let us know he's made it. He sends Nina birthday and Christmas presents and her little eyes light up and they're always things she would never use, you know, or choose herself, but she just absolutely treasures them. He got her perfume and body lotion when she was a toddler, you know? And last year a plastic toy set. A plastic toy set and she is ten. And I see his bloody baby online all the time, like they just share his little face online constantly, and it's just a baby but I hate it, you know? Like, I don't want to be with him or anything, but he never shares Nina's face online. He didn't have to glue a million bloody sequins onto her leotard. He didn't even know that he had to do that, you know? He didn't know that that is a bit of what parenting my girl is.

I thought he was boring, I say. I thought he was nothing at all like you. I hope that this will make her feel better but she just says: That isn't really what it is about, though.

This time it is my turn to open my arms to Nance. She falls into me. Her perfume is even stronger tonight. I wrap my arms around her.

I am really happy with my life, Thomasin. But when he shows up he makes me feel as though I shouldn't be.

Over her shoulder, I watch the television.

Part V

Kate in a Dream

1715

my first late-summer night out
under the sky without a roof
is as bland as oats
a world away and dirt
between my toes
I am gross
but now I like it
thank God for me
queen of the forest, or the rock and stone
and of sacrilege
I long to lean into witch
even though I am not one
I long to vomit chicken feathers and
small pieces of bone
and glittering jewels
and clumps of wet mud
and hair from a dead girl
wet, too
and whole pig's feet
trotters they are called
but they are more like feet with their
one big nail
these are the things I think of
how the trotter would be as wide as my throat is
wider, even
and I would stretch to accommodate this big new thing in me

always I stretch to accommodate and
maybe that is better than my throat just closing up
the girl stretches to accommodate too
to accommodate the thing within her
that is me
there she is in my town
her town
with the grey creature
she does not tempt me to her
but in my dreams I go
and I wake up in dirt and do not think
anywhere but here
because The Big House is my anywhere but here place
and the mouth of the forest is the wet mossy mouth of my
    mother saying
crawl inside, my child, and sleep a while longer
be a little witch and visit that girl or some other
I am starting to think I have some sort of control
over where I tread
over the things I vomit and accommodate
in the evening I sick up berries red as blood
and smear my hot red fluids on my skin
again and again, things happen here and
I know that
I can exist.

Thirteen

The forest starts on the edge of town, past the fields and the farmhouses, and spreads across the landscape further than she has ever been or even been able to see. Since leaving her home she has used the Knock hill as a sort of marker like her mother told her to – the further she gets from the Knock, the further away she is from the town and so the safer she will be. She moves through farmland then forest with difficulty. Her shoes have always been uncomfortable, and she doesn't really like walking, the constant drudge of it. She thinks of her brother, chasing her in a meadow, her feet taking off so she is not running but flying. Maggie is running alongside too, screaming: Kate, Kate, come down, and now Kate thinks this was probably just a dream. A good dream. Heaven. Maggie, tackling her into the grass.

But now, this monotonous placing of one foot in front of the next, the creeping fear of being followed. Avoiding big roots, hauling her sack, stopping to turn and stare as the Knock becomes a lump in the distance. Kate does not cry any more, but as she walks she relives those final moments with the Laird again and again in her head. Hot tea cold milk his old thin legs arms reaching out silverware silverware her feet faster than they've ever been a child's cries and screams of witchcraft. What even is witchcraft? If Kate was asked to define it, she is not sure she could. She does not know how it relates to her, and she is angry too, because the Laird can do a million wrong things and not be labelled WITCH. Kate does not yet fully grasp the horror of this accusation, does not know how rare such accusations are now, has never known of anyone in her town being branded a witch. Yet, she feels the injustice of it, and the frustration. She does not want to be made to defend her very being.

She starts to worry that her mother will be accused too. And Maggie. Even Archie's Elizabeth. Archie himself? Stop. Instead, Kate tries to think about what she will do when it gets dark. What she does know is that out this way there is not just uninterrupted woodland. There are other towns, roads that lead further than that, even. Kate needs to find one of those roads. She knows about the city of course, although she has never been.

Now the sun is dipping beneath the Knock and the sky is orange. Kate sees it from between the trees, even as the cover of the canopy thickens. She waits for the darkness to scare her but it doesn't. Darkness brings anonymity. There could be men walking not ten steps away from me and they would be no wiser, she thinks. I could be the one lurking in wait to pounce. She realises that there is power in darkness.

Kate scrambles through thick undergrowth. She is deep enough into the trees now that light doesn't matter. Even if the sun was shining it could never reach a place like this. She catches her foot on a root and tumbles down a ravine. She winces but nothing hurts too badly. She scoops up her pack, which has mercifully remained closed. She is about to thank God and then she thinks: Why?

The ravine is a long muddy corridor cut into the forest floor. Little roots push out between gaps in the rock face and they brush her as she hobbles along, feeling her way with her hands. Eventually she turns a corner. It is like I am in another world, she thinks. Kate creates monsters for herself in this world. Can you believe it? Kate says to the one with the silken tendrils, pallid skin from lack of light. It is unjust. I did nothing. I mean, I held my tongue as well as I could. For so long I held my tongue. Stone sprites shiver beneath her hands. And then I didn't hold it any more, and I'm glad of that.

Eventually, Kate's ravine opens out into a large room, partially covered by a rocky outcrop and tangle of tree roots overhead. It is a cave of sorts and Kate thinks: I will sleep here tonight and then I will keep moving.

She rummages around in her pack and finds bread wrapped in cloth. She bites into the loaf in its entirety and it is a freeing act. She has never really eaten like this before. Unobserved, with total abandon. Bread around her face, crumbs down her front. It is dark and anyway there is nobody there to see. Kate finishes the entire loaf. There is only one other in her pack and this enthuses her because it means surely she will see her mother again soon. Mother would have packed about a hundred loaves if she thought I'd be away forever, is what Kate reasons.

A stifling day becomes a cold night. Kate knows a fire takes flint and steel and she thinks her mother might have packed these things but it is too dark to see. She finds herself wishing she really could do magic, and then is angry at the blasphemous thought. She tries not to care, to curse her God fully and dramatically, but she can't shake the fear that He is somehow watching. Or someone is watching. The girl. Kate kicks her shoes off and lies swathed in her brother's shirt, her nice dress a blanket. She imagines herself hiking her skirts up to her waist of her own volition this time and leering at the Laird and his stupid son and his snotty grandson and those who came before and those who will come after. She unfurls the blue jersey and presses it to her face and then gently brings it down, down, past her mouth and onto her neck and then her chest and then back to her face, where she smells the familiar unfamiliar smell of the other town. On her back, through the holes in the knit, Kate looks beyond the opening of the cave and into the trees, where bats dart from branch to branch, little spiky silhouettes.

On the surface, in the town and the surrounding area, there are men combing the landscape for Kate McNiven. The witch is loose, they say, but not for long. They storm her mother's tiny home and check the cellars of the houses that have them. Not that any of the neighbours would harbour a witch. They are scared of Kate too, now.

Her mother is enraged. She cannot stop the men who enter her home – neither can her son, who is beaten badly by the local boys. Archie who, with a face so bludgeoned he no longer resembles himself, has to hold his mother back to stop her trying to hurt the men who hurt him.

When Sunday comes, the mother and the son will refuse to attend the Kirk even though their neighbour, the owner of Madam the dog and the last person in the area who will speak to them, advises against their absence. She urges them to keep up appearances and the Widow McNiven says: Why?

All she can think about is how she slapped Kate, how that is the last thing she did.

It wouldn't have mattered whether they attended the service or not, though. People cross the street so they don't have to walk past the McNiven house and the minister talks of demons and how the girl who worked at The Big House snuck out at night to lie with the Devil – the Devil, who more than likely secured her position in the Laird's household in the first place – and how she steals silverware and eats babies and he licks his lips when the crowds gasp.

Kate's mother forces herself to be calm. She tells herself Kate is safe, tells herself fighting the town would only hurt her daughter. She wonders whether she and her son will be dragged in for questioning. She worries she will break if she is tortured but she is comforted by the fact that her daughter could be anywhere. They can kill her if they want but she can say nothing.

Someone leaves a dead stray on their doorstep, its throat cut. Red blood is matted in its grey hair and Archie throws up when he sees it.

Elizabeth attends the burial of the stray against her family's wishes. She appears at the door without a cap, her face drawn.

They do not want me to see you any more, she says by way of greeting. My mother and my father.

So don't, says Archie. The condemnation of his sister has made him suspicious of everyone in his life.

But Kate is not the only young woman in this town, and there is anger in Elizabeth's eyes.

If you think I told them anything, she says. And then: If you think they would even ask me.

Come in then, says Archie.

Kate's mother buries the dog in their patch of garden.

Elizabeth puts her hand into Archie's. Both hands are rough from work. She gives him a squeeze, her face solemn.

Should I say a prayer? she whispers.

Archie says: I don't know.

Elizabeth says: I don't know either.

Archie's mother sets the stray down into the earth. Goodbye, sweet thing. I am sorry that this happened to you. She is quiet enough so no one hears, so her son and the girl can only see her lips moving quickly over the open grave. She hammers a small wooden post into the earth to mark the spot.

The neighbour leans over the fence and says: That is a heathen practice, burying an animal like that.

I curse you, you old horse, and I curse your dog Madam too. The woman recoils.

After the burial, Elizabeth walks home calmly, slowly, with her chin raised and her loose hair slapping against her back. She lets herself in the back door, quiet as ever, and folds herself up into bed alongside her younger sisters, who knew she was out and where she was, and whose waiting limbs encircle her and draw her into their warmth of flesh and linen and home.

The trees have rotting, unfriendly fingers. I am scratched, I stumble, I feel the hole leaking somewhere far away, but right now I know whose body I am in. There is a dirt path and then thick undergrowth. I am in her and then I watch her as though from above. Am I God, then, as she understands God to be? I am sleeping, I turn over and the camp bed creaks, Kate fumbles in the dark, I pull the covers around me tight, we move in each other.

When the dream settles into a hazy sort of reality, I am standing in the trees and I see Kate from afar – just her two grey hands as they emerge from a cave cut into the ground, as they grab moss and ferns and find traction. I wonder where we are, why we are in a forest, why she is crawling from the earth. Finn is with me but then he begins to wander. He moves nimbly between roots and rocks, he sniffs the air, he sees her and I expect him to rear up, horse-like and howling, but he continues to sniff, to meander. I know that soon she will see us too, so I try to grab him, pull him back to me, but in the dream he wears no collar and I can't.

Finn moves towards Kate, who pulls herself up onto a rocky shelf, falls to the ground, breathes a sigh of relief. My face is flushed from her exertion. I take great gasps of the forest air because I realise she needs it. I worry that if I try to speak, my voice will come out of her mouth again.

Kate lies on her back, panting, looking up at the dense canopy. I feel her close her eyes – maybe I close mine too, briefly. From where I am, it looks as though she is the one dreaming, not me. Kate in the forest as I saw her that night, the woods on the outskirts of town and not this dreamscape, she was cold and she was clean. This Kate is streaked with dirt and as she was on the screen, but seeing her in this way now, as I sleep – it is maybe the first time I have found her flesh to really, truly take on the form of a real girl.

I lunge for Finn then. In the uncanny space of this dream world he is both right next to me and right next to Kate, although we are so far away from each other. I grab at the wiry scruff of his neck; I wrench him back to me and he howls like he howled when we first met.

I'm sorry my baby I'm so sorry, I say or I think, but still he howls and howls and when Kate sees my sweet dog she smiles like she knows him, she pulls herself up onto her knees, holds out those little grey hands to him and then she looks past him and she sees me.

Oh, she says. Oh, Thomasin.

I pull at Finn again, this time so hard I am ripped back into myself.

Finn is on the bed with me and my hands are tangled in his fur. He is awake and he looks at me with deep, sad eyes. I wonder if I have really hurt him.

It was her, I whisper to him, not me.

Nance comes in, her bright dressing gown, her hair unbrushed and puffy around her shoulders, looking young and tired with no make-up on.

I thought I heard Finn barking, she says. I thought I heard him crying. Is everything OK?

I untangle my hands from him and he slinks from the bed. He does not look at me, goes to his mother and nuzzles his long snout into her outstretched hand.

Is everything OK? What happened, Thomasin?

It was her. It was her, not me.

Nance takes Finn out and I sit there on the camp bed for a while picking at the mushy skin around the hole. I decide I have to leave because everything is too real now. I sit there for so long staring at the wall, my hands, the hole – I feel as though I am still trying to wake up.

When I do eventually get up, I pull back the bedsheets to inspect them for blood. Instead, there are sticks, shredded leaves, little piles of dirt. I don't know what to do so I make the bed back up around the forest.

Thomasin, says Nance when I go through to the kitchen in the later morning. What is this? She is holding up one of my work polo shirts. It is bleeding, or rather, it has blood on it.

I thought nobody could see it, I say.

I am awkward talking to my aunt in a way, still. The reservoir made things awkward from the start. The clothes torn from their hangers, ash on the bed. These things make me a bad niece and more. She laughed at my mention of the witch before, I think. The thing is, I barely remember bringing her up. I remember the suggestion of her, hanging between us.

I thought it was just ketchup. Or jam or something. Is it not ketchup or jam?

It is blood, Nance. Because something is trying to kill me. Or someone.

Your dad thinks it's yourself that's trying to kill you. She is still holding my shirt. You know, I get my period too, Thomasin, you don't need to be coy about it.

Wait, I say, my dad has been messaging you about me and stuff? I can't picture him in the house thinking about me.

Well, no. I mean obviously not. But I just know. He was my brother once, remember. Maybe there is some sort of sibling interconnectedness that doesn't just vanish.

There were people killed in this area, I say next. Like, in the town.

She doesn't say anything. She puts her hair up in her tortoiseshell claw clip. The frazzled ends splay out like a flower atop her head.

Weren't there?

Thomasin, my aunt says eventually. Are you trying to use this all to distract from the fact that you are struggling mentally? Because, you know, it isn't exactly a big secret. That's why you're here, you know? And then she says: I just don't want you to feel like you have to hide behind anything with me.

Nance collects glass hanging lamps and vintage clothes and fantasy romance novels and if I didn't know her, I would expect her to take my witch haunting at face value. Like, yes, I am a bit sad but also Kate McNiven has slipped into my dreams or my life and she is dancing there, I would say, and my aunt Agnes would reply: Yes, I get it. Together, we will vanquish her. OK, honey?

Instead, there is silence and I fill it by saying: I know I was going to leave in a couple of weeks when term starts but I think for, you know, for my health, I think I'm going to go now. As in, as soon as possible, or whatever.

Oh, says Nance, you don't think we are good for your health? This place hasn't been good for your health?

I think she is offended. Again and again I offend her. Now I plead with her: Nance, it's not you or anything. It is all this.

This?

The upside-down wallpaper birds watch me. They look greasy and confused, coated in years of kitchen grime.

I know you don't believe me and I know you think I'm attention-seeking and, OK, I am, but I am also a bit haunted here, Nance.

When she raises her eyebrows, I say: I mean, you can't have lived in this town for as many years as you have and not think there is something at least a bit off about it. Kind of, like, otherworldly.

Otherworldly? says Nance.

Yes. Or maybe not otherworldly. Maybe so completely of this world that it hurts.

Otherworldly, Nance is saying. Most people think the town is just a bit shit so I like that you'll be leaving with a sense of otherworldliness, at least.

She isn't smiling, but I can get her there.

I suppose I'm leaving to escape the otherworldliness, actually. This place is just way too exciting for me. And also, you know, you did ask me to leave.

Well, Thomasin, I've changed my mind. I don't want to ever have made you feel like you're not welcome here. You are welcome here, absolutely whenever.

I don't know what to say and then she is asking me not to leave yet, to give it a few more days at least. Pink lips splitting, yellow teeth, relief rushing, my Nance again.

Go on, she says, for me?

I agree in a split second, which makes me wonder if it was her love and not the actual going that I wanted all along.

Instead of throwing my top in the wash, she rubs salt into the fabric and leaves it to soak in a plastic basin of cold water. This is the trick I use, she says, and then doesn't mention the blood again so it is like we have had a conversation about it even though we have not, not properly anyway.

And then she asks me to walk her to work and I say: OK, sure, I'd love that, yes, please.

I text Evan: Nance likes me again I think. She is asking me to walk her to work. Lol. XXX.

Evan says: Oh, weird. Also not weird, I guess. Does she want another chum? XXX.

I feel like there are moths in my stomach, beating furry wings against a light.

I say: Pick me up after? XXX.

Instead of waiting at the hotel for Evan I wander aimlessly until I reach a cul-de-sac on the outskirts of town. The low houses are pebbledash with plastic window frames and thick double glazing that looks almost hazy in the dull light. Potted plants line the curving street, little painted signs naming the ugly houses nice things like Robin's Rest and Pansy Cottage and Daughter's Way. The last one offends me. I can still see the Knock in the distance on the other side of town. Other hills press in all around and, close by, the motorway rumbles.

There is a clear bird feeder stuck with a plastic sucker to the window of Daughter's Way. It is filled with seeds and a squirrel is clinging to it.

I've never seen a bird use that thing, says an old woman. It is like she has appeared from nowhere, and she crawls by, clinging to a metal walker.

What? I say and she says: It's always the little ground rodents. One time I saw a rat hanging off it, just swaying in the wind. Not a cute little field mouse, but a big black sewer rat, hanging on and nibbling for its life. I watched it for ages because I was interested as to how it got there and how it would get off. I watched it for so long that I fell asleep and when I opened my eyes it had vanished.

She laughs fondly as though remembering a childhood memory. His little coat was slick with slime. It is creatures like that who will outlive us all. They want to survive more than anything.

The squirrel clings for a little while longer and then lets go. It flops onto the ground and seeds spill out its hands and it eats them off the patio instead. For it, the urge to survive is not strong enough, I suppose. Or it knows it can come back for more tomorrow.

I feel my phone vibrate in my pocket and I take it out and there is a message from Leo: Been thinking about us. I am going to buy a flat. Move in with me? I will charge reduced rent. No matter what happens I really do feel like it's meant to be you and me. XXX.

The old woman is just staring at the window even though there is nothing there any more. Beyond the white picket fences, wilder trees sway. Inside me, Kate kicks like a baby. Her little white foot lands on the hole and I feel it push out.

You really do live on another planet, I say to Leo. All this time I thought it was me but it is actually you.

The old lady makes her way past and I stand on the kerb for a while, swaying. I realise I should get back for Nina and I realise, too, that I have no idea where I am. I send Evan my location and wait. No cars drive past. Nothing really happens. I think about the way the town smells. Here, there is undergrowth and school dinners.

Eventually, Evan appears in her car. She abandons the car in the middle of the road and jumps out.

Are you not getting in?

Me, swaying like those trees and the trees in the forest of my dreams. Kate clinging to me, surviving.

Evan wraps her arms around me and presses her small elven face into my shoulder. She drives me home and this time I invite her up, and Finn remembers her from the pub, and likes her even more once she has offered him his meat strips, likes her so much he jumps up with his huge paws on her shoulders, which makes Evan and Nina both scream and laugh, and I don't think I've seen Evan laugh properly before, I realise, and I tell her that I never thought she would be an animal person, for some reason, and she says: I'm not, and plants a kiss on Finn's leathery snout and I heat up leftovers for us to share and we all sit together at the table to eat.

Fourteen

When Kate sleeps, she is back at The Big House. She crouches by the last candle in the chamber, burning the hair she has just combed from her head. The candle flickers, smoke spurts from the flame. The room smells of beef and burnt hair and surely the other women will wake soon and scream her name in anguish. Kate holds a fluffy clump of hair like a moth to the flame and it smoulders then flares up. She clutches the burning ball in the palm of her hand until the hair turns to ash that settles in her calloused creases. Burn the hair that is combed or cut from your head, Kate's mother used to say to her, otherwise birds will take it for their nests and your head will ache forever and ever and ever. As she pulls hair from her head to kindle the fire, more grows in its place and soon she is surrounded by bright burning balls and ashes and she thinks upon her mother's strange ways fondly rather than with her usual embarrassment and, as she sits in her ring of fire, she longs for Sunday and home.

Now Kate is preparing to climb up and out onto the forest floor again. She wonders if Thomasin will be there again, the dog as well, but she knows somehow that she is alone. She is exhausted and thirsty but she has to keep moving. Kate thinks of the city, the things she might do there. She remembers the lofty aspirations she used to have – to be ridiculously beautiful, disgustingly wealthy, to be loved by God and also everyone else. Everything that is not Thomasin, everything that has always been a part of Kate's life, feels uncertain now, though. She used to be able to do nothing without feeling God was watching, would feel deeply self-conscious in moments of delight or great sadness, as though strong emotions could draw His gaze, encourage His disapproval. When the Laird took her to his chamber she could feel God watching very closely, knew He was thinking her a slut.

When she fought the Laird, though, it was then that God was really seeing her, and it was then that He was angrier than he had ever been. God, Kate thinks, lives in The Big House and, like the Laird, He hates her and He wants her back.

She hears running water so she follows that sound. The stream is deep enough that she can immerse herself up to her shoulders. It is fresh and biting. Kate tips her head back and her hair is swallowed by the stream and her face is arching up towards the light as it tries to force its way through the trees and it is like she is Thomasin, drowning.

I spend my last few days in the town with Evan. We drive around, or sit in the café or the pub. Evan reads and I stare at the words as they swim on the page. Sometimes we sit in her studio, and sometimes I lie with my head in her lap and listen as she turns the pages. I want to ask her to read aloud to me, but I don't.

I tell her I am hurting and she presses a palm to my side and says, yes, you feel hot just there, and then she takes her hand away and we do not speak of it again.

I don't spend much time in the flat with Nina and Nance. Not because I don't want to see them, but because seeing them means it is true, that I am going.

When I book my bus ticket to the bigger town, and my next bus from there to the city, I feel Kate's nails digging into my flesh, trying to tighten her grip.

I spend my nights wrapped in blankets on the floor of Evan's studio. I start to wonder if she ever goes into her house.

One very early morning, I watch Evan curled on her chair sleeping, bony knees tucked in beneath her chin. I reach for my phone and look at her social-media pages. It is not the first time I have done this.

There is a picture I like of her against a plain white wall, smiling in a jumper she has made. The picture is taken with flash and her eyes are red and the wall looks like it is glowing. There are mirror selfies of her in ripped tights and handmade dresses and videos of her making things and film photos of summers past and everything is the same colour — a sort of lovely faded orange that is the colour of her too. There are close-ups of her freckled face, ribbons in her hair and clumps of mascara under her eyes. Captions all lower case. Hundreds of likes on the photos of her creations and thousands of likes on the photos of her. Her bio has a link to an unfinished website.

She is waking up as I am watching her get dressed online. She starts the video in her underwear and there is whispery music in the background and she puts on a miniskirt and some knee-high boots and a baby-doll top and slings a handbag over her shoulder and she is smiling at the camera and pretending to walk away, but I know she is just in her studio, walking on the spot. The video is really popular and her caption reads: get dressed with me. everything is second-hand.

The Evan from the video climbs out of the screen and stretches herself out beside me, lithe limbs like a cat. She rolls onto her stomach so she can look me in the face and then she starts to shuffle up towards me until she is on top of me, arms propping her body up, breathing into my mouth. The velvet ribbons in her hair trail on my cheeks.

I have always wanted a body like yours, I say.

OK, she says.

Because I want her to say something more, this video Evan – because I want her to say something like: No, what do you mean? Your body is a beautiful, very valid body – I push it. I have always wanted a body like yours, Evan.

Video Evan thinks for a moment. I reach up to take one of the velvet ribbons into my mouth. Hot on the tongue, smelling of her hair which smells of dry shampoo and sun cream.

What's wrong with the body you have?

I feel like there is too much of me and it gets everywhere. I want to be nimble enough to vanish.

OK, is all she says, and the imagining is out of my control because Video Evan is disappointed and suddenly, I want to appease her, impress her with my honesty, bare everything.

And there is this, and I am lifting my top. This is what is wrong with me too.

When the Evan from the video reaches her hand down to touch the hole in my side for a second time, I think it is maybe the softest touch I have ever felt in my life.

There is absolutely nothing wrong with this, she says.

Now the real Evan sighs and changes position and her long legs flop off the chair, and when she sees me through narrowed eyes, she smiles and says: Good morning, Tom.

When I do eventually go back to the flat, it is the day before I am due to leave. It is the early morning and I have my last shift at the hotel in the afternoon. I am here to change into my uniform, to pack my things so I can go. I remember Nance screaming, her dirty room, and me thinking I would go and just leave everything. Now, though, my things feel sacred, even more like they are a part of the town, and this is why I want to take them with me.

Nance is up – maybe she never even went to bed after a late-night shift – and she is watching a programme about people who get married to someone they have never met. A bride in a tight satin dress is shuffling down the aisle and a man in an even tighter checked suit is standing there stiffly with his hands clasped behind his back. The man is handsome in a boring sort of way. A brown-haired Leo. Both sets of families, relegated to separate sides of the room, are crying. The screen cuts to the bride's mother in a nondescript room and she says to the camera: Well, his mother looked about a hundred but he looks like a nice-enough lad. I'm still not sure about the whole process, though. As a mum I just – I can't have anyone hurting my Becky.

He can hurt me any day he likes, I say, sitting down next to her.

What? says Nance.

Sorry, that was sort of a weird thing to say.

Oh, the groom? Oh, I didn't even get a look at him, I was barely even watching.

Are you OK? I ask her.

Yes, says Nance, I'm good. Just tired. Nina is being a lot. She keeps asking for her dad. I also don't think she wants you to go but, you know, I don't think she knows how to tell you that.

That's really nice to know. I mean, it's a pain for you but it is really nice for me.

Nance's eyes flick back to the screen so I say: Give her a few days though and she'll be completely over me. You're, like, her idol.

Nance shrugs her shoulders, ash drops onto the sofa. I am surprised it has never been set alight. Nina is everything to me, obviously, and I can't imagine life without her. But having a daughter is hard. Everything I do becomes her. Sometimes I wish I didn't have that responsibility.

My aunt Nance is so beautiful. Her peroxide hair, the dark brown stripe at her roots, her long elegant hands, the sun spots on her décolletage and her wide wild eyes.

Since being here, I say, I have had fantasies about you being my mother.

I'm not sure I know exactly what to say to that.

Nothing weird. Just, like, nice stuff. You stroking my head at night or putting pictures of me up in the hall or whatever. To me you are, like, the best mum I have ever encountered because you are so kind and so normal and so yourself.

Nance clasps my hands and I can tell she is trying to look into my eyes but I can't meet her gaze and I feel suddenly naked and embarrassed. I mean, I don't know. I think I am chatting shit.

Nance kisses me twice on my forehead. One at either side, where horns might grow. It's going to be strange without you, she says.

Or maybe it is going to be normal.

Nance sighs. You have a weird opinion of yourself, Thomasin. You're not always as bad as you think you are.

I say nothing and I think she expects a response but I can't give one and she says: You'll come and visit us again, won't you? Have a stint in the sticks next summer?

Of course. I really mean this. Of course of course of course, like a million times over.

Oh thank god. I was sort of worried we'd scared you off. The weird side of your family, you know?

I have no other side of the family, I say, and she says: Well, yes.

Also, when I come back, I will really only be coming back for my baby.

We are standing up now and Finn is standing between us and I crouch down and wrap my arms around his neck and nuzzle my face into his ragged head. I have never had a pet.

There were snails in the garden and I used to take them from the undergrowth and put them in Tupperware boxes filled with dry leaves and twigs and I would tell them that this was their home now. I would watch and hope they would settle in and maybe have children and I could be the patron of a great snail lineage. Then I would get bored and they would shrivel into themselves and I would be riddled with guilt for a day and then I would do it again because this time, this time I would do it properly.

I leave them in the living room, the gentle mess, and I go through to get changed for my shift. When I pass Nina's bedroom, I hear a scratching coming from inside. If Kate is in there playing with my cousin's toys or pressing her sharp nails into the walls, gouging the plaster, I decide this time I will be brave and kill her. I will grab her from behind and the two of us will plunge to the floor, me on top, and before she even realises she has been caught, I will – I will what? Claim her instead of her claiming me? Even as I think it, a sigh escapes me. I am so tired. I edge the door open.

Inside, Nina is standing in the middle of the room in her school shirt and tie and her Sanrio pyjama bottoms. She is hacking at her hair, the scratching sound the brush ripping at her. In the light I see pale brown hairs falling from her head and floating down all around her.

Stop, Nina, I say, and she does not.

Brush brush hack hack, the hair she still has sticks out in every direction and a lot is stuck in the brush and more is falling.

Stop.

No, Thomasin, she says quite calmly. It is still tuggy.

I reach for the brush, expecting to have to wrestle it from her, am surprised when she gives it up easily. I set it on her chest of drawers for the Hello Kitties to guard. The brush bristles are no longer visible because there is so much hair around them.

I smooth my hand over her head and she says: Don't touch me.

She says it in a nice way, slightly guiltily even, and I completely understand. Sometimes I don't want to be touched either – I just don't know how to vocalise it.

OK, Nina. You don't need to brush it any more, though. You are sufficiently detangled.

She sits on her bed, legs swinging, and I pick up the strands of her hair and I am not sure what to do with them because Nina doesn't have a bin in her room. It would be wrong to throw these pieces of her away anyway, I think, and I am not quite ready to leave her yet, so I stuff the hair into my pockets and join her on the bed. I sit at the opposite end, where her pillows and stuffed toys are. A sun bear ogles me with massive glittery eyes.

Eventually, Nina edges closer to me. She says: I think I am fine now. And: Would you be able to sort it?

I braid Nina's mousy hair into two small, neat French plaits. The braids look intricate and perfect, that small line of pink scalp running down the middle, and Nina marvels at them in the mirror as she packs her school bag.

It is one of the benefits of not having a mother, this ability to do hair – on myself, on others, in the early mornings or late at night. The lines of schoolgirls, all eager to be my friend, all saying: Oh, Tom! Usually my mum does my plaits for me, I could never do them myself, but even she doesn't plait as well as you do!

Now Nina says: I am sorry you are going. I love you.

I say: It's OK. I'll come back. I have to. I love you too.

In the spare room, I pack my things. I pack some of the books Nance left out for me. I think maybe this is stealing.

When I reach up over the sink to get my things from the bathroom cabinet, I hear a rip and a steady stream of blood starts to pour into the bowl. I drop to my knees on the tiles, the contents of my washbag around me, and pull up my top. Maybe this will be it and I will never leave, I think. I think of Kate broken apart in a million different ways. I think of killing the moth in the bathroom with the spray from the shower head and I watch blood stain the grouting and everything comes back around so everything will always be happening somewhere, probably. A million versions of me and her and this place.

The hole in my side is now a tear and looks like this: giant yellowing gash, red skin at the sides and red everywhere now, too. Milky film, gelatinous sort of, like a sac or something and it is stretched over the wound but it has been punctured and as clear as ever inside me I see this pale white bony little hand, a delicate hand, a hand I want to hold, and it is pushing outwards and blood comes from her fingertips and my fat my flesh the sac of myself will not hold forever.

Fifteen

Kate walks alongside the stream, drying off. She stops every so often, chapped hands cupped, to sip the cool water. The day is so hot and the heat pierces through even these dense trees and dries the dark mud pale like clay so it crunches under her feet. The wild garlic is not enough and her pack is down the ravine still and she is starving and she is livid because she can feel that girl pulling herself away. Kate wants to scream and spit in her face. She sends streams of water from her mouth to the other side of the stream, laughs. She looks at God in the sun bitterly and sticks out her tongue. Demons, all of you, she says. It is everyone else who is the fucking demon and me who is something better entirely. She kicks dirt up into dust and blasphemes and pulls at her long hair and touches herself and speaks quietly yet aloud into the dense air and watches her voice curdle with the heatwaves. She is blood in milk she is a pockmark on flesh she is a pustule blooming under a breast inside a mouth a rotten tooth that turns gangrenous and festers there and turns that person purple she is she is she is.

Kate walks back to her cave and this is when she sees the men.

They are all around her. They have come from between the trees and they are starving hungry and they are salivating and they are chanting and of course the word they are chanting is WITCH.

Things like this – witch hunts and girl hunts and probably just hunts, where they skewer rabbits and the Laird gets a boar presented to him tied with rope and he can stab it in its fleshy belly and declare that he hunted it himself and he is the victor – things like this, these men love. They are chanting with looks of anger, of apprehension, because they are in character, but really a sinister sort of excitement pervades the space. They are only barely able to contain their glee so sometimes it seeps out because really, really this is all just a game and if they stop for one second and think about their fear, the way it manifests as goosebumps and teeth wet with spit and flushed cheeks and cracked voices, they will realise that what they are really feeling is delight.

WITCH WITCH WITCH.

Kate turns and she starts to run but the forest is too thick and they are everywhere. She knows she could outrun one man or two men because she is quick-footed and agile when she wants to be but she cannot outrun these men who seem as thick and numerous as the trees. She does not get far before an arm stripped with sinew wraps around her shoulders and she is lifted from the earth and she kicks and kicks but he holds her out at arm's length like she is a baby and then he slams her to the ground and this is when she hears the first of the many crunches of her body.

She has been living here, Kate hears. She has made this cave her home. Like a hermit. I'll bet she walks around unclothed and leaves her orifices wet and open for the Devil, one voice says. Many others laugh. I'll bet she lets him plunge his rancid prick into her and I'll bet she squeals like a pig when he does and I'll bet she begs for more.

Kate is on the ground and a man is holding her down but another man is saying: Don't put yourself where Satan has been don't defile yourself this way and the man lets go and Kate tries to get up but she is kicked again and she is called a spoiled unclean thing and she watches the contents of her bag be emptied out into the dirt and rummaged through and laughed at and the blue jersey is kicked into the mud but then this stops too, when that same older voice warns the young boys not to play with a witch's things because she can still curse them, can still call her evil beasts and familiars to her service to attack them, and she will be able to do this as long as she lives and we will only be able to laugh in a witch's presence, boys, when that witch is dead.

It could be in her head or in the elsewhere or aloud, in the now, but somewhere Kate is screaming let me go let me go and then she finds herself screaming let me in let me in, instead, and she is clawing through the years and the thickness of time and flesh and the girl is there somewhere and Kate says it again: LET ME IN.

Nina, Nance and I eat breakfast together and Finn sits at our feet, whining for scraps. I curl my bare toes into his fur. Before she leaves for school, Nina wraps her arms around my middle and then she pulls back and scrunches her nose: Your top smells kind of musty like an old person died in it.

It's the hotel. Everything smells like that up there.

At the hotel, I take a fresh bandage from the first-aid box behind reception. Nobody seems to care that I am rooting around in the desk looking for things to wrap myself in. Nance's old bat lifts a purple-nailed hand to me as she walks past and tells me to pick up the pace with my work today, OK.

I tell her I think this might be my last shift, or something, and she says: What, did you want us to throw you a party?

I pull my trolley into the lift and head to my floor.

The room I enter is one overlooking the foot of the Knock, so outside the window is just green. Because of all the heavy rain it is greener than it would usually be. The rain has brought earthworms to the surface, too, and on the path up to the entrance they wriggled and were squished beneath my feet. I strip a bed and I think: If I was cut clean in half would I become two separate people?

There is nothing sweeter than identical corridors of locked doors to which I have the key. Rooms upon rooms of big beds and patterned carpets and textured beige walls and cheap bathroom sets. More detritus. This time I find a single branded sock, flat and white like it is fresh out a packet. An unopened box of mini gobstoppers. An empty bottle of Coke. A little plastic bag that maybe also had coke left half pushed down the plughole of the bathroom sink. I have started to just leave these things. They have found their way into the maze – why do they deserve to be rescued? I lift a used condom up with my bare hands, inspect it and put it beneath the plastic undersheet. It is a strangely sensitive act, like I am preserving life. Maybe it won't be found until it dries, or starts to smell. Until someone loses a pretty earring in the bed and sticks their hand into its softness to discover something quite different.

In one room, I think this: There is another town. This town and the one that overlaps it, and it is by the Knock that I feel this the most. This place is a thin place, each layer of town a clear panel through which Kate looks through time at me. When I unwrap my dressing and clean my gaping wound, it is like I am cleaning someone else's gaping wound. Because of this, I am much kinder and much more gentle.

I clean the blood from the skin around the hole, which, even since the early morning, has widened into an even more ragged tear. There is not much blood any more. Maybe the hole is self-cleaning, like a little creature. I wrap the gauzy white bandage a few times around my middle. The fabric dips a little where the hole is but it does not become immediately stained because I have done such a good job. I touch myself gently all over and it is a nice reminder that I exist. I can feel it, though – the pain is less, but I can feel the actual shape of the thing disrupting the normal contours of my body, can feel something scratching at the surface, something moving in me.

I am just pulling my polo shirt back down over my head when I hear a knock.

I won't be long in here, I shout, but they keep knocking.

Go and just give me a minute, will you. My polo shirt is half stuck in my bra. I rip it out and pull it down gently over my side. I think that maybe it will be Inga at the door. Inga is young and always seems to be working when I am and sometimes she smiles and nods at me when I come in and sometimes she stares through me like she has never seen me in her life.

I squint out through the peephole but there is just the empty corridor, the walls that need a fresh coat of paint. Greasy handprints where so many people have felt their way to rooms after late nights or early mornings, fumbling with key cards and phones and room numbers they have committed to memory and then forgotten. Everything here contains an imprint I cannot clean off.

But, still – the knocking. I turn very slowly, press myself against the door. Still no one. I realise the sound is coming from inside the wardrobe.

Thomasin, says Kate.

I stay very still. I try not to breathe. I tell myself I am not really there and none of this is really there either.

Thomasin? She knocks again and again and the wardrobe door rattles. The knocks become more rapid and then they escalate into banging and it is all so sudden, and the wardrobe moves from side to side.

Thomasin Thomasin Thomasin. Her voice rising into a cry, a scream. She bangs and bangs and the flimsy wooden door shudders. There is no lock on that door.

I throw myself across the room, against the wardrobe, which shakes and threatens to fall on me. It doesn't, though, and I hear her heavy breathing, her raspy wheezes between shouts as I press myself against it. I have my arms outstretched behind me, wrapped around the wardrobe, my back against the door, the handle boring a hole at the base of my spine. The real hole throbs and screams. If this cheap piece of furniture wasn't here, we would be touching. Is this the closest we have ever been? There are no trees between us. Do my dreams of her bring us closer than this?

Thomasin, she says. Knock knock knock. Thomasin, Thomasin. Knock knock knock and everything shakes. Kate wheezing and trying to breathe sounds like someone rattling an old key in a lock.

I want to run away, or lock myself in the bathroom. But then I would have no way out. I have this image of Kate lounging on the big bed while I sit in the bath, shivering. Her pacing the room, looking at the cheap pictures in their cheap frames and admiring the garishness of the carpet and calling to me in a soft cooing voice: Thomasin, I know you're in there. I know you're in there and I can wait all day and all night for you, Thomasin. I can wait for you forever and ever and ever and ever. The Knock hunched over, looking in, blocking out the sky.

In this image, she is sing-song like a child but now she is screaming and it is not the door but the whole room that is shuddering and what was once my name is now just a throaty gargle like her mouth is filling with salt water and then she is saying: They are here THEY ARE HERE they are here for both of us and you have to let me in you have to let me in so I can get away Thomasin LET ME IN.

The banging stops. It is so sudden. I feel a great weight pressing against the wood and she is sliding down to the ground and I hear her voice slipping through the crack under the door. She is moaning now, drawn out, voice slightly cracked from the shouting.

Kate lets out something that isn't a sob so much as a low animalistic groan. She moans: Please please please please please please please.

I slide down to the ground too. I think maybe we are sitting back to back. For a while there is silence. I feel like I am drowning again. The peacefulness of it all, the terror.

You have hurt me, Kate, I say after a while. There is a hole in me that came from you.

I am shaking all over and my hands have swollen so all I can feel is a slight tingle. My fingers are purple cylinders and my silver rings are disappearing into the flesh. Everything smells of disinfectant and sweet rot.

I hear her on the other side, deep inhalations like she is trying to regulate her breathing. I imagine she is oxygen-starved, and then I wonder if she needs to breathe at all, or if she simply does so out of choice or habit.

I am sorry, Thomasin, Kate says. I don't really understand. All I understand is that we do whatever it takes to survive. And then, in a voice so soft it is nearly a whisper: Let me in. It is so small in here. I cannot see and I cannot breathe.

No, I say.

Let. Me. In.

I will never let you in.

Kate howls. She claws at the door and it is like the wardrobe contains a huge creature not a girl and she is probably taking great gouges out of the wood on the other side and she is screaming my name and then, again and again: LET ME IN.

There are quieter moments too. Moments where I feel her breath in the slit under the door, feel it on my back, and she is hissing through that little hole: letmeinletmeinletmeinletmein-letmeinletmeinletmein and her lips are probably touching the floor of the wardrobe, all the shit that collects at the bottom.

The hole is throbbing dully and my cheeks are wet with tears. I think it has been just minutes but it feels like forever.

They are here, Kate says again. She knocks once more and I feel her fist on the inside of my flesh like she is knocking from within the hole too. The sound is no longer a hand on wood but a hand hitting against a wall of flesh – a muffled, wet thud.

I say nothing. I close my eyes.

Eventually I am sick of the silence, of only my own rattling breath. I stand and edge the wardrobe door open. If I'd been brave enough to do this when Kate was screaming, I wonder what I would have seen. A straw witch? A burning woman, charred flesh falling off the bone? A sweet pale girl in a long white dress? A girl who looks like me, wearing my clothes? A stupid haunting bitch who stinks of wet earth and rot, who screams and moans – who whines, who whines – because she does not get what she wants and what she wants is me or my life, or something?

Instead, there is a broken hanger, a greyish white sock with a hole worn into it at the toe, a curled-up fire-evacuation notice, a ball of lint-rolled Blu Tack.

There is also the blue jumper. It is muddy, has been stretched and pulled at, twigs and wet leaves caught in amidst the fluff. The inside of the wardrobe smells mulchy, the air thick and very old. The mohair has come apart at the cuff and as I reach in and scoop it out, cradle it in my arms, I am careful not to let that slender blue thread unravel any further.

I take the jumper and nothing else, abandon the trolley in the room. I leave the hotel beside the hill even though my shift has only just begun and I walk to the flat where my packed bag waits and I do not look behind me as I go.

Outside the flat, I realise I don't have my keys so I buzz and buzz and eventually Nance answers and she says: Oh, Thomasin, honey, and just hearing her voice makes me start to sob. I am tired of being numb. Inside, I walk past her and straight to my room. I should feel bad doing this, but it makes me feel as though I exist. Like, this is my house and my room. Storming is something a daughter can do.

I flail in the middle of the room. I grapple for my case. I do nothing, I stare up at the ceiling. I realise that the ceiling is textured. How interesting that I never realised that before. My eyes get wetter and everything blurs. I leave the door open because closed doors leave things to chance, now. Kate could be anywhere, behind everything, and it is like she is closing in on me.

Nance is in the doorway. Honey, she says. Did something bad happen at work? Did someone say something nasty to you?

I don't talk. I stare up at the ceiling. The texture has morphed into holes and those holes are filled with dirt or little seeds or pus so it is like the whole room is made of my skin.

Nance comes to me, presses a cool hand to my forehead, frowns.

Eventually, I say: I know it was meant to be tomorrow, I know it wasn't meant to be today. I'm sorry. I'm sorry, but I have to go.

Are you sure? she says. You don't seem well.

I just have to go, I say. I'll feel better if I just get back, I think.

Thomasin, she says, and I say: Please?

Nance tells me she is hardly going to hold me here against my will, though she looks hurt. She prises the blue jumper from my shaking hands and folds it up in a plastic bag so the dirt doesn't get everywhere and packs it into my case. She peels my fringe from my wet forehead, ruffles the hair. She lifts my case down the stairs for me, walks me to the bus stop, tells me what stand the bus to the city will be at when I get to the bigger town, writes it on my hand so I don't forget: Seven, in inky black biro.

Nance holds me tightly and kisses me hard on each cheek and then she leaves me.

On that bus and the next one, I don't say anything to anyone and I stare straight ahead at the plastic back of the seat in front of me and I don't look out the window and I don't look back.

Thomasin's bus leaving is a cord ripping. In the abyss, Kate tries once more to reach her. But Thomasin is not there and Kate can reach no one else – has never been able to reach any one else – and soon Kate starts to feel as though she, herself, is not there either. Wherever I am, Kate thinks, I am completely alone.

Part VI

The Hole

1715

I am in the place between places
I am something taking flight
I'll shout that to the trees, then:
I am I am I am I am I am I am I am
but the Laird is too
and now he has multiplied so as to grab me
at every angle, in every crevice
many men screaming silverware
it was there one day and then it wasn't
and the prison they build me is one of knives and spoons
and there is no mention of what the Laird has done and tried to
    do
only knives and spoons and seductions
and witch from every pair of raw salmon lips
dragging out my kitchen girl who says
(skinnier than in my dreams, shaking, promised more more
    more)
that Kate, she is a witch, or something
I swear I saw her make the silverware disappear
I am beneath the canopy still when I close my eyes
and then
growing as tall and as wide as it
peeking over the tops of the other great trees and seeing just
    this
just everything
sunlight refracted through water

a silver-finned fish which has not yet been caught
which slinks at the river's bed
(let us search for the Devil's mark, then)
(her skin is disgusting, so rough and grey)
stab me till my burst moles bleed
and I become pulp
(pull and shave where the occasion shall serve
search her body all over
for the Devil doth lick the strangest parts)
and I, in the ground, ripping at myself in fear
not Kate McNiven but a witch without skin and hair
and I cry and cry and cry
and so does my kitchen girl and at home
my mother and my brother
and the leaves which dance on the hearth
and my dressing table
and all my nice things on it
and the town I used to wander into and the paths I took to get there
and the animals with lolling pink tongues I thought were telling me:
Kate the angel, Kate the clever girl
join us, stand swaying in the sun in this field
life is bliss, life is fine and my mother from the doorstep:
come on, inside with you, or, well then, a little while longer, I suppose
you look so happy out there, Kate
and the Lairds say: Well, we have corroborative evidence
more than enough to go on
you are dangerous
and a whore too, so the Laird of The Big House said
the Devil tempted you to tempt him
you were his vessel

whose vessel?
their words meander around me like licking flames
blood and water fill my eyes fill this stifling pit
and worse things will happen before I am dead
in the end, I will confess:
I lay with the Devil. I am a witch.

Sixteen

The bus pulls into the city. I stand under the plastic awning in the station for a while. When I am at home, I am kind of evil and desperately lost, cruel to the people I love and cruel to myself too. I feel nervous, and I want to delay my return.

I watch a big family with lots of little children and they have their suitcases piled up around them like a fort. A little girl has a small case with four wheels and she sits atop it and rolls back and forth, back and forth. Sometimes she looks over at me, to check I am still watching. An airport bus pulls in and they board and it takes ages and the man is fumbling with tickets printed individually on A4 and the woman is watching the girl rolling back and forth and she is the last to get on the bus, the woman, hauling her daughter and the plastic case up the stairs with milky eyes, a very vacant sort of look. I watch them as they pull away, and although the windows are darkened, I can see their outlines and their smiling mouths. Tired and clinging to each other and going somewhere or maybe going home.

I toy with staying at the bus station forever, or going back to the town, or going somewhere else. But – Kate. I am shaken, still in a bad dream. Here, at least, I feel the stretch of miles and miles between us. Soon, I hope, I will feel nothing at all.

I walk in the direction of my own home. My dad's home. The girls don't know I am back and I don't want to see the bathroom of the flat again. Sometimes, I would think about killing myself in there, but it was always some romanticised version of death where my red blood would spray across the white tiles and it was never what death actually is, which is just gross and horrifically sad. Also, I haven't replied to their texts for so long that I think they probably hate me.

Out of the city centre and towards the suburbs, I pick up a bunch of flowers from the corner shop. I plan to present them to my dad. My dad likes to care for flowers. He likes to trim the stems and put them in a vase of tepid water and into this vase he also pours flower food from a sachet and it makes the water foam up like the flowers are sitting in soap. People who know him know this about him so they bring flowers when they come to the house. He is thankful for this, I know, because otherwise he would have to buy them himself and justify his feminine purchase to the supermarket cashier. These are not for me, by the way, I imagine him saying to some spotty teenager. These are for my wife girlfriend fiancée mother grandmother my daughter's unborn daughter not yet conceived sister niece the bitch along the street and by bitch I mean female dog next woman I see on the walk home last woman I touched first woman I kissed the graveyard the headstone of my dead mum these are to throw into the abyss or toss up to heaven or give to my daughter. Breathe.

I don't walk through the meadows. I take the main roads instead because this means I don't have to walk past Leo's family house with its pressure-washed patio and astroturf lawn and shining uPVC windows.

When Leo took me to his house for the first time, it was after we had been together for two months. One day he said to me: I have decided I want you to meet my parents now, as though he was unsure up until that very moment.

I said OK and then there I was, standing outside the door as though I had been lifted up and thrown there. Leo went in first, by himself, carving the way, and I stood there wanting to pick at something. When I am in a garden, I like to rip up handfuls of grass but I couldn't this time because the grass wasn't real.

Are you going to come inside, dear? said his mum, poking out a head as blonde and pink as her son's. She looked as though she really, really didn't think I was a dear and I wondered if she was the sort of woman who might see me as competition for her only son's affection.

In through the plastic I went.

Leo's mum would later tell me she was a boy mum, which was more of a mentality than a physical state. She would say: Before I had my son, I didn't know what true love was.

We sat at their big dining table, which was covered by a shiny grey tablecloth. The chairs were white faux leather. Leo's dad, a small man with the build of a rugby player, in a shirt from his local club, got us Diet Cokes from the big American refrigerator. There was bottled water in a cellophane stack of four in the centre of the table too. Even then I found Leo's inability to drink from the tap to be absolutely grotesque and repellent. One of the first things about him I was brave enough to hate.

Now I stop in the middle of the pavement for a moment to watch a woman with seven dogs walk past me, the one million leads turning her into a strange sort of roving spider headed towards the city centre. The dogs are all small and fluffy – the sort people want to adorn their first-floor flats and pruned back greens – and they don't pull and they don't bark. Already I miss Finn so much it hurts. I even have a sudden compulsion to run after the woman and tell her: I have one of those too, let me get out my phone and show you some pictures. I don't though, obviously. I watch the great beast turn the corner and vanish from my sight and then I turn in the opposite direction and walk home.

My house smells strange. I think this as soon as I walk in. It is like a hotel, but not the hotel beside the hill. One of those nice ones where you actually want to steal the soap. Maybe it has always smelt like this. And because people's houses rub off on them, I would have smelt like it too. Leo probably loved me for my sanitary scent. Clean but not necessarily fresh – cloying, maybe. Now, I hope, I will smell like Nance's flat. Stale smoke and cheap perfume and microwave dinner and dog. I want to smell of things that repel. Also my flesh, rotting – the most repellent thing of all.

The cream lampshades in the living room are furry with dust but the cream carpet is freshly hoovered. The mirrors are misty but the TV has been wiped down. The kitchen is clean because it is bare, apart from a bunch of bananas and a metal bowl of nuts on the side and some milk and yogurts in the fridge. One mug and one bowl and one spoon sit in the sink. The same pictures are up that have always been up, even the one at the end of the hall of me as a child. It is a little picture from a film camera and I am about two and I am smiling in a stripy summer dress with ice cream on my nose. My hair is sun-bleached and thin and curly in the way that children's hair so often is. We are in Spain, probably, all-inclusive. It isn't the holiday that is a memory I hold dear but the picture itself, seeing it on the wall every day for so many years.

Coming home is being thanked for flowers and being asked these two things: Will you go back to your flat soon, then? Will you go back and visit Agnes next summer, too?

Coming home is being asked, too, not to touch anything. I have everything just the way I like it, says my dad. You know that about me.

My dad's eccentricities aren't strange instruments or weird food experiments or mid-life-crisis hairstyles. My dad's eccentricities are loading the dishwasher in his own particular way and recycling with precision and eating the same few healthy foods while watching the same genre of documentary every night.

Coming home is realising that my dad might be a bit sad and lonely and feeling only resentment towards him about this. If you would look at me, Dad, you would see that I am here and always have been.

My dad is trimming the ends of the stems and selecting a vase from the tallest cupboard. The neighbour gave me a nice bunch of carnations last week. To apologise for the building work. They are getting an extension and every weekday there is just brown dust and banging. Nice bunch of carnations. And they have lasted well, too. Make sure you look at them when you're in the dining room, Thomasin.

OK, Dad.

The neighbour is a woman, says my dad. I can't mind her name but it's too late to ask now.

Do you remember when we went to Spain?

What?

The picture in the hall? I think it is Spain.

We didn't go. You did. Agnes took you, just you and her. It was quite a bit before she had her wee girl with that – what was he called? Matt, he was called, wasn't he?

Oh, I say. Oh, I don't remember that at all.

Well, you were very little. It was just after your mum – you know.

Went, I say. I say it to fill the space his half sentence has left rather than out of any sort of spite towards the woman who birthed me. My mum, who sends me carefully wrapped gifts on some birthdays – sensible things, cashmere socks and good-quality hair products and crisp textbooks only vaguely related to my degree and much too dry and challenging anyway – and FaceTimes me with her awkward, boy-like partner – a professor of something or another at a university down south, like her – on some Christmases. I don't blame her for just leaving. Not everyone is supposed to have children and not every woman should be made to stay. I sort of like that she forced my dad into the awkward situation of being my sole carer. Also, when I close my eyes and think of my mum now, I see Nance, the white and turquoise and pink cloud of her, the sofa stained and the car door flying open, her weird clothes on my body and her arms around me.

We went away too, though, Dad, didn't we? Me and you.

The holidays I do remember with my dad were me sitting swinging my legs on a Travelodge bed while he took business calls at the laminate TV stand or the orange wood desk by the tiny window looking out over the car park. Run down and get yourself some breakfast, he would say while on hold, and I would because he told me to, and in the breakfast lobby with my watery eggs I would watch the other families and would wonder if we, too, were going to do something fun like go to a water park or a museum.

I would take my dad mini pastries wrapped in napkins and he would never eat them so, after we had been on a walk or a drive or to an Italian buffet or whatever else was nearby, I would wait for him to fall asleep in the adjacent room and I would keep eating until I felt sick and even after that, I would eat until all of the mini pastries were gone.

Do you remember how we would always go and stay in a hotel for, like, a long weekend and I would always steal all the breakfast pastries from the buffet and we would share them later, while we were, like, at a museum or a water park or something?

Yes, says my dad, I did have to take you on some business trips back in the day. Thank god for retirement, eh? He smiles at me.

Do you remember the pastries and all the things we would get up to, though? I ask.

Sure. And then: You know what, I do remember the pastries. You would get up at the crack of dawn and run downstairs so you could get at them before anyone else did. You liked the ones with jam the best.

I am delighted that he remembers it this way. Although I desperately want to continue the conversation, I don't have anything else to say because there is nothing else about that time I remember.

I didn't realise Nance took me on holiday, is what I eventually come up with.

Oh, he says, yes. That wasn't the only time. Before she had her daughter she was always stealing you away. Which was nice, you know.

Why did she stop?

Stop what?

Stealing me away.

We didn't get on so well, she and I. I mean, when we were very little, we did. She was my big sister, she loved me. He takes a weird, shaky breath. When Agnes first moved up to the town, you know, she'd come down and see us, you remember that, but I suppose I didn't want her around you all the time. I suppose – he trails off. And then she had her daughter, you know, and if she wanted to come to the city she would've.

Did I see her as a sort of mum, though? Like, when I was a child did I think she was my mum?

No no no, says my dad. It was never anything like that. You didn't think she was your mum. And then, changing the subject slightly, he says: Is she a good mum, though? Just out of interest? To her daughter?

My hand drifts to the hole, which has hurt less in the short time I have been in the city. I have an urge to feel something familiar, like the inside of my body, but when my hand drifts under my top, something doesn't feel right there any more.

Her daughter is called Nina. And she is good, yes.

Kate is in a witch pit, a dark black hole ragged with stone. It is nothing like her safe cave. It is where they put condemned people many years ago but it has been a long time since a woman has been a witch here in the town. Witch, the very concept of witches, is starting to become this old thing. It is not the seventeenth century any more, or the sixteenth, even, when there was a real witch fanatic on the throne. People know witch means paranoia and anger and they know it means neighbour-on-neighbour fighting and dead cows and rejection, or rape if rejection isn't an option. They know these things, but people, even the ones who played with Kate as children or sold goods to her at the market or sat near her at the Kirk, reason her murder away as divine justice, as the way things are and most likely should be, and then they think little more of it. This is later, though – for now, Kate the witch shakes the town and makes it more alive with chatter than ever. People walk or ride from other towns, too. It is so completely wonderful to have something to talk about.

At first, Kate's mother and brother do not know she has been captured. Her mother strokes Archie's hair at night and whispers: All is well, my boy, all is well, she is safe and away. Archie does not bat her away and broaden his shoulders. He doesn't want to take up the mantle of man any more because surely a man would be able to swoop in and ensure his sister's safety, surely a man would choose to go with her and protect her. They could be on the high seas right now if he was a man, Archie thinks.

My girl is safe, I know it, his mother is saying. If she wasn't safe, God would let me know.

There is a banging on the cottage door. It is Archie who answers. It is a stable boy from The Big House, a boy Archie has known his whole life.

Friend, says Archie, thank goodness.

The boy does not stand on the porch but far back. Oh, Archie boy, and he cannot meet his eyes. Oh, I am sorry.

At first, Archie does not believe it. We will fight it, he will say, and the boy who was his friend will shrug from all those steps away.

Fight what? Is it not God's will, Archie boy? I know it is a dear shame and a personal tragedy, but overall it is God's will, I am sure. Go to Him instead of her, trust in Him.

Archie says: I will go to God, then, and I will kill Him and I will not live in His world any more. It comes out hoarse and loud and the boy yelps and retreats, back towards the neighbour's house — the house she will later fortify with stone walls and high fences and shrubs that she will train up over the windows that look out upon the McNiven home — and then past that, back to the safety of his own home.

Archie drops to the ground, where a long time ago his mother scattered straw. He remembers Kate coming home one Sunday and seeing the straw and scrunching her nose and grabbing the broom.

This is hardly a barn is it, Mother? she said, and then, inclining her head to Archie: We have but one pig!

When Archie was much younger, he remembers, he would watch as Kate collected the straw instead of sweeping it out onto the step. She would gather it in her arms and stuff it into their mother's spare shift, tie it shut with string. Look, Kate would say: A lady to dance with.

Now, Kate can see flickers of light from the metal grating above her — it was the grate that she was dropped into and she fell down down and she cracked her ankle and now it is bent at an odd angle and she can't put pressure on it– and she can hear voices above so she thinks she could be in the town. She hears children, sees the flash of little forms above her. They are daring each other to goad the witch. Go on, says one. Go and have a look in.

Kate thinks that if she was up there with the children, she would want to goad the witch too. Or just see her, maybe, have a peek at total evil or something like it. I can barely see the wretched creature, says a young high voice. His fluffy head is blocking out the light entirely now. He is pushed aside by a bigger figure, an older boy. I can see it just fine, says a voice on the verge of breaking. Squeaky then gravelly and back again, like her brother. Kate watches as the boy leans over the grate and makes a strange sound and moments later a globule of spit lands on her head. It slides down her forehead and, gagging, she wipes it before it falls into her eye.

To make a woman a witch you must do this: Prick her all over with bodkin needles to see if she bleeds. Remove bits from her – her teeth if you like, but you absolutely must remove the nails. Shave her head with a blunt knife. A witch will come alive against the tip of the blade. Get as close to the skin as you can. Let the blood run in her eyes. Use her body against her. Or, if you cannot take her body, destroy it. The boys know this. This is what happens to Kate.

When they take the nails off her right foot this hurts the most because her ankle is broken and they slide a hot metal clamp under her big toe and they pull and when they do, her whole foot is pulled, the ankle bent back the way it has come and she feels bones cracking again and howls and wills the nail to just slide out and the skin has swollen so much it is purple, inflated around the nail so it is just a little sliver of pink peeking out from puffy bruised flesh and when they do eventually rip off the nail the skin seems to close up around the wound before her very eyes like a fleshy wall so there is barely any blood.

I press my nail into the soft flesh of my hand. The nail is ragged and it cleaves the skin like a peach. I go in through the layers until I reach the bone and then I wake up, uneasy in my childhood bed.

I text Nance: Everything OK with you guys? And then, because this message feels so wrong, so abnormal, I send another and it says: Also thank you for having me. I don't think I've really said thank you enough. XXX.

In the next room over, my dad is watching TV and the sounds seep through the old walls.

Now I am in the city, I am starting to wonder whether any of it was real. The grey of it all tells me I am mentally ill and the town exacerbated it and I was never really punctured by a witch's finger and now, here again and safe and cosy between big buildings and new things, I can see that it was all a bad dream I have woken up from. I should make up with Leo and get fucked on my springy mattress in the student flat or on the soft memory foam of childhood and eat tea with my dad and kiss my friends on the lips in the pub they insist on calling our local and I should probably kill myself one day too, just for continuity's sake, but only after I've got a half-decent final grade at university so at least my dad might cry at my funeral. She was a good girl, he might say. She had potential. None of this is real none of this is real but really all of it is in such painful high definition that it is sharp and it cuts deeper than sweet vicious Kate who is nothing like me because she wants to survive and I have no idea if I do.

I think I am feeling these feelings because the hole is starting to close. It is still a hole but the film over it is thicker and whiter, more of an opaque lining now, and the edges which have been wet and pulsing and taut and shiny and red and pulling ever outwards are shrivelled, the skin slackening, the wetness drying up and scabbing over. This is fascinating to me, but also terrifying because it is like I am losing a limb. I am losing this, I think. I haven't seen Kate since coming back to the city. She can't reach me here. Which is good, obviously, which is exactly what I wanted. And yet.

Maybe she just missed the bus, is what I tell myself next. Maybe she'll turn up later, out of breath, laughing. I have never really seen Kate in this playful light so I wonder why I do now. Where is she when she is not in me?

Seventeen

I wake up to a man standing over my bed and at first I think it is some man I have never seen before in my life. Actually, it is my dad. He is holding a cup of too-strong tea and he holds it out to me but keeps his distance, still, so I have to awkwardly sit up and shuffle myself back towards the headboard. I am wearing pyjamas from when I was about fifteen, the plastic decal on the front morphing into something grotesque against my chest.

When you were little I would sometimes just stand and watch you sleep, he says. When I could get you to sleep, he adds. Because you were so bad at sleeping. And when you did, eventually, I would stay up all night anyway just watching you tossing and turning.

Why?

Because you were my child. I was responsible for your life.

I take a sip. The tea is slightly cold. I wonder if he made it for himself and then decided to give it to me, or if he made it for me but stood over me for so long that it cooled. Thanks, I say, holding up the cup to him.

I'm not – he stops. I mean, I am. I can be here.

Do I have to reassure a man who is nearly sixty that he is loving enough and good enough? Would that be the kind thing to do? To drink his tea and tell him he loves me. You love me, Dad. I know that.

I drink his tea and I tell him: You love me, Dad. I know that.

It is exactly what he wants and this gives me a momentary

flush of happiness, like he is accepting flowers from me again. I have so much to give, I think. I think too how funny it is that we have really always just been the two of us, but we have never been a unit of two. Father and daughter, separate entities under the same roof, just passing each other in the corridor. We drifted past each other even when I was young enough to reach only his stomach, then his chest, his shoulders. Now I am as tall as him and maybe a bit taller than that, even.

Do you need any money? Is that why you're here and not at your flat?

Oh, I say. I mean, no. Like, I was working over the summer in the town.

Yes, Agnes told me. That's good. So you don't need any money?

I'm OK.

You're sure?

I mean, maybe a bit of money.

Oh, he says, and he looks sort of relieved. Oh, that's great. I'll transfer it into your bank account.

He leaves the room and I sit there in bed for a while. The hole has continued to scab over, and the amount my skin has closed up overnight is sort of shocking. I have tried to scratch it open in my sleep, I know, because I can see nail marks across it like a wild animal has been at me. My sleeping self is not willing to let it close and I have no idea, really, what my waking self wants.

Kate's capture is the best gossip the town has seen in a lifetime. Everyone is enthralled by the witch.

Archie walks to The Big House every day. He rattles the doors and windows and screams until he is dragged away by the Laird's men. At first, they treat him gentler than the local boys did, and then they beat his teeth out. You are no good to

Kate like that, Archie, his mother says, but the next day she joins him at The Big House. Screaming for the Laird, she throws rocks at the building, howls for her daughter's life, demands to know where she is. They are escorted from the premises back to the cottage and the men are sent to stand outside to prevent further attacks.

Kate's mother feels like she has lost everything, but she has not and she clings to Archie and she presses her face into his hair and her children's heads have always smelt the same so, with her eyes closed, Archie might be Kate and Kate might be Archie and they are all together and all is well. She can still feel Kate's flushed cheek under her palm, can hear the echo of that slap. She cannot stop wondering what might have happened if she had barricaded her daughter in their home instead of sending her into the wilderness and although Archie wants to comfort his mother, he is angry, too, and he has no words for anything any more.

For a time, there will be rumours about the old Widow McNiven being a witch like her daughter, and people will lick their lips and try to provoke the grieving family, but the Widow McNiven stops speaking and her son gets bigger and sterner and, eventually, people get bored and something else happens and they are left alone.

For now, though, in the darkness, mother and son grip each other. The Laird's men stand outside their cottage. Sometimes Archie can hear them joking, laughing, sunning themselves on the porch. He feels his prayers are met with nothing, but still, he prays with his mother. It is all they can do. There is no one they can fight and the town is against them.

It has rained overnight so the witch pit is like a well and Kate wonders how long she will have to be here for and she longs for interrogation, longs to be anywhere but here, in the damp against rock and so, so aware of her own body.

Kate closes her eyes and tries again to reach the girl Thomasin, but she has no idea where she is. She tries to imagine the girl in the pit with her, and after a while these imaginings become so vivid that she can feel Thomasin's soft hands stroking her hair and Thomasin is saying to her, voice hushed so the people above ground can't hear them: We can go to the city together, and further than that. I have been to so many places, we have so much to show each other.

In some of these fantasies, Kate has Thomasin marry her brother so she is locked into their little family forever, and it is the three of them and their mother who travel to the city. In other fantasies, it is just the two girls, their bodies becoming one without pain. Looking at you is like looking in a mirror, Thomasin is saying to Kate.

Kate has a vacant smile on her face. She is in this fantasy but she isn't really lucid and her mind drifts away and when it comes back Thomasin isn't standing next to her but far above her, looking through the metal grate and laughing down at her and the girl has a spiteful face now, and Kate has no idea who she is.

Thomasin scrunches her lips together and balls saliva up in her mouth and then she spits.

I meet Leo for dinner. He offers to come to the flat or my dad's house but I can't have him in those spaces because he has been in them so many times that they feel like his and that means I am vulnerable there. We are in a little late-night café just outside the city centre, the ground floor of a pale stone tenement with a terraced garden out the back. There are candles everywhere. It is very romantic. It is a warm night and I dug out one of Claudia's long floaty dresses from the back of the wardrobe in my dad's house for the occasion. A body made up of lots of different parts of other people's bodies, this is all I really am.

I order a sandwich with soft aubergine I don't even need to chew, oil dripping out from the holes in the bread and pooling on the plate. I get a coffee that comes in a tall glass with a tiny handle. Leo asks for water for the table, but bottled not tap because he just can't drink that stuff Thomasin, you know that. He does not order anything to eat. I am watching my body right now, he tells me. Cutting. Instead, he watches me eat.

So, he says. You're back.

For now, I say.

He asks me if classes have started yet and I tell him that, yes, they will next week.

So you'll be around until next week at least? He says this with a smile and a laugh like he is making a joke.

What is funny about that? I ask.

Oh, nothing, nothing. This summer you've been hard to grasp. You were bad before you left but we were good, at least, the two of us, and now you're back and you're bad, you're worse, and we're bad now too.

I get what you're saying. I bite my sandwich. The bread is so soft and chewy and the aubergine is salty and wet and the coffee is so mild it tastes like warm milk and I am taken back to the petrol station and the town and everything and I think I even close my eyes and tip my head up as skylights like little yellow dots stain the inside of my eyes. You should try some of this, I say. This sandwich, with the aubergine.

I am cutting, Leo says. Did I not just tell you that?

Hmm, I say.

For fuck's sake. This is such a fucking shame, Thomasin.

I rip a piece of crust and swirl it round in the oil. When I put it to my lips, the oil trickles down my chin. I catch it before it drips down onto the dress. Now that would be a fucking shame.

It's like you don't care about any of this. Like you don't care about us any more, what we had, or me, or anything.

If that's how you feel.

It's infuriating, Leo continues. It's devastating. You think you don't love me any more but you don't know what you're letting go of, how much you will regret letting go, and it's so frustrating because I can see it and you can't.

There is something weak about Leo, I realise. Sort of pathetic. In many ways I think I will always fear him and what he meant to me at one time but also he is pitiful and he really does look like an American actor and he is always just playing a character and clinging to those around him so they can legitimise him and make him real and I pity him, yes, sort of, but I envy him too because he is so unaware of his own selfhood that I think in many senses he is really truly happy. Leo needs people and their affirmation to survive. I wonder if he would exist without me in his life. I was his project and every time he was holding my hand or my hair I was willing him into existence and supporting him and being what he needed and I cannot be that any more for him. Clinging to Leo, afraid of him but afraid to let him go and before the town I would phone him up whining in the middle of the night begging him to come over and I would analyse the things he said and repeat back his opinions word for word and watch him smile and say: Yes, well said, my girl, and he didn't make me feel good exactly but he made me feel secure and normal, attractive even, and sort of proud like I could say, yes, he is mine, I did this, this one good thing I did but now I don't think I need that sort of validation because in the town I have done so many strange things and had so much strangeness thrust upon me that I no longer resemble a functioning person, a person who presents as normal and so has to keep the grotesqueness of their self within and I no longer have to care about things like Leo.

Thomasin, says Leo. You're not listening to me.

I think it is interesting, though, that Leo still cares about me. This would have made me so happy in the past because it would have given me that sense of power that I craved and never possessed in the relationship – partly because I didn't want to, I think, because I liked to watch Leo while he was driving and he liked to be watched – but now I really don't feel anything other than a vague sense of annoyance and I am not addicted to whatever it is he gave me any more, so I don't think I will go back to that place that is him, ever again.

Thomasin, Leo says. Thomasin Thomasin Thomasin. I don't know any other men who would put up with what I've put up with. Who would love you like I love you, who would love you at all. You do know that, right?

He sounds almost sad.

I take the last bite of my sandwich. I lift the plate and bring it to my face and lick it clean. The plate obscures my vision entirely so I do not see him, only the salty fragrant oil, the last chunks of aubergine stuck to the ceramic.

Right now Leo should be telling me I am disgusting and I have no manners and he should be telling me to stop in a firm voice, looking around to see who is looking at me, but he is silent. He is being careful, placid. Leo can be silent or make a scene if he wants, I realise. I can make a scene if I want. I do not care. He can stand up and shout at me in front of all these people and they will see him for what he can sometimes be or he can walk out and cut me off or he can cry and lick the oil off my fingers and pay for my dinner but these things do not matter to me any more and I have drawn a line between us so he cannot touch me.

It is over, Leo, I say. And I really mean it.

He opens his mouth to speak but he doesn't speak. I look at him and I know my expression is blank. I have caught him off guard. Did he think this was going to be some sort of reconciliation? He is looking at me but he cannot look into my eyes. I watch him put on his jacket, which is crisp and denim and one I have begged to borrow many times, and then I watch him leave.

I order more food. I feel empty without the thing that is Kate within me. It is a foreign feeling to not flinch every time I move, to feel no pain, see no blood. I have to fill the pit in me with something else and I want to fill it with food. I order a bottle of sweet white wine, fried rice balls with tomato sauce and melted cheese at the centre. They are on a bed of rocket and their heat has caused the rocket to wilt and turn dark. A plate of spaghetti, wound tightly into a saucy ball. Ice cream in a tall glass and I ask for every sauce so it looks sort of like a murder scene but tastes so incredibly sweet and I can feel my teeth aching and tingling and my brain seizing up but I keep shovelling everything in. I lick every plate and platter. I ask for the bill and it arrives with some little heart-shaped chocolates wrapped in shiny pink foil. I put them into my bag for later. I will always, always be hungry again but for now my stomach is rock hard and swollen.

The nights are getting darker but people are still out and everyone is still in summer clothes and the city is lit with streetlamps and blue light and I walk through the meadows and it is only at the last minute that I decide not to go to my dad's but to the flat instead. When I get in the lights are off and their doors are closed and I am not even sure if Claudia is back, and I sleep between bare mattress and duvet because Elaine stripped my bed when I was gone.

I decide to text Evan: I have broken up with my boyfriend. Properly this time. How are you? How is everything in the town?

She replies: Thank fuck. Don't break. He might try to win you back and you have to hold firm.

I think we're finally past that, I say.

She replies: Everything I know about love comes from TV and books and you and it seems like love sucks!

Love sucks love sucks love sucks love sucks love sucks love sucks love sucks!

I type: Does it? I don't think that was love. What I had with Leo was something else. I think I know that now.

I hover over the message for a while and eventually I send it.

Evan sends me a paragraph of hearts and happy faces. At first I think she is making fun of me, but then she says: I really hope we see each other again soon, Thomasin. XXX.

I wake up feeling weirdly joyous and weirdly empty. I can't remember my dreams.

The hole isn't a hole any more, it is just a mark like it was when Kate first touched me with her straw finger, and this makes me feel weirder, like everything is going backwards. It isn't fully healed – there is still a dip in my skin and some scabbing in the very centre – but I can no longer stick my fingers inside myself from that point of entrance, which is sort of disconcerting. More reassuring, though, is the fact that nothing can come out of me. I had got quite used to not being a contained vessel and instead being some sort of multi-purpose gelatinous lump spilling out everywhere like over-risen bread dough. A person without holes does not leak, and nothing seeps in.

I pad through the old tenement, go down the hall into the old kitchen. It is a kitchen designed for students – laminate counters and faux-granite surfaces – but it also has the original cast-iron range, a massive black structure now used to store university work and the fruit bowl and envelopes with ever-increasing bills, and letters from Elaine's gran, who addresses her cards to all three of us.

Elaine is making breakfast. My first thought is: She is back at it again, sort of cosplaying family life. Elaine loves having us in the flat but, and Claudia and I have discussed this, she makes us feel like visitors because she is always cooking us meals and cleaning up after us and playing hostess and she is always smiling. Maybe she is just happy, I suggested once, and Claudia shook her head and said: It is so intense and overbearing, though. Sometimes I feel like she is laughing at us.

I embrace her and she tells me how delighted she is to see me. She tells me that Claudia is back too, and grumpy already, and she puts avocado toast with scrambled eggs and sesame seeds and cherry tomatoes down in front of me. She has chopped the tomatoes into little segments as though she is worried I will choke on them if they are whole.

I have an urge to shock and upset her and am about to reveal the break-up with Leo, when she speaks first.

Do you know, says Elaine, I've started to pick out my eyebrow hairs.

What? I say.

It started in summer. Just a few and at first it was sort of deliberate because it was relaxing or whatever but now it's compulsive, like, when I'm trying to watch TV or when I'm studying and then I look down and there's all these little hairs in my hand. I just want to tell you now in case you notice and feel awkward about it, or whatever.

I don't know how a person is supposed to reply to something like this. I want to say the right thing but because I am thinking of what that right thing might be, I don't say anything at all. I think of Elaine holding my hand and changing my sheets and being my friend and still I don't say a thing.

You can't tell because I've started filling them in. At least I hope you can't tell. The pencil is a bit dark maybe but you can't tell. Or maybe you can. And it's like, I still go out and do everything the same as I did before but now I rip out my eyebrows too.

Elaine is not usually candid. She is quiet and smiling and she tries to please people and she listens and she does not ever want to be jarring and this is what I know about her, but none of these things are really attributes, they are just other people's perceptions. Elaine gives advice, Elaine makes my breakfast and puts up with Claudia's barrage of texts and my radio silence.

Elaine, I mean, Elaine, you need to try and stop.

She picks up the string of her herbal teabag and drags it around the rim of her cup. The yellow liquid inside sloshes.

If I stop, I worry that I will stop functioning altogether. Like, maybe this is keeping me sane.

You could shave them, remove the temptation entirely.

God, she laughs, and then what? Move on to my hair? Maybe my eyelashes first.

Grow your leg hair really long and rip that out, I say.

I'll consider it, she says, and now she is smiling.

I can see it when I look at Elaine, now I know that it is there – the little gaps between the hairs that she has tried to fill in with that too-dark pencil. The over-exaggerated arches that are slightly different and much too high on her face. She looks a bit surprised. I can see it all now, and I really have no idea how I didn't before. I wonder what she would look like without hair. Maybe she would still look pretty. Probably not. Maybe her baldness would be good for my self-esteem.

Any time, I say, any time you need to talk you can come and talk to me. Do you know that, Elaine?

Yes, she says. You're my friend, Thomasin, I know that. And I'm talking to you now.

Yes, and any other time. I'll be there.

Before I walked in she filled the cafetière and I think it must be just about ready to pour now. She has left two little cups on the side with the frothy milk already in them. I push down and watch the granules vanish. I pour the syrupy brown liquid and the contents of the cups bloom. The smell is wonderful and it fills the room. I pass a cup to Elaine and she holds up her tea and tells me the coffee was just for me and Claudia. I take a big sip, smile wide.

Coffee is divine, really, I say, and it has a nostalgic taste to it.

Hmm, says Elaine.

Which is strange, you know, because I was never allowed it as a child.

Hmm, she says again so I say: Anyway. I am there for you, OK? You know that. You'll be fine. I promise.

Yes, Thomasin, thanks.

I drink my coffee, let out a sort of satisfied grunt and watch my friend's face contort – or maybe it is the eyebrows that are making her weird like that – and then I go through to my room and this is it, isn't it, for now, but all the while I or some part of me is saying: I don't exist I don't exist I don't exist I don't exist I don't exist I don't exist I don't exist and is this me slipping back into something good or bad and is this the light at the end of the tunnel or a return to the worst possible state of being?

I hear Claudia walking along the hallway from her room into the kitchen and instantly she says: What the hell have you done to your face?

And I wonder if it really is possible to hate your friends and love them and want to be them or be with them and I wonder if Kate feels any of these things towards me.

Claudia, Elaine and I spend the rest of the day in our separate rooms, or maybe they go out, or whatever – I don't know. I take a long shower, I draw moths on the steamed-up glass, and we reconvene for a takeaway in the early evening. I wear the dress I took from Claudia an age ago, even though we are just in the flat, even though there is a streak of oily aubergine down the front. I am challenging her to challenge me.

Instead, though, the conversation is focused on Elaine. I root around in my cardboard pot of noodles, spear spring onions on my fork, half listen.

It's not the café, Elaine is saying, I like the café. It is stressful but good. I needed it this summer.

You should've told us. I would've come back earlier.

It's nothing serious.

It's a compulsion.

Not a serious one.

I let a strip of red pepper in thick brown sauce fall onto me, pick it up, roll it between my fingers, put it into my mouth.

Thomasin? Claudia is saying.

I say: What?

You seriously weren't listening to a word, were you? This is our first proper night together again after summer. I mean, care a little less, god.

Elaine says: Don't, just leave it, it's fine.

I tell them I was thinking about other things, get up, look back at them from the doorway. I don't know what I'm supposed to say, to be honest, I tell them.

Elaine says: Anything, Thomasin. We're here for you too.

I say: Elaine, some of your eyebrow pencil has rubbed off just there. I can see the bald spot.

In the hall, I hear them still. Claudia says: That's not your dress. Fucking take it off. And Elaine, in almost a whisper: Don't, just leave it, it's fine.

In my bedroom, I press my face into the pillow and wonder if the summer changed anything about me at all.

Later, when I am under the covers, Claudia comes into my room. She doesn't knock. She sits at the foot of the bed with her hands clasped in her lap. She is wearing a beautiful pair of silk pyjamas.

I've just been with Elaine, she says. For, like, a long time. She has been crying, obviously.

Oh, I say.

Thomasin, you made her cry.

Maybe I did make her cry. I want to feel sad for Elaine and her eyebrows but I can't just conjure feelings from the ether if they don't already exist inside me.

Claudia tries to meet my eyes. I stare at her pyjamas instead. There are little shiny birds on them, their claws entwined with rose-bush branches.

Can you leave me alone? I say eventually. I'm trying to get some sleep.

Claudia sighs, stands, walks to the door, which she closed behind her when she came in as though we were going to be having deep discussions late into the night.

Goodnight, I say, and it makes her turn around and face me again.

Thomasin, you know there is going to be a time when you have pushed away all the people who love you or like you or even know who you are and you will have no one left and however you feel now will be nothing compared to how you feel then.

OK, I say, whatever. Claudia doesn't know that I am not alone, that there is a witch inside me, pushing on my organs, tugging especially on my heart or maybe my stomach. She sits on my lungs sometimes, too, I think. Or she did in the town, where she was heavier and the hole was deep. Since coming home, I have tried to avoid thinking properly about the absence of Kate.

Claudia's face softens a bit: I don't see why you can't just let us in.

I am really sorry. I am sorry to both of you. But I just don't think I can.

Sleep well, Thomasin, Claudia says. Have happy dreams.

I listen as she pads across the hallway, into Elaine's room instead of her own. I hear the creak of the bed as she gets in. I lie still for a minute but I am no longer comfortable. I feel so lonely. I get out of bed, out of the room and across the hall, stand outside Elaine's for a moment. I knock and push open the door and I think maybe I will say something to them but there is nothing to say.

Claudia in her silk and Elaine in her fleece move over to make room for me and I slide into bed with them and Elaine lets me share her pillow, so our noses are almost touching, and Claudia straightens out the duvet so it covers us all and we stay like that until the morning, clinging on, and I have the best sleep I have had for as long as I can remember.

Eighteen

I spend a week in the flat. I unpack my bags and I wash some of my clothes, even. The blue jumper shrinks a little when I put it through but it still fits well enough and the last of the mud and the last of Kate is gone. The girls love the jumper, and I relish in telling them it was handmade for me by my new best friend.

We just got so close in such a short space of time, I tell them. Like, she really helped me through some stuff, you know?

Claudia sceptical, Elaine leaning in, both of them nodding their heads, listening. It is almost scary how easily I have slipped into myself again. I feel a bit like me before I was mentally ill to the point where it made me unlikeable and repellent. The me who wouldn't stand in the shower crying – at least not too often, and even then I only did it because it made me feel tragically beautiful. I start to feel more and more like that version of myself who is always being perceived, and not by some otherworldly being but by everyone and everything around me.

My new mantra before I go to sleep is nothing to do with Kate, no begging her not to haunt me or asking her to keep me company, it is this: I am happy I am happy I am happy I am happy I am happy I am happy I am happy!

I put up colourful posters on my landlord-off-white walls so the room resembles Nina's colourful one and I buy throws from the home-bargains store and spread them on my bed and I even use hangers instead of dumping my clothes at the bottom of my wardrobe and I even buy a big plastic folder to organise my university work and all the while I am telling myself how happy I am and I am telling myself, too, that this is self-care. I don't go out with my friends because I am doing face masks in the candlelit bathroom with spa music playing and I start reading again but the books aren't the ones I love, they are self-help books stolen from Elaine's room, and when Claudia bangs down the bathroom door because: Oh my god Thomasin I need to pee I have needed to pee for like the last half hour, I tell her to just fuck off because I am practising loving myself, finally, and can she not just be happy for me?

The days pass and the hole in my side seals up completely and I rub scented moisturiser into the red skin, rub my whole body in oils so I resemble a seal and with my new soft shining skin I slip between my freshly laundered sheets alone and I think about who I will be and sometimes I say to Kate: Maybe you never really existed maybe summer was my lowest ever point like my proper mental breakdown and I had to create you to show me the light, or something. Is that, like, a possibility? I realise I could look her up but never do because I don't know what I would do if she were real, or not real.

I bake a cake using a recipe from social media with no sugar and no butter and the strange flavourless spongy thing sits on a plate in the kitchen for a few days before it mysteriously ends up in the bin. I interrogate the girls and they both deny it. Elaine looks terrified.

Claudia says: God, I forgot how sort of despotic you were. The energy in the flat is unbearable.

Elaine clasps my hands. Maybe a ghost ate it, Thomasin, or, like, maybe a ghost chucked it in the bin?

It is the ghost bit that sends me into a miniature spiral because I think, yes, that could very well be possible from my point of view because a ghost has done much worse than that to me before and I storm off into my room and resolve to stay there for the rest of the night to punish them, but I get hungry and as always I give into that hunger so I come crawling out.

The girls both hug me and pour me tea from a pot on the table and I see the glance they share and know they have made some sort of private agreement to just be nice and this frustrates me even more because it makes me feel fragile and left out and I want so badly to be let in.

But: I am happy!

I text Evan. I text my dad. I go on long walks with my headphones on and watch dogs running in the meadows. I wander round campus with an acquaintance from one of last year's classes and he insists we get bubble tea and I finish mine in five minutes and have to spend the next few hours watching him painstakingly sucking each individual black ball while I tell him again and again how good this summer has been as a healing journey for me.

I am happy!

Nance sends me a picture of Nina and Finn at the café on the high street with the caption: At his ripe old age, Finn finally made it to a café without knocking over any tables or savaging any customers. Here is photographic evidence.

I am happy!

I feel as though I am seeing my physical form with a new clarity. I resolve to lose weight and get hot and start washing my face before I go to bed. I do yoga from video tutorials in my underwear with the blinds shut. I resolve to buy nicer underwear so I can do it with the blinds open.

I am happy!

I check my bank account and see the money from my dad. Because I am a good daughter, I text him again, this time to thank him and ask if he wants to have dinner with me at some point in the next week. He replies: No, sorry, I am a bit busy Thomasin. But use that money to buy yourself something nice on me, OK? I have a panic attack in the shower and it feels like my chest is closing in on itself and I turn off the water and try to regulate my breathing and eventually I manage and I can take in air again and I wipe the steam from the mirror and stand there looking at my tear-streaked face and eventually I start laughing at my reflection and this, I think, is what healing is.

I am happy!

I arrange to meet up with a man I met out one night many months ago through a friend of a friend, who goes to one of the other universities in the city. It is me who finds him online and messages him. This is the sort of thing people do after a break-up, I tell myself. I ask Elaine to help me compose the message and she looks at me in confusion. I realise I still haven't told her Leo and I are finished. I go to the man's student accommodation where he works as a support representative for younger students. His flatmates have all moved out and the new cohort hasn't yet moved in, and I stand with him in the kitchen as he mixes rum with ginger beer, talking about nothing, still wearing his bright red STUDENT SUPPORT T-shirt branded with his university's logo. I tell him I'm just going to nip to the loo and walk out the door and down the hall and get lost for a while in the endless bright white maze of it all, the metal banisters, the blue plastic carpet, the layers of posters for society events and student bands and spare rooms for rent like layers of flaking skin. Eventually, I find the big glass front door and burst out of it, collapsing on the tarmac. He doesn't come looking for me, even though I crouch there for ages.

I am happy!

I come up with a short-story idea for the first time in a very long time. A girl goes hiking and a tick latches on to her leg.

She goes to remove it but falls in love instead. She can't bear to separate herself and the tick. It sucks her and she kisses its bloated body and swells with joy as it swells with her blood. I toy with the idea that she might be sexually attracted to the tick, as well as romantically. I never write the short story.

I am happy!

I find out that an influencer couple I have followed for some years have broken up. It is a shock to all and the comments are furious. We didn't see this coming, says one. They each release separate videos about the break-up and I watch both of them. I find myself tearing up when the influencer man says, through his own tears: She was the best I ever had and I'll always love her, don't you guys worry about that. We will continue to make content together, but we won't be together any more, says the woman. Don't you guys worry about that. Next, I watch a video of a man squeezing a blackhead on the nape of his neck. There is no pus – it comes out whole like a little brown stone, leaving an indent that is peach-coloured and clean.

I am happy!

I close my eyes and lift my face to the sky and feel the September sun on my face and in that moment I am connected to something out of this world and I know that there have always been Septembers in some way or another, so Kate would have once felt this very same sun in this very same way. The freedom I felt immediately after ending things with Leo morphs into a different sort of discipline. I am free to restrict, I am free to construct myself however I want, I am aware of my body and what I want it to be so I will not gorge again. Now I have left Leo, I imagine myself as a new girl. I imagine myself with longer hair, for some reason, standing up in front of a seminar talking confidently, raising my hand in lectures to provide interesting counterpoints and always, always provoking discussion. Brave and a little brazen, maybe. Uplifted, even. Empowered?

When I am not feeding my ever-dying attention span with thirty-second videos and the same safe music again and again, thoughts of her do slip in. The skin on my side that was once dropping off is nothing now. There is no hole, only the faintest mark, like a birthmark, and even that will fade. I am healed and clean. I feel relief and loss intertwined, the knot of them sitting where Kate did. I wonder where she is now and if she is OK and I know she is not because I saw her future on the cinema screen and all I can say to shift my attention away from the town is:

I am happy! I am happy! I am happy! I am happy! I am happy! I am happy! I am happy!

The days pass and then I get a call from Nina. It is very early in the morning and the ringing wakes me up. I roll over in my soft heavy sheets, in Claudia's silken pyjama top, stolen from the dirty-washing basket. Nina is using Nance's phone and at first I just hear her breathing down the line, rapid, wheezing through each breath.

Put your mum on, Nina, is she there?

The girl lets out a sob and then, to herself: Stop it, just stop it. To me she says: No, she's not here, she's out looking.

Looking for what, Nina? What is it?

For him, for Finn. He's gone. Please can you just come, can you please come today?

I don't even think about it. I move a disparate mess of clothes from my floor to my bag, my new toothbrush, a half-full bottle of water. I am still half asleep, talk to Nina the entire time about nothing much at all just to keep her on the line, listen to her breathe, only hang up to phone a taxi to the bus station.

Elaine is up. I was watching the sunrise out the kitchen window, she says. And then I just stayed up, I guess. Without make-up to fill in the features she has picked off, she looks like a Renaissance painting.

I tell her I am leaving, but that I'll be back tomorrow, hopefully. If not tomorrow, then in a few days. I don't tell her why.

Did you forget something? Is Leo going to drive you?

No, no, I'll get there myself.

Class is literally about to start. You'll miss everything.

Maybe.

I know if Claudia were up, she would fix me with a perplexed sort of look and I would fix her with a dirty one and everything else between us would be left unsaid.

Elaine puts her arms around me. She smells of coffee, her vanilla perfume, the warm milk she is heating on the stove. See you tomorrow, then.

I buy a ticket to the next town over and stand under the terminal. The roof is clear plastic and the sky rains and pours. I realise I haven't told Nance I am coming, and hope Nina has. I think of drowning, half-arsing my part-time job, of destroying her room, of getting her to pick me up, delirious, at the petrol station, the drain on her life that I was all summer. And then I think: I could be worse. I could be, like, a drug addict or a creepy woman-child who drowns kittens. She took me to Spain nineteen years ago. She loves me.

It is only when I am on the next bus, the one that will take me to the town, that I let myself think of Finn. I imagine him alone, wet, shivering in a copse somewhere, trapped between the branches of a felled tree or tangled up in electrical wiring from a pylon brought down by the storm or in a bramble thicket, his coat stained red and stuck with thorns. I imagine

Nance tearing through undergrowth and thick mud and water and anything to get to him.

The rain has cleared and the sun is out and the countryside speeds by like it did on my first car journey to the town with Leo.

There were no clouds that day but now the blue sky is speckled with them, and the grass then was flat and sun-damaged but now it is lush and meandering because of the rain. Always, this place is scorched and then comes back to life more lovely than before.

Part VII

On the Knock

1715

the Knock hill is a carcass unintelligible as any dream
a green dream a haze a captive tower
a spirit world a very living place
I have been stripped of my fabrics and my things
which were precious and few
and even my skin
doesn't look like my own, like
I am being roasted in the flesh of another
a bird baked into the centre of a pie
can I climb out and fly or dance at least?
I think of the Laird, after a party in the velvet dusk
dancers there too, girls I had never seen from a bigger town
girls from the city and me
wanting to go home needing my bed he said
I ate the pie and I will eat the dancers too
go home tonight Kate McNiven go home tonight
and I will see you tomorrow
and, morning, when I brought him tea
white morning crisp morning running through frosted grasses
cursing wet feet spilling hot tea
scalding my wrists which he held
silly girl
me pouring, him saying
I ate the dancers I ate the dancers
and his stern wife picking at tea leaves
pretending to see something that could never be there

him hanging her necklaces or his mother's necklaces
someone's necklaces that were not his to give
around my neck
the weight a comfort a wealth a
vision of me dancing with gold coins at my throat
the weight a collar
I like pretty things but
I am not his
my throat does not want to carry this
and my countryside is not a glittering jewel
I cannot pluck it from the dirt and set it in another time
    another place
where I feel safe
(that Kate's not half bad
I should've sampled her when I had the chance
that Kate will be in hell
soon dancing with the Devil so
you won't ever see her again
we aren't going to hell
lads
all those who have come to witness this lawful execution
boys who gathered the logs
our dear Father from the chapel
come to chant away the killing
good man
who lights the fire
his eldest who begs to chuck it on the pyre
you have become a man
tie her to the post and set it alight)
I am terrified but
I am angry
I am really angry
and blood from my shorn scalp leaks into my eyes

so of course I see red
and I see a mother cover her girl's ears
rough hands though gentle and neat when braiding I assume
    and
I am fervent
and why are you even taking your daughter to watch me burn
(sweet girl close your ears for the Devil hath got her tongue)
but he hasn't, I have my own tongue
this tongue in this mouth
this pink satin tongue like a cushion
rough like a foot
I walk where I want to in my own mouth
and the Laird is just a man really just a stupid man
stupid men are dangerous men I want to
live in a time where they are not
there is no time where they are not
but I will take my teeth to it all
my sharp teeth my eternal peasant's teeth my animal teeth as
    old as myself
to the town and the smoke rising up from the houses
so hearths will grow cold and men will shiver
and curse Kate McNiven with lips blued from
cold and drink from loveless long nights
poor men poor people here
and the smoke is cloying it is in my mouth in my eyes and
flames lick my feet
I have always liked my feet
I am delirious on smoke
a hedonist for air
for the very fabric of the world
for things that I can grab with both hands
for texture and colour and
the way I feel in my body

that is not mine any more but
that I love love love
eyes fixed now
on no one but my slice of world and
I am utterly and entirely convinced
that I possess some sort of magic
that my curse will slip through the gaps in time
through the ages
and slink into a new day
where it will hang
resonant.

Nineteen

Kate McNiven walks up the Knock. She is barefoot and the sun beats down on her shorn head and she cannot really walk any more and she drags that dead foot behind her, a parasitic limb. The path is treacherous, and the heat has brought the insects from their crevices so now they hum in the air and in the dried ferns and Kate sees flashes of black beetles in the tree roots. She will stumble and hit her head and she will be pushed and break bones and see the bones coming out through the skin but she will not pass out, even though she wants to, and she will realise that never in her life has she ever fainted, like her body is resistant to it and is desperate to keep her awake for every moment of her suffering or maybe it is her body clinging to life, clinging to consciousness, desperate, always, to hang on. The skin on her calves looks as though it has been peeled off. She can't remember the men doing this to her, so she thinks maybe she did it to herself. I have peeled some potatoes in my time, she thinks, so maybe I did this to myself.

The men who escort her feel special to have been chosen for this job. This day is a break from their usual toil and they will be remembered for their help in delivering justice, they think. The Laird will know them now, and their sons will want to be like their fathers. Soon a procession of others will follow, made up of more men, yes, but also their sons and their daughters and their wives. One will hold a screaming baby to her chest. They will all make their way up the Knock once the witch has been tamed by these first brave few, some of whom were her initial captors. The Laird will arrive with his wife and their grandson and a group of servants. The kitchen girl will be there – Kate will think that bringing her is a cruel trick, a final stabbing, an embarrassing demonstration of Maggie's subservience or maybe just of the Laird's dominance – and it will nearly make her cry.

Before the confession was taken from Kate, witch was still this far-flung thing. Yes, she had been accused and yes, she had run, but witch was a fiction and witch could be sorted out by her mother because witch could not really touch her. Even when they were heating up the pliers and saying, You should really just confess now, girl, confess and spare yourself all this.

Confess and you will be saved, Kate was thinking: There is no logical world in which this will not be over soon. This will all be over soon. And when the burning metal made contact and melted her flesh, when she was branded by men all over her body just for other men to arrive and call those burn marks the imprints of the Devil's red fingers, when she first felt the sort of unimaginable pain that most people will never feel in their lives, witch was not just close, witch was her. It is not weak to buckle under pain, to have it prostrate you, change you. Kate screamed and confessed to make it all stop and when she did they said: She is a witch! She hath confessed! And it all went on and on and on anyway and, really, Kate was a witch to them before she confessed and she was a witch after – it made no difference. And most of these men are boys who don't even know what witch means. Some of them harbour a secret feeling that all women are witches and that the only thing it takes to bring this out of them is a little bit of pain.

Kate leaks fluid from every part of her. It is hot – too hot. The sheer brutality of what is being done to Kate McNiven is already imprinting on the Knock, seeping down to the town below.

When the story of Kate McNiven is told after the fact, this brutality will not be enough, and townspeople claiming to be eyewitnesses will add that once she reached the top she was thrown back down again and made to walk up a second time and this, even, will not be enough, because years later others will add that she wasn't just thrown back down but stuffed into a barrel and rolled to the bottom and when she was pulled out she did not resemble any living thing but she was living, somehow, and this horror will satiate, finally, for a time, until people get bored and want again to hear the story of the witch.

When she is almost at the top of the Knock, Kate will look beyond the path and see a mottled grey figure flitting between the trees. She will recognise it, that massive creature. An ungainly dog with too many limbs and ragged fur and a sweet long face and, despite its loping gait, it will be manoeuvring between cut trunks and gnarled stumps and fallen branches and gaps in the clusters of ferns with such easy grace that, for a moment, she is able to leave herself and follow it. A little beast, like her. A canine spirit from another world, or another version of this world. Pain doesn't ripple over the body because it cleaves her into pieces.

Maybe the other world will be a honeycomb of caves like her safe one, with a different nice room for each of the people she loves. Maggie will still be welcome, despite everything. Kate does not like to think about it any more, but in the witch pit she realised that if it was Maggie accused and her on the other side, she would scream WITCH just as loud. She will have a place in my great comb, Kate decides. I will give her that.

The honeycomb of caves turns to actual honeycomb in Kate's mind, and her people are bees in the hive. We might lick the walls sometimes, to get that sugary coating on our tongue. We will never want for nice things to put on bread.

Kate, queen of bees with a giant sting.

They reach the top.

She is draped over a man now, for her knees have long since buckled beneath her, but she feels the dog too, his rough tongue gently licking one of her limp arms.

The bus pulls onto that familiar wooded road in the late afternoon and I feel it inside me, this crossing of a threshold. In the distance, I see the Knock. I cannot see the summit but on a path leading up there are the tiny black dots of bodies, scattered.

Stepping off onto the high street and the thing under my skin is returning, or maybe just awakening after a short city sleep. It is nice to not be alone in your body, I realise. I breathe as deeply as I can, but there is something like anticipation in my throat and it is making me choke. Fumbling with my phone, walking in the direction of home.

When I get to Nance's flat, I really regret not phoning ahead. This is weird, turning up again like this. Even a little embarrassing. Thoughts go round and round in my head but I cannot reach a conclusion and then I am at the front door and it is almost like Leo has dropped me off all over again except now, of course, everything is my choice.

I ring the buzzer and hear Nina's voice on the other end.

Hello?

Nina?

Oh my god, Thomasin. You have to come up you have to come up now.

I take the stairs two at a time and I can see Nina's little body on the landing and she says nothing and she takes my hand.

I feel the absence of Finn as soon as I enter the flat.

If you stay with her I will go out to look, is what she does say as she leads me into the living room.

The room is a mess – not the usual ordered chaos of their lives, the hair-covered sofas, stacks of books and vintage curios in odd places. There are cold cups of tea everywhere, each one untouched. Ashtrays sit overflowing and the windows are closed, the air cloudy and stagnant. Cereal, softened and stale, sits on the coffee table, a bluebottle rubbing its feelers together on the side of the bowl.

Nance sits on the linen sofa staring blankly out the window, motionless. Her face is red and puffy and the skin on her neck is red too, as though she has been hacking at it with her nails.

I step into the room and she turns her head to look at me but I don't think she really registers my presence.

Nina sits down next to her mum.

Mum, she says softly, wrapping her arms around Nance's shoulders. Mum, it's OK, Thomasin is here, Mum. And then to me: She was looking all morning ever since. You know. When she got back I didn't know what to do so I just made her food and tea.

Nance is still looking at me and her face breaks into a weird sort of smile and she says: Thomasin, and then she starts to cry.

Nina clutches her mum tightly and buries her head into her breast, Mum Mum Mum Mum Mum Mum Mum, and Nance shudders and heaves and cries silently.

I crouch on the ground next to them. From the mass of their bodies, Nina extends a little hand to me and I grasp it.

I try to speak in a soft, placating voice and realise what I am doing is mimicking my ten-year-old cousin.

How did it happen, Nina?

She untangles herself from her mum and looks at me. If you just stay here with Mum I can go out and look I can get my friends to help I just don't want to leave her.

No, I say. No, Nina, you just tell me where you saw him last.

Nina is running her hands through her fine hair, she is pulling at the sleeve of her school cardigan.

Mum, we're just going to go and make you a cup of tea, Mum, OK. You just stay there.

Nance doesn't respond. I follow Nina into the kitchen. She starts talking quickly, stumbling over her words.

It was me and him and Mum just the three of us this morning before school and he was off the lead and we were down near the hotel and he is a cheeky boy Mum always says he tries his luck and tries to run but he never actually runs obviously like he wouldn't really run and I was chasing him or he was chasing me and Mum was down on the bench and she was just on her phone or something for just one minute and I shouted over to her look at us is what I said and then I looked back at him but he was gone and I don't know where he went and we looked for ages for the whole morning and Mum went into the hotel to get them to look too but then she started crying, crying a lot and she wouldn't speak to me, and I was saying: Mum, we have to keep looking, but she got someone from her work to drive me home in case Finn, like, in case he walked home and she said she would keep looking but then they drove her home too and Finn won't go to them he needs me and my mum he needs us.

She is fumbling with the teabag tin, trying to get the lid off. When she eventually does, the tin falls to the ground and all the teabags fall out and she throws the lid down too and lets out a single howling scream.

Do you want a hug? I open my arms for her, I do not know what else to do.

No I don't I don't don't touch me, she is saying, just let me just give me a little second.

She grips the counter, breathes, looks at me. Don't worry. I am not going to scream again.

Let me sort this. You go and sit with your mum.

No, Nina says. I can't go back through. Can you?

I do as she asks. Entering that room again is like fighting through thick air. I start coughing and I am glad because it means that for a second I don't have to speak. I sit down next to Nance.

I need to find my boy but I feel like I can't move.

I know, I say.

I shouted at Nina. I told her it was her fault.

It's OK.

It's really not.

She knows you didn't mean it.

She says: I did mean it.

I feel like if I don't keep saying it is OK I will start to feel as though it isn't and then I will be just as useless as Nance and we may as well just stick on the TV and watch it crying while Nina brings us food and tea and the house fills slowly with rot.

She is staring out the window again and it is like she has shut down. There is a cigarette on the arm of the sofa and matches by a stack of burnt-down candle stubs on the mantelpiece. I light the cigarette and slot it between her fingers. She does not move. I know that this is the wrong thing to do because it will kill her long-term and short-term could burn the house down. But this is what I do.

I go to the kitchen, where Nina has poured hot water into seven cups. She is scooping teabags up off the floor and putting one in each and when I say her name she turns around, guilty, and says: I don't know.

You are doing a great job, I say.

I know that I have to go and look for Finn and that the sooner I do, the better chance I have of finding him. This is a small place, I tell myself. Everyone in the town knows him. He can't have gone far. Then I think of the fast cars on the route to Evan's house, the trucks that rumble down winding country roads.

I bend down so I am level with my cousin. I don't grasp her shoulders. I am going to go and get Finn now. I will go and pick him up and bring him back here, OK?

I expect her to protest, to ask me again to stay and watch Nance, but she just nods.

I will make the tea. I just need to put the milk in and then it will be ready.

Thank you, Nina.

I am heading to the door when she says: How will you know where to find him?

At first I don't know how to respond. I haven't even thought about it.

Then: You know how Finn is, like, your brother, Nina? Well, that means he is my cousin, which means we can both feel him wherever he is. It's like magic.

Her lip wobbles. But I can't feel him. If I don't know where he is does that mean that he is dead?

I force out a laugh. That is so ridiculous. Canine familiars can't die if the witch is still alive. It is impossible. And you are still alive, aren't you?

I have no idea where I have got this from. Kate, obviously, but this is the stuff of fiction spun from more than dreams. Still, it makes my cousin smile slightly.

I am still alive, she says.

She goes back to make her many teas and, no sooner than I have arrived, I am headed back out the door.

Finn was lost by the hotel beside the hill which means I have to go there too. Not to my old place of work, but the hill itself, that craggy summit, those tree-covered slopes. A weird place I have never wanted to tread. I know that Kate was brutalised there, and I am worried that the sharpness of it all could split my skin. But I also know I have to go, and in a way I am sort of proud of myself for my bravery. It is a good feeling to have people that you will do anything for. Nina, Nance. My Finn, who is sweet and has endless love to give.

I have come back to the town, then, to go up the Knock. I am almost laughing as I go because this was always going to happen, I think, like Finn and Kate have colluded to send me up there.

I slip my phone from my back pocket, I don't know why. I text Evan: Back in town! Finn is missing. Going up the Knock. I love you. XXX.

I put my phone away and feel it vibrate against my skin and I know it is her but I don't check, I just keep walking and soon I will start to scream his name and the closer I get to the Knock hill the more confident I am that he will run to me and that he will be completely fine.

My baby my baby my baby. My grey baby my colossal baby my sweet sweet baby my baby.

There is a pyre of logs and sticks and one large shorn beam sticking out from it and Kate is tied to this with rough twine. She does not wear manacles any more, so when she is burnt there will be nothing left of her body but her teeth. Maggie will pick them up when the procession is gone and keep them in a little pot like a saint's relic. She will know that this is a deeply sacrilegious act and one day when she is baking at The Big House, she will throw them into the hearth in a panic. She will clean out the hearth later that day and gasp. Again the teeth will not burn, and she will not understand why and she will kiss each individual one and then, eventually, get rid of them by pushing them down the drain with the food scraps. Maggie is meant to feed the scraps to the dogs, or she eats them when the cook turns her head, but mostly she likes to see them going to waste. Maggie will be much angrier than she used to be, and the Laird's lady will be eating much less by that point, so the scraps will be many and the drain will clog and the teeth will bubble to the surface again, shining yellowish white.

Now Kate looks out. She feels pain, she feels so many other things. She feels everything. Finn, slipped through the folds from one time to another, runs circles around her, barking. Kate will join him in his noisemaking because she is already a madwoman to these people and so she has nothing more to lose. A few people step back, confused. A mother decides now is a good time to shield the eyes of her child. Kate wonders if she could have ever been a mother, but the concept never held any appeal and especially doesn't now. Kate is a daughter and a sister, and she is herself. She lets her voice run down the sides of her mouth in wet torrents.

The dog and the witch bark. They are calling someone else to them.

Twenty

Sweet Finn, with his delicate face. He has jumped from stretched canvas, from a scene painted burgundy and set in gold. Now he has pulled me into a strange green world. My skin tingles, and it is the opening of a freshly closed wound.

I scream his name.

There are multiple paths up the Knock, all marked with different-coloured posts. I pass the red post, the summit walk, and I think of blood and nearly dead Kate's feet being dragged up and up and up. I have not seen this scene, but I know it happened. The Kate up here, though, that is not her, really. Up here, she is anonymous and intertwined with the branches, stuck through like pierced meat but also ancient in a sense, as though she fused with the ragged Knock trees the minute the saplings took root.

It has rained recently, I think, and the ground is waterlogged. I am wearing canvas trainers and they sink into the mud, into the red grasses and ferns that line the road. It is humid and I am wearing one of Leo's old jumpers – mine now – and I take it off and tie it around my waist. The plants are suffocated and my feet are so wet and hot. Everything seems dead, or dying. Unlike the rest of the town in its newfound lushness, here, no new things push out from under the earth.

The path splits into smaller paths and still I follow the red, which is now more of a muddy trail with spindly trees dripping in pale green lichen like ratty hair. Baby's breath, I think it is called, and all is silent. There are other trees too, big ones that I don't know the names of. Giants with broken hands that jut out from their trunks and stretch towards the sky, droop towards the ground. If I wasn't on a mission, I would want them to grab me, probably.

Finn, I scream.

I feel him, close, or maybe it is her I am feeling. I look for them both between the trees. I think I see her but it is a family. Two women and their child, all clad in colourful waterproofs. The child has a tiny backpack with a lead attached and it trails in the dirt as she runs, untethered.

As they pass, one of the women smiles at me. Are you OK? she says. We heard shouting.

I ask them if they've seen a giant grey dog and they say no, no sorry and we've been right to the top so if he was up there I'm sure we would have seen him. They wish me good luck and run after the child, who is ripping fern fronds from their stalks with her round little hands.

As I continue, the smiling woman shouts after me: It's forecast to rain again. Take care of yourself up there.

At the top of the Knock there is a monument. I am out of breath and I collapse by it. It is shiny, polished columns drawn together by a shallow marble dish filled with stagnant water. It is grand, it has a man's name carved at the base. Me, the idiot, thinking it could be in memory of Kate. Ha ha ha.

I expected more from this place, I think. It has loomed over me all summer and now here I am and it is just land. Hot land, dead land. I can no longer picture Kate walking these paths in tears with bloody feet. I can't see her on the pyre any more. Her, staring out into the mist, fire licking at her calves. I do not hear her voice when I set my palms against that dead man's stone. I feel strange, uneasy. I am not sure what exactly I expected to feel, what I longed to feel.

Finn, I scream, and although I am up here above everything, my voice echoes and I scream his name again and again.

I am still sitting slumped there by the monument and I feel a hot wet tongue on my face and Finn has slinked round the stone and he is licking me in a frenzy, tail wagging.

I wrap my arms around my dog-cousin's thick neck, bury my nose into his fur.

It is you, I say. Sweet guy, it is you.

I have been up the Knock and I have found Finn and nothing bad has happened, really. Already, I am thinking about leading him home and bursting through the door and seeing Nance's face, the softness of her cheek against mine, Finn on his hind legs.

I know too, though, that Finn didn't come crawling from the undergrowth. He wasn't there one moment and then the next he was and something about this reappearance is deeply wrong.

Rising shakily, gripping his collar so he doesn't try to run again.

When I stand, the Knock is not the same as it was before. There are people everywhere, and there is Kate as I saw her on the screen.

When Kate looks at Maggie, she feels a loss briefly greater than her physical pain. For a minute, she thinks only that the kitchen girl has a freckly face. She used to pity Maggie, because, to Kate, freckles are flecks of iron that have floated to the surface of the skin. Kate thinks, even now, that Maggie must be filled with metal because she is so freckly. She thinks that she could dive inside the girl and pluck out something sharp and shiny as a knife.

Maggie sways, looks like she will faint. Kate wills the girl to meet her gaze but Maggie's stares flit only between the ground and her employers. No one atop the Knock can really look at Kate and to her this is the final injustice.

Everyone from The Big House and the town and a magistrate from the city who has sanctioned the execution are up the Knock. There are the local officials too – the high steward and steward clerk, court officers and the doomster. These men have all enjoyed a drink or many at The Big House. Some of them are educated men but university can't buy them what the Laird has. The magistrate has a pointed beard and narrow buckled shoes which have long since gone out of fashion. He looks uncomfortable atop the hill. He does not look at her because the Laird and his wife and their entourage have just arrived. The Laird has a pale face. The Laird's wife is dressed all in black as always, with a large glittering brooch securing a dark lace shawl around her thick shoulders. Kate remembers wearing that shawl in her hair and dancing about The Big House in the nighttime. She was a dark bride then, and she thought she was free.

There are boys around Kate fumbling to light torches. Kate feels a bead of sweat trickle from her shorn hairline down the side of her face and down her neck and across her breast and her stomach and then down her hip where it lingers for a second on the bone before continuing its journey down her leg, to her feet, to the gaps in between her toes. This makes Kate feel alive.

Kate McNiven, says the Laird.

Kate looks down at the man who accused her.

Soon, he will have the scent of her charred flesh on his nice clothes but for now he talks to her as though she is serving him tea, again. On her knees, again.

Kate, he says, except now he is quivering a little. The Laird is sad to lose his girl. He is wondering if the accusation might be a mistake. He is trying to convince himself that he is ridding the world of a great evil and in doing so is securing his place in heaven. He has never seen Kate look so small, so childlike and broken. A wicker doll with a bald head. Still pretty, though. He wonders if – if no one else was up the Knock with them – if he would take her where she stands, one last time. He decides that he wouldn't, because blood would stain his silk coat, one of his favourites. The Laird feels the unfamiliar sensation of tears in his eyes.

He pulls himself together – he has one last gift to give her.

Kate struggles against the twine that now binds her as the Laird clumsily climbs onto the wooden plinth and reaches up. People around them gasp. He is not quite level with her, but tall enough to reach her neck. Careful not to brush her skin, he places the blue beaded necklace upon her.

You always loved this, he says. Maybe this will remind you who you were when you were a good girl.

He fumbles with the gold clasp. Now everyone is silent. His wife, in the background, sucks her teeth.

The Laird secures the clasp and steps back and Kate wants to spit on him but her mouth is so dry. Smooth cold blue beads like eyeballs. She feels the weight of this thing around her neck.

The Laird steps back and Kate sees Thomasin, standing there as clear as the town below, and this is when Kate knows, truly, that the Knock is the thin point between places.

The boys light the pyre. People stand back, faces blank. A child cries.

Kate looks out at the town, and then at Thomasin. And then she commits her last great act as the witch on the Knock.

Kate bows her head as though in prayer but what she is really doing is biting down on one of the big blue beads and it is cool and heavy in her mouth and the fire is catching well now and Kate jolts her head up with the force she has left in her and the Laird's necklace breaks and the beads pop off and fall about the pyre and the Laird steps forward, hands raised, and Kate looks him in his bland eyes, and she spits out the big blue bead that fills her mouth and this, this is when she curses the town.

She doesn't need to say anything to anyone here, and she is sure she can no longer speak in words intelligible to any man anyway. In her head, she tells her town that she still loves it, it is where she grew up, where the people she loves live, and although she wants to burn it all down now, she knows that want won't last forever. Instead, she vows to imbed herself into the very existence of it, and this curse is not vengeance but permanence. It is the will to endure longer than any of the people around the pyre, longer than The Big House, even, which has stood for hundreds of years already. She will immortalise herself in the things she knows, and these things are not big buildings of old stone but heaped straw in a warm house, and familiar clothing, and girls like her, and the soft pliability of flesh.

The bead she has spat hits the Laird and he jumps backwards, clutching the side of his head as though he has been hit hard. She sees the gleam of her spit on him.

Kate feels this brief satisfaction because, finally, she has touched him and he cannot touch her any more, but then she is consumed by a pain unlike anything she has ever felt.

Kate McNiven is burnt as a witch on the Knock hill in the year one thousand seven hundred and fifteen. She is the last woman to be burnt on the Knock, and one of the last in Scotland. She does not know this, and if she did it wouldn't matter to her anyway.

Kate, I scream.

Maybe this is the first time I have said her name aloud.

I scream it again: Kate.

In the smoke and the flames, she reaches for me.

I go to her. Smoke gets in my eyes.

It is OK, I've got you, Kate. I've got you, Kate, I say again, and nothing is as real as this and our hands touch and I feel her in me more than I ever have, so much that the weight of her little body in my bigger one sends us crashing to the ground and we are there, together in a way we have never been before, in the wet grass on the Knock flecked with ash from another time.

The fire has died out and the pyre is ashes and blackened logs and shiny teeth and blue beads and Kate has cursed the town and, now, she is with me.

I am on the ground with Finn, still grasping his collar and unwilling to let it go, and I can't see Kate but I can hear her and I can feel her.

I feel winded, I am panting. Holding my dog as tight as I am is maybe the only thing tethering me to this place.

Look, I hear Kate say.

The old man from the reservoir, from all those months ago, is standing on a grassy knoll. He is peering at the ground as though he is looking for something. The first thing I think is: Maybe he has lost his glasses. The second thing I think is: Oh my god that is the man. He is stout and clean-shaven with a shock of white hair and he is everything I remember. Get your clothes off, and suddenly we are at the reservoir again. I just want to see what's underneath, or something.

Part of me didn't want to see but part of me absolutely did. That was what he said of my half-naked form. I remember him winking, mostly. Innocent fun, the way old men are. I feel my body getting hot all over. I am sweating and it is like I am burning and shivering too.

How did he make it here? I feel Kate ask me. How is he in the same place as us?

Anger is not something I expected to feel at the top of the Knock, but it comes to me in freezing waves. Leo's jumper sags and falls from my waist into the dirt, my vest is sodden. I am livid. For Kate, for myself.

I am not sure whether I can make it over to the man. I am on the ground still, at the very summit. Finn pants in the heat beside me. I want the heavens to open and I want water to fall out. I need this, I realise. We are both done with the heat. Maybe I could crawl, but I do not want to crawl.

In the distance I see manor houses bordered with stone walls set apart from the normal world. Beautiful, formidable buildings with ancient roofs gilded in sun.

My side is open again and a pale slender hand is pushing out. I do not resist it any more. I don't know that she won't hurt me but I need to see what happens. Under my skin all over, things crawl. Stretch marks split into tiny slits through which I see that translucent other skin, wriggling.

Look at him, says Kate.

Instead of crawling, I scream. The man stands up and looks around and he sees me. I beckon him over. Sweat drips from my fringe into my eyes.

Finn rears backwards when the man approaches. I let go of his collar but he stays close.

Is everything all right, love? I thought I heard– He trails off. And then: I was just looking at broken glass in the grasses. Do you know teenagers come and break bottles and leave them here? Disgusting behaviour, in this beautiful place.

I look up at the man through my wet hair. My teeth are gritted. He does not really see me at all.

He says: It is our job to look after our town, don't you think?

I hear: I just want to see what's underneath.

Do you? I say now. The sheer exertion of keeping my

body together just for a moment longer is costing me the clarity of my vision, which is spotting, making his pink face swirl.

Do you? I say again. Want to see what is underneath?

Are you sure you're quite all right, love? the old man asks. Love love love.

Come, I say to him, and then, to Kate: Come out.

He bends down over me and I grab him. The sudden movement rips me open and now I really feel Kate stirring, Kate who has been in me all along. Kate, who is a vengeful beast who can be feral, like me. Since I came to the town we have been two parasites fighting for control of the same host but now we are one perfect grotesque form, a half-woman strange being and we look the way men see us, I think, and Kate thinks: Now we are a witch in the worst and most terrifying way.

With the first hit, he tries to shake our grasp and scramble to his feet. After the second hit, he lies there motionless. We don't stop.

I scream and then the screams turn into something different and inhuman and as I beat the corpse blood sprays up across my face and it is hot and it tastes like metal and we don't stop and I think our screams are being swallowed by another world.

Kate thinks he is the Laird but this is not justice for the past, really. This is just a thing that happens. A bodily thing, a thing with no morals beyond the physical. It is a catharsis.

We beat and bash everything that has been done to us into the soil into him again and again until his face is a hole and he turns to mush at the summit, that place where Kate was burned that is now a place between places, so maybe what we have done will slip into elsewhere, and we let out howling screams again like dogs like wolves rabid untethered we smash our hands into flesh until our hands go through and we are touching the earth.

You don't own this any more, I am saying. I am surprised to hear my voice is calm, measured. You are gone and you can never come back but Kate is here and always will be.

I roll over onto the grass, stretching my red palms towards the sky, pushing them down into the green. I am a burning woman soaked through.

Finn licks blood off my fingers, licks his jowls and comes back for more.

When Kate McNiven crawls out of my skin she does not leave me behind like an old dress, a discarded sack of flesh, a leather bag for a better girl. It is a gentle birth, and we both get to survive.

It is painful in a pleasant way. The sensation is a strange pulling and creamy whiteness oozes out of me and it is her leaving my body so I can just be myself again. Kate's hands come into the world first, those long pretty fingers that have moved under my skin for so long. They prise their way out and one hand grips my stomach and the other the ground and they push gently and I look down and I smile when I see her head breaking above the surface.

She gasps for air, the rest of her sliding out still half covered in a milky caul. I help pull it from her torso as she kicks her legs free.

I look down at myself and am surprised to see just that familiar hole, stretched a lot and torn around the edges but I am not halved in the way I thought I would be. These wounds will heal to circular scars and stretch marks and most of this blood is not mine or Kate's anyway, it is the old man from the reservoir's blood, or the Laird's blood, or the blood of the cursed town, or whatever.

Kate is wringing out her hair, which is covered in fluids from the sac.

Her eyes meet mine and this is the first ever time we are meeting, really, in the same time and the same place.

Kate, I say, and she says: Thomasin.

Kate stands on the Knock for the first time in over three hundred years. Everything looks different but also the same.

She knows this town intimately, is part of the then of it and the now of it too – she has lived here, in this now, every night in her dreams for a summer. She misses her mother but she knows her mother will have died almost three hundred years ago. She knows her home is chalky dust under a ploughed field, helping things grow. She knows there will still be some of the buildings of her girlhood, and some of the trees, the ones that are now the tallest and the thickest, stretching up towards a sky that is near enough the same as it was then. Soon Kate will find out that The Big House no longer stands, that the biggest house in the town is now the hotel, which was Thomasin's place of work instead of her own, which was – which still could be – another thin place where things can bleed together.

Did we kill that man?

I don't know, Thomasin says. Would it bother you if we did?

Kate doesn't need to think about it. No.

Kate, on the grass atop the Knock, eases into her first movements, the discomfort of them, the assuredness of that discomfort and the long slow stretch of someone easing out limbs that have been locked in place for so long.

Kate is Kate as she was before she was burned in many ways, but there are traces of her death on every part of her body. She has hair she can run her hands through although it is short and she can see the stubs of nails on her fingers and she has teeth and can bite but there is a darkness under her eyes and a yellow sallowness to her skin that her mother would tend out of her with hot broth and rest by the hearth. I am dead, she thinks. Then she feels sorry for herself so she thinks instead: I am not completely dead, I am also alive.

But Kate does not know how alive she really is. She is undead, yes, but the body she moves in, although it is a version of the one she has always moved in, does not really feel alive. What is it to be alive? Kate wonders. Is to be alive the same as to live? Will the form she exists in age or will she be a witch in a girl's body forever, until long after Thomasin and the woman and the girl and the dog are dead?

The two girls stare out over the surrounding hills and the fields and the deep black reservoir and the forests, at the town nestled in among it all. Then up to the sky. One of them says: It looks as though it is about to rain.

Thomasin looks at Kate closely, reaches for her hand.

It is strange to be here in the flesh together, Kate says.

She takes Thomasin's hand. The other girl squeezes her tight and Kate thinks that maybe their minds are still connected in some way even when their bodies aren't so when Thomasin squeezes her hand tight again Kate feels the pressure of that squeeze in every part of her.

Now she sees their futures splitting off into separate winding paths.

When I was in you. Kate pauses. She is still painfully aware of Thomasin's recent hatred towards her, her anger and fear. This new way of being together is as disconcerting as it is ordinary. Kate begins again: When I was in you, I felt how loved you were. I saw that and I felt it.

Thomasin looks surprised. She smiles. Come with me. You could do anything now. You can stay with me and my friends until you get on your feet, if you want. Not that you ever have to get on your feet. What is getting on your feet, anyway? I hate when people say things like that.

Kate finds her words: In truth, I am just so tired. I am nineteen but it has been three hundred years. I just want to rest awhile, I think.

At first Thomasin doesn't understand what she is saying. You fought so hard for your life. To become physical again. To exist.

I think that means I can exist in a way I never had the chance to before. I can exist however I like. A big part of that was in you releasing me.

If you don't come with me, where will you go?

Kate doesn't know yet. Instead, she lifts the hem of Thomasin's top up, up. She touches the hole in one brisk tap. It is still raw and red but it no longer pulsates with the promise of life.

Sorry, she says.

Don't be, says Thomasin. Although, it feels weird in here without you. Sort of cavernous. Lots of room to breathe, I guess. Then she says: I'm sorry too.

Don't be, says Kate.

After a while, Thomasin says: If you really can do curses and stuff, I have a really bad ex. Before Kate can respond, she says: Just kidding. Sorry. Not funny. And then: If you're not going to come with me, I don't know. I can't just leave you.

It's not your decision to make.

Kate McNiven has grown up in the shadow of the Knock. It is not just the place she died but the place she has lived, and decided to come to life again. She is what she has always been, what she became again when she clawed her way out of Thomasin – a girl, a physical form, pushing through. But this is not all there is. There is more and she is more. She can always return to the Kate of flesh and blood. She will, maybe.

Now, though, she thinks she might exist everywhere for a while, and the Knock hill will flicker green and brown and orange in the distance and in her, a lovely wild place still, and the site of an awful thing still, but a place that can preside over her no more.

Kate thinks about the curse she screamed at the summit, the blue bead she spat at the Laird three hundred years ago. Three hundred years, a day or two – it is all the same. They killed someone in that same place today, a man, pushed him into another time or ripped him out of this one, maybe. This is not the sort of thing that is happening to Kate, for whom time is no longer a constraint, a concern. She can feel something happening though – she is making something happen.

Kate McNiven has unpicked the fabric of her life and of time, and now of her physicality too. Her curse is a curse of permanence, and she claims the Knock.

It isn't really hers – it belonged to the Laird once, and now a hotel chain – but it can be her and everything can be her, and she gathers the town in her arms, the place where her mother and her brother lived and died. The town and the hill and the fields and the paths – they are not hostile places and they are not boring places, they are filled with life and some of that life is Kate, and she decides she will live it all and live in it all and, at last, she is home.

I hold Kate close until it feels as though I am holding nothing. When I hold her, I feel partly like I have wrapped my arms around myself.

I say: Will I see you again?

The skies open. A question answered. The rain is freezing against my skin. It cuts through the ripples of heat and the haze of older smoke and I can still see the town below, a bit. Blood runs over my eyes but then it is washed away.

Twenty-one

I imagine a version of everything where Kate comes back down the Knock with me, where I take her to the flat and we sleep limbs entwined in the tiny camp bed, her skin still smelling like ashes and wet straw. When I wake alone the day after the events on the Knock, I feel at first as though she is still here, although not within me any more, our bodies glued together only by sweat and dried blood.

When I first saw Kate in the flesh I thought I could care for her gently as though she was my own little creature, nurture her and show her the world. But I am angry at the world. It is not really a respite for burned people to escape into. Part of me wished that Kate had just taken my body and lived my life for me so I didn't have to. Mostly, though, I just looked at the texture of her skin, the smattering of spots of late teenagehood, her shorn colourless hair, her eyes flickering under her eyelids as she became used to the light.

It is the morning, but out the window some solitary old men are standing in a line outside the pub, beers in hand, staring at nothing, smoking, thinking of conversations to start. I expect all the straw figures to be gone now, but there is one there, still, half destroyed by the storm and slumped against one of the fold-out chairs under the pub awning, its face pressed into an ashtray.

I wonder if we really have beaten the man from the reservoir into the earth or into another time and I wonder whether that time is Kate's time. If so, will the people there cry for him as they would their Laird? Maybe he was the Laird, or some other version of him. When I left the Knock he was gone as though he had never even existed. People go round and round and they come back, sometimes. I realise that I will have a lot of time to think about this because I am not dead and I don't even feel slightly dead.

I read the text from Evan. She says: Back in the town? Ew. Why? I want to come to the city and stay with you so go back there please. Does next week sound good?

The thought of her sitting in her little studio waiting for my next response excites me.

I reply and she replies again and we are talking as though we are in the same room and it is this ease, I realise, that I have never before been bothered to cultivate with my friends.

I love you, I type. I send it.

She replies: I really love you too. XXX.

I fall back onto the little bed and narrow my eyes so the bright room fades to a soft blur, let myself lie like that just a moment. My top is raised to my chest and I feel the hole Kate crawled from, which is already closing to a purple oval, only the very centre still wet with blood and milky fluid. It will one day just be a white circle, slightly raised from the skin, the centre blushed the palest pink. The body heals and the body remembers.

In the kitchen, I rinse some cups of cold tea, make coffee with lots of milk, some juice for Nina, set them on a greasy tray. Greasy, because Nance's house hasn't magically cleaned itself overnight. Her reunion with Finn was a joyous one – Finn running in, tail wagging, Nance screaming, standing, tea and uneaten biscuits and ash and cigarette butts and literal hair that she had ripped out falling around her.

Nina, attaching herself to me, small hands around my middle, serious little face looking up.

Nance, handing me a towel and telling me to pat dry my hair and the rain goes on all night.

A meal scraped together with leftovers. Slimy chicken thighs then breakfast cereals and yogurt and fruit. Me, gnashing at bones and licking my plate, then my head in a punnet of slightly soft strawberries, red juice around the mouth.

Now the cups slip on the tray. I take them through to the living room where Nance tiptoes around discarded dishes, a ball of tea towels under one arm. Nina and Finn are curled on the linen sofa. Smoke swirls in the air and cushions are scattered.

Over bitter milky coffee, Nina in her turquoise leotard performs the part of her dance routine she can remember. Indeed, she has been selected to stand in the front, surrounded by all the other children in gold. She is happy but she does not smile as she dances across the living room, lit by the sun through the bright orange curtains, because she is focusing on getting all the moves just right.

Later, I return to the bus stop.

The high street is quiet and the first leaves have started to fall and drift over from the forests and field edges to the pavement and they are damp and soft so my footsteps are quiet too.

My goodbye to Nance and Nina and Finn was a proper one. Finn, licking my fingers and my face again and again and always. I tell them I will be back in winter, when the Knock and the forest around it are laid bare. When Kate is snow on the branches and the compact glittering earth.

Now, from the bus, I see Kate in the sun between the trees, the white water crashing against the dam wall, the orange ferns and the wych elms, the ramshackle shops and the low, sighing cottages. She is here, I am thinking, and it starts to rain again, and the wind picks up and rattles the windows. I am laughing as the bus is leaving, and I look back at the town and everything in it and then I am thinking: Here she is.

In the town, in the early summer, people make straw figures and dress them in their old clothes. It is a tradition so old that no one remembers how it started. On the corner of the high street, the children dress the witch. Up the Knock, the scent of a story, burning, still clings to the trees, unaware the narrator has returned.

Acknowledgements

Little concrete information exists about many of the women supposedly convicted of witchcraft in Crieff and Strathearn. There are so many different iterations of Kate's name and life, with the first mention of her in writing dating from as early as 1818. Some stories of Kate are told through poetry, a version of her name appears on a 1938 'Calendar of Cases of Witchcraft in Scotland', some sources place her as early as the mid-16th century. There is no solid historiographical evidence of her existence, although she lives vividly in local tales, and I see this book as an entirely fictional building upon that folklore, or at least my own version of it. As a basis for this work, I primarily used *Perthshire Crieff Strathearn Local History*, a decade-long blog project by my late grandfather, local historian Colin Mayall. His research into witch trials draws together local legend and existing archival evidence to present the stories of women who may have been. I want to thank him, firstly, for inspiring my writing.

Thank you to my brilliant editor, Charlotte Robathan, for bringing so much insight and so many wonderful ideas to this project, and for really getting to know Kate and Thomasin as well as I do.

Thank you to my agent, Sara Langham, for her constant support, encouragement and enthusiasm.

Thank you to my mum, Elise, who is from Crieff and grew up around stories like this one, and to my dad, Fraser. Also, to my little brother, Fin, and our beloved dog, Otis.

Thank you to my granny, Sheila, who gave me my love for books and stories and would write them down for me when I was too young to write myself but knew exactly what I wanted to say.

Thank you to all my lovely, funny friends – especially Lillian, my wonderful writing partner, and Ellie – for their endless support and love.

Also to my friends at the Faber Academy and our tutor, Peter Benson, who read some of the earliest iterations of my first chapters, and to the University of Glasgow English Literature and Creative Writing department, where *Last Witch* was born in the form of a dissertation.

Finally, thank you most of all to Jamie. I love you.